Wait For Me
Yesterday in *Spring*

Every day, when school got out,

we'd go sit and talk down on the seawall,

whiling away the hours until dinnertime.

He was the only one who could talk to me about nothing

and make it feel like everything.

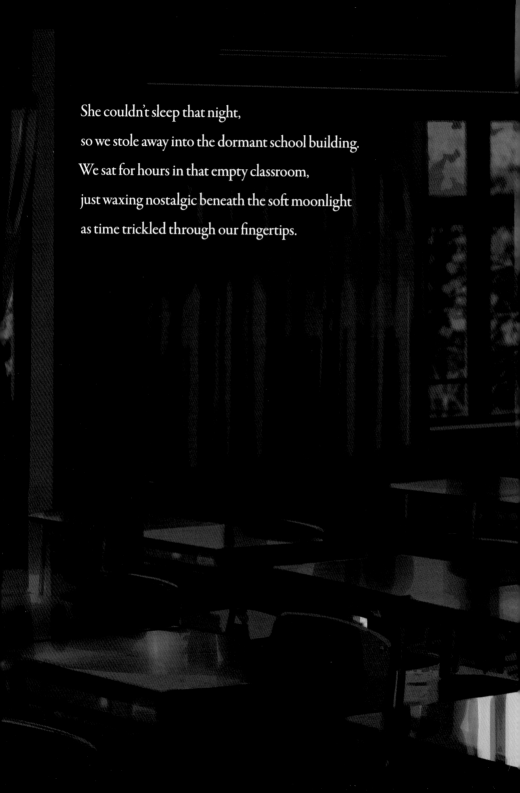

She couldn't sleep that night,
so we stole away into the dormant school building.
We sat for hours in that empty classroom,
just waxing nostalgic beneath the soft moonlight
as time trickled through our fingertips.

Akari Hoshina

Kanae Funami

CONTENTS

Wait For Me Yesterday in Spring

KINOU NO HARU DE, KIMI WO MATSU by Mei HACHIMOKU
© 2020 Mei HACHIMOKU
Illustration by KUKKA
All rights reserved.

Original Japanese edition published by SHOGAKUKAN.
English translation rights in the United States of America, Canada,
the United Kingdom, Ireland, Australia and New Zealand arranged with
SHOGAKUKAN through Tuttle-Mori Agency, Inc.

Seven Seas press and purchase enquiries can be sent to
Marketing Manager Lianne Sentar at press@gomanga.com.
Information regarding the distribution and purchase of
digital editions is available from Digital Manager CK Russell
at digital@gomanga.com.

Seven Seas and the Seven Seas logo are trademarks of
Seven Seas Entertainment. All rights reserved.

Follow Seven Seas Entertainment online at
sevenseasentertainment.com.

TRANSLATION: Evan Ward
COVER DESIGN: H. Qi
INTERIOR LAYOUT & DESIGN: Clay Gardner
COPY EDITOR: Jade Gardner
PROOFREADER: Rebecca Scoble
LIGHT NOVEL EDITOR: Katy M. Kelly
PREPRESS TECHNICIAN: Melanie Ujimori
PRINT MANAGER: Rhiannon Rasmussen-Silverstein
PRODUCTION MANAGER: Lissa Pattillo
EDITOR-IN-CHIEF: Julie Davis
ASSOCIATE PUBLISHER: Adam Arnold
PUBLISHER: Jason DeAngelis

ISBN: 978-1-63858-409-4
Printed in Canada
First Printing: July 2022
10 9 8 7 6 5 4 3 2 1

Wait For Me Yesterday in Spring

WRITTEN BY
Mei Hachimoku

ILLUSTRATIONS BY
KUKKA

TRANSLATION BY
Evan Ward

Airship

Seven Seas Entertainment

CHARACTERS

KANAE FUNAMI
The protagonist. A seventeen-year-old boy who has run away from his home in Tokyo.

AKARI HOSHINA
Kanae's childhood friend. A girl who attends the local high school in Sodeshima.

ERI FUNAMI
Kanae's fourteen-year-old sister. Lives in Sodeshima.

AKITO HOSHINO
Akari's older brother.

SAKI HAYASE
Akito's ex-girlfriend.

HAVING ANGUISHED AND LANGUISHED till I could anguish no more, I grew fed up with the notion that over-analyzing my anxieties would do me any good and turned my head toward the sky as if to mark a clean break from this pessimistic spiral. To my surprise, the azure expanse of air above was every bit as clear and tranquil as the serenity of mind I craved. A lone black kite painted figure-eight shapes against the firmament, its doleful whinnying call ringing out from on high as it scanned the earth for its next meal. Beside it hung the receding moon, still and placid in the morning sky like a single drop of spilled milk.

I sucked in a nourishing breath of crisp, coastal air to provide my weary brain with a fresh supply of oxygen. Nostrils now lubricated from the sting of brine on the breeze, I picked up the slightest hint of plum blossoms amidst the usual scent of sea salt.

It was the spring before my final year of high school. I was seventeen.

I brought my gaze back down to the road ahead and resumed my homeward saunter along the coast while waves crashed against the seawall beside me. It was by no means the most direct way home, but that suited me just fine—I needed the extra time to think.

I thought back to last night—that fateful occurrence that had been the catalyst for all of this but also an ending of sorts for me in particular. The reality of it all still had yet to fully set in. I could only play back the events of the night before over and over in my head, asking myself ad infinitum whether this was truly the ending I wanted or if there was something more I could have done; a different choice I could have made, a better outcome. The more I thought on it, the more it began to feel like my mind was being swallowed up by quicksand, each attempt to break free only dragging me deeper into a mire of my own regret.

I nevertheless continued trying (and failing) to cram my disparate thoughts into a single cohesive shape that I could wrap my head around, until before I knew it, I was standing outside the door to my house. I strode through the entryway, kicked off my shoes, and headed straight for my room without even announcing my return. I couldn't muster up the willpower to do much of anything, so I threw myself down on the bed and tried to expel the unending flood of distressing thoughts with every labored sigh that passed through my lips. It wasn't long before the feelings of exhaustion began to set in. It made sense, given that I hadn't slept a wink since the night before last.

No sooner had I closed my eyelids than did a stream of memories begin to flash against their undersides in quick succession, like a series of slides on an overhead projector—memories of Akari, and of the past few days we'd spent together. She'd be laughing in one, crying the next, blushing up a storm in yet another. As these images played out against the backs of my eyelids, like individual freeze frames in time and space, I realized just how blessed I'd been to share each of these precious, fleeting moments with her. Just having her in my vicinity—speaking, listening, existing—was enough to make me feel content with my sorry little life. That was exactly why, regardless of the choices I might have made, or the ones I'd make in the future, I swore to myself I'd do whatever it took to—

Before I could finish that thought, my mind finally succumbed to my body's pressing demands for sleep, and I lost consciousness.

CHAPTER 1
April 1st, 3 p.m.

FOR THE FIRST TIME in nearly two years, I was sitting aboard a small but familiar passenger ferry, letting the slow undulations of the waves rock me gently from side to side. From my seat by the window, I could survey almost the entire indoor seating area. There were a hundred-and-some-odd seats on this vessel, if memory served, yet you could count the number of actual passengers on one hand. I glanced up at the old hanging wall clock and noticed that it was 3 p.m. on the dot, meaning it had already been well over six hours since I left Tokyo. With my elbow braced on the windowsill for support, I rested my head against my palm and let out a short, wistful sigh.

I'd run away from home, and for a pathetically clichéd reason, no less. Try as I might to purge the unpleasant thoughts from my mind, they came rushing back after every attempt. I was partially at fault, to be fair. It wasn't okay for me to have skipped out on my spring break supplementary classes, and I only worsened things by trying to cover it up with a lame excuse when my dad caught me red-handed playing hooky at a local bookstore (I'd tried to play it off as though the pulpy sci-fi novel I was leafing through was, in fact, teacher-recommended studying material for its practical applications of physics concepts).

Those two initial blunders aside, I genuinely believed the vast majority of the fault landed on my father's end of the table. As far as I was concerned, the way he lashed out at me as soon as we got home—calling me a waste of his money, a "high school dropout in the making," a disappointment to the family, and just a plain-old hopeless case—was extremely uncalled for. A lot of it was straight-up verbal abuse.

I knew it was wrong to skip out on my classes. I fully admitted that. It was my father, though, who insisted I take supplementary courses in the first place. I certainly wasn't enthused about the idea of having to spend my spring break in school, but he wouldn't hear otherwise. Yes, he had indeed been footing the bill for my tuition and living expenses, but it was always *his* idea to invite me to live with him in Tokyo. Yet I simply stood there, eyes downcast, letting him verbally berate me for what felt like hours on end, all the while resisting the urge to call him out on just how unreasonable he was being. That last, almost casual quip he made—I doubted he thought before saying it, to be honest—was the final push over the edge:

"I knew it was a mistake to bring you back to Tokyo with me."

That single line hit me so hard, it felt like I'd been bashed over the head by a baseball bat. After two or three seconds of dumbfounded silence (maybe it was longer, actually—hard to say), I stomped off to my bedroom and slammed the door behind me. Ignoring my dad's incessant yelling, I crammed a few changes of clothes and some bare necessities into an overnight bag, and as soon as I woke up the next morning, I ran out the front door. More than half a day had now passed since the altercation, yet thinking back on it still made me grind my teeth in frustration.

"...Stupid asshole," I cursed under my breath, the hot air fogging up the window pane.

I knew it wouldn't do me any favors to keep reliving these events on a loop inside my head, so I chose to abandon this line of thought and gaze out at the open ocean, its waves shimmering brightly beneath the midafternoon sun. The deep blue waters were fairly choppy today, causing the little ferryboat to rock back and forth and teeter from side to side. It was actually beginning to make me feel a little bit seasick, though it was possible the turbulence had nothing to do with that. I might have brought the nausea on myself by way of anxiety alone.

I stood up from my seat even so and headed toward the front of the ship to get some fresh air. The moment I stepped out onto the deck, a blustery wind snatched up the hood of my sweatshirt and sent it flapping furiously against the back of my neck. The early spring air felt slightly icy against my skin, more so than it would without the added wind chill, but it gave me exactly the refreshing jolt I was looking for. The frigid breeze snapped me right out of my depressive cycle; I was already feeling more alive again.

I looked around, but there were no other people standing out on the windswept deck. With measured steps, I made my way toward the bow, where I leaned over the railing at the front of the ship. Straight ahead of us, I could see our destination: the tiny remote island I once called home, yet hadn't even visited for two entire years. Sodeshima.

We soon made port at Sodeshima Harbor. I slung my overnight bag over my shoulder and prepared to disembark. As soon as I stepped off the ferry and exited the harbor, however, I spied someone I recognized walking down the sidewalk on the other side of the street. Though his hair was a bit longer than it had been two years prior, I could have recognized that dusky crew cut and imposing stature anywhere. I'd spotted Akito Hoshina.

Back when I lived in Sodeshima, he was about the closest thing to a celebrity the small island could claim. With his extraordinary athleticism and baseball skills, he single-handedly led our no-name high school's baseball team to nationals at Koshien—an achievement that made him the talk of the town for quite some time. He was the guy that every young boy on the island wanted to grow up to be, myself included. Considering he was three years my senior...he must be twenty years old by now. I wondered what he was up to nowadays. We'd had a couple of very brief interactions in the past, so I considered calling out to say hi, but by the time I made up my mind, he'd already disappeared into the ticket office for the outbound ferry. I'd officially missed my chance.

"...Oh well. Maybe next time."

I'd make a point to be more assertive in approaching him if another opportunity arose, I decided. I turned away from the ticket office in the direction of the one place I knew would put me up for a while: my grandmother's house.

After passing through the few blocks of tourism companies and traditional-style inns that centered around the harbor, I headed inland up the steep and narrow residential streets. Though I was born in Tokyo, I'd spent the majority of my life in Sodeshima. I now lived a life indistinguishable from any high-school-aged Tokyoite, but it was here in Podunk Sodeshima that I attended elementary and junior high, my most formative years. Sodeshima was more of a hometown to me in that respect than Tokyo would ever be. One could practically say that this wasn't a case of me running *away* from home but a kind of home*coming*... not that that distinction changed anything.

Speaking of things not changing, I thought to myself as I glanced up and down the streets of Sodeshima, noting the surprising lack of much development over the past two years. Everything was for the most part exactly how I remembered it. Nothing but old Japanese-style houses lined the streets of these neighborhoods, with nary a modern building in sight. This was a level of eerie stasis that went way beyond evoking nostalgia, straight into the realm of mind-numbing stagnation.

After hoofing it uphill for close to ten minutes, I came to a stop before a two-story wooden house with the nameplate reading FUNAMI posted on its gate. I was home. As I struggled like always with the rickety door that fit poorly in its jamb, I called into the house, and my grandmother quickly walked out from the living room to greet me.

"Welcome home, Kanae," she said, the deep wrinkles in her face stretching and shifting into the form of a broad and soothing smile. She was already in her late eighties but stood upright as ever, arrow-straight. By all accounts, she was extremely spry for her age; her excellent health was the one thing I was grateful to see had stayed the same over the past two years.

"Hey, Grandma," I smiled back. "Long time no see."

Before I let myself get dragged into a long conversation, I headed upstairs to set my things down. I stepped into my old bedroom to find that everything—my bed, my bookshelves, my desk—was almost exactly the way I left it two years ago. The only noticeable difference was that someone had been cleaning it regularly, as there wasn't a speck of dust to be found. My bed had also been dressed in a thinner springtime comforter now that winter was over, which was presumably my grandmother's doing.

I set my overnight bag down on the floor and then exited the room. Heading back down the stairs, I made a quick pit stop in the traditional Japanese-style sitting room to pay my respects at my late grandfather's altar and let him know I'd come home before heading into the living room. I sat cross-legged on a floor cushion at the low dining table across from my grandmother and cut right to the chase.

"So, yeah. Like I told you over the phone this morning, I'm probably gonna be staying here for a little while," I began.

"Because of that little kerfuffle with your dad, I take it?" she replied.

"Yeah... Wait. Did I already tell you about that?"

"No—he gave me a call not long after I got off the phone with you. Said you might be heading this way and to keep you out of trouble if you did."

"Oh, he did, did he...?"

"Sounds like your old man's got you all figured out," she teased, cackling like a mischievous storybook witch. That my father had so easily predicted my every move filled me with an odd mixture of shame and indignation.

"...Knew I should've run away somewhere else."

"Oh, please. As if you'd even have anywhere else to go! Besides, it's not like you have anything better to do with your spring break, do you? Just take it easy here in Sodeshima for a while. The big festival's coming up, you know!"

"I'm not going to that stupid thing, Grandma. You know I hate big crowds."

"Yet you still wanted to live in Tokyo. I'll never understand it."

"That's a totally different kind of crowded, Grandma," I said dismissively, picking a mandarin up off the table and beginning to peel back the skin. Before I could pop the first slice of orange into my mouth, I heard the front door rattle open.

"I'm hooome—Uhhhh, what?"

Sure enough, it was my little sister Eri who now stood in the living room doorway with her mouth agape. She'd grown a bit since last I saw her two years ago—which would make her fourteen now, come to think of it. Her once-frizzy braids had developed into something more hip: a low-hanging side ponytail. What drew my eyes more than anything, though, was her sailor-style schoolgirl uniform. My little Eri had ditched her dorky red elementary school backpack and was now a full-blown teenager. As her older brother, it was definitely a strange feeling.

"Hey, Eri," I said. "Been a while, huh? You back straight from a club meeting or something?"

"Why are you here?" she replied tersely, her eyes narrowing.

"Wow, okay. That's one way to greet your loving brother you haven't seen in years, I guess. Didn't Grandma tell you I was coming?"

"She did. I'm asking *why* you're here."

Her words were sharp. It was clear that she wasn't happy to see me—which I could understand. She'd resisted the idea of me moving to Tokyo to the very last. We left off on fairly negative terms two years ago, and I hadn't tried to get in contact with her since.

"C'mon, don't glare at me like that," I said. "This is a reunion worth celebrating, right? Here, sit down and eat one of these mandarins with me."

"Last time I checked, those aren't yours to give away, *Kanae*."

Now that one stung. Granted, it wasn't the first time she'd called me by my actual name, but she only tended to use it when she was extremely pissed off at me. All the rest of the time, it was "Big Brother."

"Anyway, you didn't answer my question," she demanded. "What brings you back here to Sodeshima? State your business."

"I don't have any business. I just ran away from home, so I'm gonna lay low and mooch off of you guys for a while."

"How long is 'a while'?"

"Maybe a week or so. It's April 1st now, so...maybe until the 8th?"

"I see. And *why* did you run away from home, exactly? Did you get in a fight with that deadbeat?"

I turned back to look at my grandmother across the table, but she shook her head. Apparently, Eri had guessed that one all on her own—she was a sharp kid. I had no reason to lie, so I fessed up.

"Yeah, that's about the size of it," I replied. "You got it in one."

"See, this is exactly why I tried to stop you from going with him. I told you that man isn't right in the head."

"Yeah, well... You may have been right about that. Definitely regretting it now."

"See? You never should've gone to live with that deadbeat in the—"

"Eri," my grandmother cut in. "Stop calling your own father a deadbeat."

Eri puffed out her cheeks and scowled at this rebuke.

"Well, I'm not gonna call him my *father*, that's for sure. Not when he hasn't done anything to deserve it..." she grumbled.

I could definitely understand where Eri was coming from. Originally, the four of us—me, Eri, my dad, and my mom—all lived together in Tokyo. When I was six, and Eri was barely three, our parents got divorced because it came to light that my mother was having an affair. I never heard all the dirty details, but suffice it to say, my mother had completely lost any potential attachment she had to our family. She was more than happy to foist full custody off onto my father.

Mind you, I wasn't sure whether my father actually *wanted* custody of the two of us or not. I preferred not to think too deeply about that. The fact of the matter was that he didn't waste any time in sending us to live in Sodeshima with our grandmother while he stayed in Tokyo, where he proceeded to neglect us altogether for nearly a decade. I totally got why Eri felt he was a deadbeat, seeing how he hadn't lived with us since she was practically too young to remember. To Eri, he was hardly any different from any old stranger off the street.

I never felt that way about him, myself, at least not through my junior high years. When he asked my eighth-grade self whether I'd be interested in going to high school in Tokyo, I took him up on the offer and moved to the big city right after graduating from junior high. To be clear, though, my decision had less to do with me wanting to rekindle any sort of father-son relationship and more to do with me becoming just generally disenchanted with Sodeshima on the whole.

"Come on, now, Eri. Have a seat with us," my grandmother pleaded gently, and Eri obliged, sitting down right beside her. "I'm going to go brew some tea for us; you kids feel free to catch up a bit while I'm gone, okay?"

Eri nodded silently as my grandmother pushed herself up and headed over toward the kitchen. I sat across from my sister, who was now hanging her head low in shame. She'd always been a huge Grandma's girl, so it probably came as a shock for her to be chided like that. As far as Eri was concerned, Grandma and I were the only family she had, so it made sense that she was so desperate to stop me from moving to Tokyo. I actually felt quite sorry for her when I framed it that way.

"Aw, c'mon. Don't let it get you down," I tried to reassure her.

"Says the guy who started it... This sucks," she pouted.

"Why don't we change the subject? You're in junior high now, huh? Hard to believe. Doing any sports or after-school activities?"

"Like you even care. How come you never called or came to visit in the past two years, if you're so curious about my life?"

"Well, I mean...it felt kinda awkward, y'know? Especially after you fought tooth and nail to stop me from moving to Tokyo. Wasn't sure you'd wanna hear anything I had to say."

"Wow, I didn't know you were such a wuss," she sneered. "Yes, talking to people can be pretty awkward sometimes, *Kanae*, but that doesn't mean you should go cutting a family member out of your life. I can't believe you're so dense. We're not even talking common courtesy here—it's just common sense."

"Sheesh, did you really miss me that much?"

"Huh?" she scoffed. "What are you, stupid? Of course not. See, this is exactly what I'm talking about: you have a chronic case of always picking the worst possible thing to say in any tough situation. I'm guessing you probably don't have many friends over there in Tokyo, do you?"

"*Excuse* you?" I snapped, more annoyed that she was right than anything. "Look, I'll admit that I should've tried to stay in touch. Sure. The same can be said for you, y'know! You knew my phone number. You could've called me up whenever you wanted, but you didn't."

"Sorry? Why should it be *my* job to reach out to you when *you're* the one who ran off and ditched us? Anyone with half a brain would agree that it was your job to bury the hatchet, *Kanae*. You really don't have a sensitive bone in your body, do you?"

"This has nothing to do with me being insensitive, and you know it. Anyway, would you quit saying my name in that condescending tone of voice? '*KUH-NYE.*' You sound stupid. It's time for you to grow out of this little rebellious phase and go back to calling me 'Big Brother' like a good little sister. Or should I say, 'Big *Bwudder*'?"

"Ew, what?! You mean when I was, like, five?! Don't make me puke. If anyone's going through a rebellious phase here, it's you. Aren't you a little old to be running away from home 'cause Daddy made you mad?"

"Sh-shut the hell up! You don't know what happened! He forced my hand!"

"Oh, please. You probably just got caught skipping school, and he called you out on it!"

"It wasn't *school*! It was just a supplementary course, okay?!"

"*Would you two knock it off already?!*"

My grandmother's booming voice reverberated like a clap of thunder as she reentered the living room, carrying a tray with some cups and a small teapot.

"Eri! Stop trying to get a rise out of your brother like that!"

"Wha... No, he was the one that..." Eri stammered.

"And you, Kanae! You're her older brother; you're supposed to be the mature one here! You can't let yourself be so easily provoked!"

"...Fine. Whatever you say, Grandma," I sighed, then stood up from the table and headed for the doorway.

"Where are you going?" she called after me.

"To cool off for a bit," I replied without even looking back at her, then quickly slipped my shoes on and stepped out the door.

"Welp, I sure didn't waste any time making things awkward..."

I muttered to myself as I made my way back down the hilly road outside our house. How ridiculous was it to have gotten myself in another argument less than an hour after I arrived here? Eri was one hundred percent right about me, and there was the proof. I didn't want to admit it to her, so I got heated and tried to deny it.

I was kind of a loner at my high school in Tokyo. That was already the case when I was at junior high here in Sodeshima, though, so I couldn't blame it purely on the culture shock. My relative lack of social skills meant I didn't have many friends growing up, but then, in eighth grade, there was an incident where I stood up for another classmate who was being bullied that caused all the "cool kids" to start ignoring me and spreading nasty rumors behind my back. Eventually, even the bullied kid I'd stood up for jumped on the bandwagon out of fear that they might turn their attention back on him. It was at this point that I first developed some (admittedly pretty mild) trust issues.

Still, it wasn't as if I learned nothing from that unfortunate experience. The most important lesson my junior-high years taught me wasn't anything from the curriculum, but that insulating yourself in an echo chamber of people who are too afraid to speak out or go against the grain only breeds narrow-mindedness. That was why I was so eager to take my father up on his offer to move me to the big city. My primary goal was to get away from insular, single-minded Sodeshima. I figured that in a place with as much diversity as Tokyo, the city I'd originally been born in, I was sure to find *somewhere* I could belong, *some* group of people who would accept me into their niche. Alas, those hopes were quickly dashed.

At first, people at my new school were extremely interested in me because my remote island lifestyle was something they couldn't even fathom. Their curiosity didn't last for very long. My natural awkwardness shined through soon enough, and my difference in life experience made it hard to relate to my fellow classmates, so I gradually became an outcast all over again. Then, after I failed a few tests in a row, some students started treating me as though I was some illiterate country bumpkin. There was nothing good about my time there. I persisted anyway, in the hopes that one day I'd meet someone who would be willing to accept me the way I was. Instead, my frustration continued to build and build, I grew more and more impatient, and with the incident last night, it all reached a boiling point.

"I knew it was a mistake to bring you back to Tokyo with me."

When those words left his mouth, it felt like the entire city of Tokyo was sneering at me, ridiculing me for thinking I would ever fit in. I couldn't bear to stay a moment longer, so I ran away to my grandmother's house in Sodeshima as quickly as I could. Now here I was, running away from the place I'd run away to.

"Man, I wanna go home…"

Not to Tokyo nor Sodeshima—to some undefined concept of the word "home," to some place out there where I could feel like I belonged. Where on earth that place might be, I didn't know. Probably somewhere beneath cool linen sheets on a brisk spring morning, where I could sleep the day away in spite of the world. While I knew full well that that was a pipe dream, I still didn't feel like going back to my grandmother's house anytime soon. Luckily, there was plenty of daylight yet remaining, so I decided I'd wander around the island for a bit.

I moped around feeling sorry for myself for a while, until eventually I came to the concrete path that ran along the coast. There I was greeted by a powerful gust of saltwater wind that made my little hairs stand on end—both on the back of my neck and inside my nostrils. As with most small islands, the winds around Sodeshima were pretty intense all year long, mainly due to the lack of any significant land barriers to impede them. The open ocean was where strong winds were born, after all, which made Sodeshima a sitting duck right in the middle of the tempest.

As I walked along the shoreline, bracing against the blustery gale, I eventually came upon a young girl sitting on the waist-high seawall, her legs dangling out over the ocean as she gazed in longing toward the mainland. She wore a thin, slightly over-sized sweater and a pair of plain, black comfy-casual pants. Her washed-out chestnut hair was styled in a shaggy, mid-length bob, and I could tell just from seeing her face in profile that she had a smooth bronze complexion. Except I already knew that her hair was only so washed-out because of chlorine bleaching, and that her skin color was not the result of any artificial tanning but the natural pigment she'd been born with. Her name was Akari Hoshina. She was the younger sister of the island's star athlete, and also my best friend growing up.

"Aka—huh?"

I started to call out to her but then stopped short—because as the first syllables were leaving my lips, I noticed that there were tears streaming down her cheeks. There was something captivatingly natural about the way she was crying too—she wasn't sniffling, wasn't making any attempt to wipe her tears away, and hadn't even blinked as far as I could see. I had to second-guess whether calling out to her now was truly a good idea. Still, I couldn't very well walk right past and pretend not to notice her, so I slowly walked up behind her and called her name once I was a few feet away.

"Akari...?" I asked. She immediately whirled around, so fast that the centripetal motion sent teardrops flying off her cheeks.

"K-Kanae-kun?!" she said, gasping with genuine surprise as she shot up to her feet on the raised part of the seawall. "Wh-what are you doing h—ah, wagh!"

"Whoa, careful there!"

Perhaps due to how quickly she'd stood up, Akari lost her balance right away and nearly fell backwards into the ocean.

Thankfully, my emergency reflexes kicked in. I shot forward to wrap my arms around her thighs (which were at eye level) and pulled her back in. For a split second, I could feel her body heat against my cheek, even through the thick cotton fabric. As soon as I made sure she'd regained her balance, I pulled away with urgency. That was one brash maneuver on my part—even if it *was* just to make sure she didn't hurt herself. As I stood there, desperately praying that I hadn't made things ten times more awkward, she hopped down from the seawall and brushed sand off the butt of her pants.

"Sorry about that," she said. "You startled me, is all."

"Yeah, my bad. I shouldn't have snuck up on you like that. You all right?"

"Yep. A little frazzled, but beats falling to my death! Thanks for the assist!" she grinned teasingly. She didn't look like she was planning to hold my jamming my face between her legs against me. As I let out a sigh of relief, I remembered what I meant to ask when I first saw her.

"Hey, Akari? Not that it's any of my business, but...were you just crying a minute ago?"

"Huh? Ohhh, yeah, uh... My pollen allergies have been *really* acting up lately, you know how it is. Kinda annoying, but what are ya gonna do? Ah ha ha..."

She rubbed the corners of her eyes with her fingertips as she tried to laugh it off, but it hadn't looked like a case of pollen allergies to me. I was convinced that there must have been another reason she was crying, maybe over something bad that happened today. Even if that had been the case, I wasn't brazen enough to try to drag it out of her. Especially when this was our first time seeing each other in two years. I decided it might be best if I changed the subject.

"...Well, so long as you're doin' okay, I guess. Anyway, it's good to see you again!"

"Yeah, good to see you too! We haven't really seen each other since graduation, have we? You home for spring break?"

"Yeah, more or less. Planning to be here in town for a week or so."

"Cool, cool. Plenty of time to get a little R&R in, right?"

"Yup, that's the idea," I said uninterestedly, then looked down at Akari's legs. "So what's new with you? I'm betting you're still on the swim team?"

"I mean, yeah... What about it?"

"Oh, nothing, I just, uh... I could tell from your thighs, that's all. No way they'd be that tight if you weren't getting *some* kind of workout in every day."

Akari stared at me like a deer in the headlights for a solid five seconds and then suddenly burst out laughing.

"Ah ha ha ha! I'm sorry, *what*?! Who are you, and what have you done with Kanae-kun? Or did all the red-light districts over there turn you into a massive creep?!"

"What?! C-c'mon, that wasn't *that* creepy, was it?! I mean, I guess I see how you might take it as... Okay, yeah, it sounds pretty bad, doesn't it? Look, forget I said anything! Sorry."

"Nope, too late now! I'm calling you 'Kanae the Thigh Guy'

from now on! Or how 'bout this: 'The Femur Fetishist'? ...Wait, no! I've got it! 'The Crural Connoisseur'! Ha ha ha ha!"

"Please, no. I will do literally anything."

The two of us sat down on the seawall, facing inland this time, and shot the breeze for a good, long while. Akari was not only my closest childhood friend but also my very first crush. There wasn't a specific moment or anything that made me fall for her— it was more like one of those things that you just kinda realize after a while. Sadly, my hopes came crashing down one day in junior high when I overheard her say something to another girl in our class:

"Me and Kanae-kun? Not a chance. We're just friends. There are zero feelings there, believe me."

I tried to convince myself it was a good thing I found out before I confessed to having a crush on her and made a fool of myself—key word being "tried." After that, we maintained the status quo and never grew beyond platonic friends, until eventually we went our separate ways when the time came to move on to high school. It wasn't uncommon for childhood friends like us to grow apart after a while—how many people could say their best friend at eight was still their best friend at eighteen? Not many, and I didn't think there was anything wrong with that. For me, it was enough that we could get together and reminisce about old times like this every once in a while. I couldn't wish for anything more.

"Man, oh, man, Kanae-kun," she said after a while. "I've gotta say, I'm relieved to see the big city hasn't changed you all that much. Here I was half expecting you to come back with your hair dyed and a whole bunch of crazy piercings."

"Please tell me you don't think that's how everyone in Tokyo looks," I groaned.

"Well, no, obviously. But it's one of the fashion capitals of the world, right? Bet you ran into all sorts of cute girls and models and whatnot, didn't ya?"

"I mean, maybe compared to Sodeshima, yeah."

"Oh yeah? Do tell. You got yourself a little girlfriend over there, big guy?" she asked, turning her head to the side to look up at me from below so she could gauge my reaction. Part of me wanted to say I did, for the sake of sheer bragging rights, but if she were to call my bluff it'd only make me seem more of a loser than I already was. She would never let me live it down, either. I decided to answer honestly.

"Nope, I sure don't. Sorry to disappoint, but my social life over there has been preeetty boring so far."

"Yep, figured as much."

"Wow, okay. Didn't realize I was getting roasted here," I grumbled sarcastically. Akari snickered. I decided to turn the spotlight on her, even though I knew it wouldn't be much in the way of payback. "You haven't changed one bit either, you know that?"

"Really? You don't think?"

"I mean, your hairstyle's exactly the same, for one thing. I could tell it was you from a mile away."

"...Really? I feel like I've changed a lot..." she mumbled to herself before looking dejectedly down at the ground.

If that was really how she felt, then surely *something* about her must have changed. I gave her another good once-over; obviously, puberty had done its work on her, but something told me that wasn't what she was referring to. And on the off chance it was, I had no idea how I was meant to respond to that.

I brought my gaze back up to her face, which was when I finally noticed something about current Akari that junior-high Akari definitely lacked, albeit a pretty minor detail: there were faint black circles under her eyes. As I stared at them, wondering if perhaps she hadn't been getting much sleep lately, she brought her own gaze up to meet mine, and our eyes locked.

The old me would have surely looked away immediately. Hell, I would have expected the new me to do the same...but I couldn't. There was something in Akari's eyes—some fathomless, murky darkness, as if someone gathered a skyful of rolling black clouds in the midst of a thunderstorm and somehow distilled them directly into her pupils—and it made it impossible for me to look away. Like I needed to find out what it was, or it might consume me too. In the end, Akari was the one who looked away first.

"...Okay, you can stop staring now. This is officially awkward," she announced.

"Huh? Oh, uh... Sorry. I didn't mean to," I flustered, turning away as the embarrassment set in at last. I tried to sneak another peek at her out of the corner of my eye and saw that her face had gone beet red too. A few moments passed, and then she jumped up to her feet with a "Hup!" and spun around to face me.

Then she tucked her hands behind her back and leaned forward, bringing her face closer to mine.

"Hey, um. Kanae-kun?"

"What's up?"

"Have you decided what college you're going to next year?"

"Yeah—U of I. But you knew that already."

The high school I was attending now was a feeder school specifically for U of I hopefuls. My admittance would be guaranteed so long as I didn't get held back a grade.

"Yeah, I know... Just thought I'd double-check since we haven't talked in a while, y'know? Anyway, I should probably start heading home."

"Okay. Hope I see you around."

Akari flashed me a quick smile, then trotted off. I remained seated there on the seawall for a moment, stretching out my back. That was the first time in a while I'd talked to another person for such a long time, and it felt good. Somewhere in the tiniest recesses of my mind, however, the thought of that darkness I'd sensed lurking in her eyes kept gnawing at my brain.

I pulled out my cell phone to check the time. It was 5 p.m. I still wasn't ready to go back and face Eri, so I decided to kill time for a little while longer. I slid my cell phone back into my pocket and stood up, doing a few arm stretches as I pondered over where to go. Then I spied a plum tree in the front yard of a nearby house. Its deep red flowers caught my eye and made me realize I hadn't seen any cherry blossoms yet this spring. Since today was April 1st, they should be in full bloom—and I knew the best spot on the island for cherry blossoms was the temple grounds outside of the Sodeshima Shrine. Thinking that might be a good way to kill another hour or so, I chose to make my way over there.

I took my time walking down the vacant streets and enjoying the pleasant spring air. When I passed by the old tobacco shop, I saw a police officer on a bicycle at 12 o'clock, pedaling his way toward me. As soon as he noticed me standing right in his trajectory, he slammed on the brakes. He was one of the few law enforcement officers stationed on the island—a man in his late thirties with an oval-shaped face.

"Well, look who it is," he said with a mischievous grin. "Thought I recognized you. Long time no see, huh?"

He hadn't changed one bit either—still the friendly jokester he'd been when he first came over from the mainland, way back when I was in elementary school. Everyone on the island loved him, kids and adults alike.

"Yeah, it's been a while," I replied.

"You visiting for spring break? Man, I miss being a student."

"What, police officers don't get a spring break?"

"Heck no! You kidding me? They work us year-round till we can't take it no more. It's a rough life, believe me," he complained. I was about to make a quip about how he couldn't be that busy if he had the time to stop and make small talk with me, but then he went on: "Heck, I just got done handling another stupid call."

"Oh yeah? Some sort of incident?"

"Yeah, nothing serious, though. Couple of crotchety old folks got into a bit of an altercation up at the shrine. Had to go over there and break it up."

"Oh, I was on my way over there now. Were there a lot of people there?"

"A pretty decent number, sure. The Sodeshima Senior Society's having a meetup there today. Think they're playing some croquet right now, if you wanted to go up there and join in."

I gagged. Suddenly, I'd lost all interest in seeing the cherry blossoms.

"Yeah, thanks but no thanks... I'd have to be pretty desperate to want to spend my spring break knocking balls through hoops with people five times my age. No offense."

"Ouch, kid. I mean, I get it, but ouch."

"Man, aren't there any events aimed at people my age around here? If they don't start trying to appeal to a younger demographic, this island's gonna be a ghost town before you know it... What with the declining birth rate and all."

"Weh-heh-hell! I see someone's been studying up on social politics over there in the big city. 'Demographic,' huh? That's a pretty big word for a guy your age!" the officer exclaimed with a hearty chuckle.

"All right, I'd better get going," I said, turning on my heels so that I wouldn't have to endure him talking down to me a moment longer. I walked off in the exact opposite direction of the shrine, determined not to let my precious spring break go to waste.

After waving the officer goodbye, I wandered aimlessly around the island for a while. I didn't want to risk bumping into any senior citizens, or even any of my old classmates, so I chose one of the least-trafficked roads on the island and began making my way down it. Before I knew it, I was walking through alleyways in between rows of old, dilapidated houses. This part of town was virtually in ruins; none of the islanders I knew ever came around these parts anymore.

There'd been a fairly booming mining industry on Sodeshima about fifty years ago, which apparently increased the tiny island's population by several orders of magnitude for a time. Once the tin supply dried up, though, a majority of the populace moved over to the mainland, leaving entire neighborhoods of empty houses in their wake.

When I was a little kid, every grown-up I knew tried to warn children not to go playing in this part of town, sometimes saying it was too dangerous, other times claiming it was haunted by ghosts. I'd always been a good boy and done as I was told, so this was actually the first time I'd set foot on these streets. The further in I went, the more obvious it became that all of these houses had been deserted. There were weeds poking up out of the concrete, and you could tell at a glance that most of these buildings hadn't even been entered in decades, let alone lived in. Yet while I grieved for the island's ever-decreasing population, I also couldn't help but enjoy the streets' eerily tranquil atmosphere. This kind of absolute peace and quiet always calmed me down, and even more so now that I lived in a place where I had to bump shoulders with people every day just to walk down the avenue.

I saw that the sun was now beginning to set, yet still I pushed onward, heading deeper down the labyrinthine backstreets. After passing through a particularly narrow alleyway, I came out into an open clearing where a small, abandoned park still stood. There was a rusty swing set, a jungle gym adorned with a big sign that read "KEEP OFF", and a sandbox full of weeds; all these elements combined to exude a bittersweet aura of nostalgia as they sat there, forgotten, waiting for the day they'd be demolished. A day that never arrived. It had likely been many years since the laughter of children at play was heard here. In stark contrast to the sorry state of the playground equipment, the park itself was surrounded on all sides by strikingly vivid cherry blossom trees— along with a single, massive tree right smack-dab in the middle of the park—all of which were in full bloom.

"Whoa... This is crazy..."

The majestic blossoms were so overwhelmingly gorgeous that they seemed magnetizing, and my feet started moving toward the central tree of their own volition. Each step forward brought its majestic grandeur and radiant vitality into a sharper, clearer focus, to the point that I genuinely wondered if this single tree might be the true culprit responsible for sapping all the life from this area—it was *that* breathtaking. A shallow layer of fallen petals formed a moat-like ring around its trunk that crunched beneath my shoes with each successive footfall. As I drew closer and closer, a sudden gust of wind sent a flurry of fresh petals dancing and fluttering through the amber evening skies. For one fleeting moment, the park was draped in a soft pink veil, and the rich scent of cherry blossoms filled my nostrils. It was like several years' worth of spring scenery, all condensed and refined into a single instant.

Man, I had no idea this place was even here. Talk about a hidden gem... Hm?

I stood there, marveling at the splendor of it all, and as I did, I caught a glimpse of a small wooden structure hidden on the other side of the tree. Circling around to get a better look revealed that it was an old miniature shrine, so small that the tip of its roof only rose about a meter off the ground. On its front face were a small set of double lattice doors, one of which was hanging open. Curious, I crouched down to take a peek inside, but all that lay within it was a single rock that was about the size of a rugby ball. A deep fissure ran right down the center of it. I could only assume this was some sort of sacred relic: a stone thought to hold spiritual power, or at least religious significance to whoever built this tiny shrine to house it. For whatever reason, I felt weirdly entranced by the little rock. I reached out a hand to feel the texture of the thin, dark crevice in the middle of it.

Just then, an unexpected burst of sound came blaring into my ears, and my heart nearly jumped out of my chest. Even after reflexively pulling my hand back, it still took me a few moments to calm down enough to realize what it had been. A melody muffled in static. *Greensleeves.* It was the six o'clock chime that played out over the island's emergency loudspeakers every evening. Still, I was surprised by how close it sounded, so I straightened up and took a look around. It didn't take me long to find the source of the siren: one of the aforementioned loudspeakers was perched atop a telephone pole in a corner of the park. No wonder it was so deafeningly loud.

I always hated this melancholic melody when I was growing up on the island, and I still hated it now. I didn't like how effortlessly it could pull at my heartstrings and put me in a bittersweet mood, even when I had nothing to feel sad about or to yearn for.

The mystery solved, I crouched back down and reached my hand out to touch the stone inside the shrine once more. The blaring loudspeaker had definitely shaken me up, but not to the extent that I lost interest in the strange rock altogether. As the loud melody continued to blare through my ears, I slowly brought my hand closer and closer...until eventually, my fingertips landed on the jagged crevice. The moment they did, something electric shot through my body like a static shock, and my consciousness shut off in a single blip—like my mind was a TV and someone had abruptly pulled the plug.

INTERLUDE I

THINKING BACK ON IT, I realized that Kanae and I had been friends for more than ten years now. I couldn't remember when our first interaction was, exactly. I guess our friendship had a lot to do with the fact that my last name (Hoshina) came right after his (Funami) alphabetically, so we'd often get grouped together and placed next to each other on the class seating chart. So naturally, we grew more comfortable talking to one another over time. It also probably helped that since there were so few kids in our school, we pretty much stayed together with the exact same class all throughout elementary school and junior high.

I always loved hearing what Kanae had to say. Because he lived in Tokyo before he moved to Sodeshima, he knew all sorts of things I didn't and would tell these crazy stories that always sounded unbelievable to younger me—like about how everyone in the city power walks everywhere all the time, or how in Tokyo, there's a mini-mart on every street corner. I was spellbound whenever he talked about it, hanging on his every word, never wanting to miss even a single unimportant detail.

Still, my initial impression of him was that he was some regular, smart kid who also happened to be a very good storyteller. It wasn't until second grade that my perception of him began to change. At the time, I was kind of an introverted kid, and a grumpy pessimist, to boot. I haven't really changed on either front, mind you, but back then I had virtually no social skills to speak of—which was probably why things ended up playing out the way they did.

It was lunchtime, and I'd finished eating my food. I was flipping to the correct page in my schoolbook when one of the boys in class came up to me and shoved his finger right in my face. I could still remember his exact words:

"Hey, you. How come your skin looks so dirty all the time?"

I couldn't say a single word. My biggest insecurity back then was my naturally darker skin, and how I didn't look like the other girls. I sat there, unable to *try* to think of a comeback. I must have been in shock, to be completely honest. The boy noticed this, which only emboldened him further, so he proceeded to deal the finishing blow:

"I mean, when was the last time you took a bath? Never?"

I felt my face go red hot. To make matters worse, the boy said it in a loud enough voice that it echoed through the classroom, and now everyone around was looking straight at me. I could hear snickering coming from various directions, broken up by whispers like "Ew, gross," and "Dare you to go sniff her." I did remember hearing one girl telling people to knock it off, but the majority of kids had already made their choice to take shots at me. Meanwhile,

I was so frustrated and mortified that all I could do was sit there, biting my lip and looking down at my feet. No matter how hard I tried to stay strong, I couldn't block out their cruel words, and eventually tears began to well up in my eyes. Right as the dam was about to burst, I felt someone grab me brusquely by the arm.

"C'mon, let's go," they said.

I was in disbelief—it was Kanae. At the time, I never would have expected him to jump to my defense like that.

"I said, come on!" he implored again.

There was a hint of anger in his face and voice that made me quick to obey. He dragged me out of the classroom the second I was on my feet, and paid no mind to the jeers from our fellow classmates as he pulled me down the hall at a brisk pace. I could still remember the feeling of his hand gripping my wrist as he led me down the outdoor staircase—firm to the point of being painful. It wasn't until we reached the landing that we came to a stop, and he finally let go of my arm.

"Okay, I can't hear them following us anymore," he said matter-of-factly.

The very next instant, I gave in and broke down, and all the tears I'd been holding back came cascading down my cheeks like a waterfall. Kanae was visibly confused and panicked by this, stumbling over his words as he tried to ask me why I was crying. Between sniffles and sobs, I told him exactly how I felt:

"I hate my stupid body. I *hate* it."

"Aw, c'mon. Who cares what those idiots say? They're trying to mess with you, that's all."

"But now everyone thinks I'm gross and I stink!"

"Trust me: you're not gross, and you *definitely* don't stink."

"You're just saying that! Don't lie!" I said, raising my voice so high that Kanae recoiled a bit. He didn't even let that deter him, though. He shook his head and tried to reassure me.

"I'm not lying..."

"Yes you are! You probably think my skin's dirty too, don't you?! You think I'm some...some nasty girl who doesn't know how to take a bath!"

With that, I plopped myself down on the ground with my head between my knees, covering my face with both hands. As the tears came streaming out, an intense wave of regret washed over me. I was rational enough even then to tell Kanae wasn't lying, and yet I still lashed out at him, and why? Because I couldn't fathom why he was being so nice to a misfit like me. That confusion meant I couldn't accept his kindness as genuine. The more I thought about it, the more guilty I felt. I should never have taken my anger out on the one person who went out of his way to rescue me from that situation, no matter my logic. So I cried and I cried, until I could cry no more, and the guilt gave way to self-loathing. But then, when I lifted my head again, I saw that Kanae was still standing there in front of me. His gaze met mine. I could see the genuine concern for me in his eyes.

"A-are you okay, Akari?"

"...Yeah."

"Look, I'm not good at this stuff, but...cheer up, okay?"

"...Okay."

All I could muster were one-word, noncommittal responses. Kanae clearly was not satisfied with this, because he continued to stutter and fumble his words as he tried desperately, albeit in vain, to make me feel better. Eventually, after a moment of silence, his face lit up as though he'd hit on a brilliant idea.

"Hey, Akari. Give me your hand for a sec," he said confidently.

"Huh...?"

I had no idea what he had in mind, but I held out my right hand regardless as instructed. He proceeded to grab it and, after a hesitant pause, crammed my fingers straight into his mouth.

"Eek?!" I gasped, yanking my hand back in surprise. At first, I was utterly dumbfounded as to why on earth Kanae would ever do such a thing, but then he looked me straight in the eye to say something that would stay with me for the rest of my life.

"See? You're not dirty at all," he proclaimed with confidence. Then, in a slightly more bashful tone, he added: "...I mean, *I* sure couldn't taste any dirt, at least."

My jaw dropped. There was a long pause—and then I started laughing hysterically. Kanae looked down at me like I was a crazy person, but I couldn't help myself. I mean, I'd heard people describe things like linoleum floors as "so clean you could eat off of them," but to *actually* put someone else's hand in your mouth, just to prove it wasn't dirty?! It was so absurd, I couldn't take it! I laughed so hard that tears were coming out of my eyes again—so hard that my stomach started to hurt, and I completely forgot why I felt sad in the first place. The next thing I knew, I was in love.

CHAPTER 2

April 5th, 6 p.m.

WHEN I SNAPPED BACK to my senses, the first thing that registered in my brain was the somber melody of the six o'clock chime flowing into my eardrums. Then, as soon as the long-hanging final note of *Greensleeves* fell silent, all the turmoil and confusion came rushing back into my mind like a shot of adrenaline.

What the hell just happened to me?

I'd never passed out before in my life, but these symptoms sure seemed to fit the bill—all my thought processes came to an abrupt halt without a hint of prior warning, and then the next thing I knew I was someplace completely different, scrambling to figure out how I got there. To be more specific, I was no longer standing beneath the big cherry blossom tree at the abandoned park—I was down by the coast again, sitting on the seawall with my back to the ocean. Right in front of me stood the island's resident patrol officer, holding his bike at his side as he looked down at me with concern.

"Hey, you all right, kid?" he inquired. "C'mon, say something."

"...Officer?" I mumbled drowsily.

"Uh, y-yeah? I'm still here, pal... Didn't go anywhere," he joked, but with an awkward laugh that said he was as confused as I was. Not that there was anything strange about him stopping to talk to me, of course. I was still floundering to figure out how I got here and how long he'd been standing here in front of me.

"So, uh... Is there something I can help you with?" I asked, trying to be nonchalant.

"Whaddya mean? Thought we were makin' small talk."

"We were...? For how long?"

"...You sure you're all right, kid? We've been chatting it up for, like, the past five minutes. Did you have a stroke or something?"

Five minutes? I definitely wasn't sitting here talking to him for that long... At least, not that I could remember. I took another look around to confirm what I already knew: this was *not* the last place I remembered being. This was the Sodeshima seawall, not the abandoned park with the cherry blossom trees. Weirdly enough, the sky was still the same deep orange it had been when I last looked up at it—so I couldn't have been out for *that* long. I fumbled around for my cell phone, wanting to check the time, but it wasn't in my right-side pocket like it was supposed to be. Panicking, I tried to remember if I'd simply forgotten it at home but then belatedly realized that I was already holding it in my left hand. Relieved, I was about to press the button to make the screen turn on when another question took hold of my mind: If I was passed out, how could I have pulled my cell phone out of my pocket?

And that wasn't the only thing that didn't add up—the clothes I was wearing now were totally different from the ones I'd been wearing earlier. I specifically remembered sliding my hoodie on this morning, but now here I was wearing a regular crewneck sweatshirt. One that definitely *did* belong to me, for the record, but I had no memory at all of changing into it. Or was it possible that I'd somehow been wearing the crewneck the whole time and simply mistaken it for my favorite hoodie this morning? Surely not. They weren't even the same color.

"Hey, c'mon, kid! Don't clam up on me again," the officer said, calling me out for getting distracted. I quickly shot my head up to look back at him.

"Sorry, officer. I'm a bit confused, I guess. About what time it is, and the clothes I'm wearing... Stuff like that."

"If you say so... Well, I can't help you with your wardrobe, but you should know what time it is, at least. Think about it: Didn't you hear the six o'clock chime go off?"

"Huh? Oh, riiight... Yeah, okay. Must have slipped my mind..."

That only raised more questions in my head, but I decided to leave it at that and shove my cell phone back into my pants pocket so as not to seem like I didn't believe him. And to give the guy some credit, I *had* heard the six o'clock chime while I was sitting here—but I'd also heard it back at the abandoned park. Which shouldn't have been possible, unless I was somehow magically teleported here in the blink of an eye... No, even then, the officer claimed I'd been sitting here talking to him since at least 5:55. So what the hell was going on? No matter how hard

I racked my brain, I couldn't come up with any sensible explanation for it.

"Look, kid," the officer began, "if you aren't feeling too hot, I'd be happy to give you a ride home. Or take you over to the clinic to get checked out, if you'd prefer."

"No, no—you don't have to do that... I can walk myself home. Thanks, though."

"You sure? Well, okay... Look, I know it's been a rough few days, but try not to overthink things, all right? It wasn't your fault, and you did everything you could. Anyway, I've gotta get going, but I'll see you around."

"Wait, *huh*...?" I stammered as he straddled his bike and put one foot up on the pedals.

"Oh, and one more thing," he added, looking back over his shoulder at me. "No more late-night rendezvous for a while, yeah? I know you're young, but you've gotta dial it back."

And with that, he pedaled off. I sat there for a good, long while trying to figure out what he meant by "late-night rendezvous," and how it had been a "rough few days," but I honestly had no idea what he could be referring to. Still, it seemed like he was genuinely concerned about me, so I must have *really* looked like I was at the end of my rope. Which wasn't that far from the truth, in honesty—I hadn't felt this confused and gaslit in a very long time. The struggle to wrap my head around it was starting to make my vision blur. It felt like I was being made the victim of a cruel joke.

That thought gave me pause. What if it really was some prank? Today was April Fools' Day, after all. Maybe someone predicted that I'd finally be coming back this spring break and got the whole island in on some super elaborate plan to make me feel like a crazy person... No, there was no way. I shook that ridiculous conspiracy theory from my mind. I needed to stop overthinking this—it was making my brain hurt. Plus, it was getting dark out. It was about time I made my way home.

By the time I made it back to the house, the sun had completely dipped beneath the horizon, and there was no longer much light outside at all. When I opened the front door, Eri came out from the living room in her school uniform, and we made eye contact. It wasn't until that moment that I remembered she and I got into a fight earlier, and my stomach dropped. I wasn't sure if I should play it off like nothing had happened or be the bigger person and open with an apology. But in the end, she broke the ice before I could even make up my mind.

"You're home pretty late. C'mon, hurry up and get inside," she urged.

"S-sure, one sec," I replied.

She was acting perfectly normal; I couldn't hear any hint of anger in her voice. I always thought she was the type to never let a grudge go, but maybe I hadn't given her enough credit. I still needed to apologize, though; it seemed like the right thing to do, especially since I was the older sibling. I slid off my shoes and stepped up into the hallway, stopping Eri as she made her way toward the bathroom.

"Hey, uh... Eri?"

"Yeah? What is it?"

"Listen, I'm sorry for all that stuff I said before. That was really immature of me."

"Huh? What are you even talking about?"

"You know. We got into that argument, and then I basically stormed out of the house...?"

She squinted her eyes and looked at me dubiously for a moment, then let out a soft "Ohhhh," as if I'd refreshed her memory on some irrelevant factoid she'd long since purged from her mind.

"Yeah, don't worry about that," she said. "I'm over it. Besides, I said some stuff I probably shouldn't have too."

I was extremely taken aback by this response. This was the same girl who would never dream of apologizing, or even back down the slightest inch, no matter how mad you got at her. This, more than anything else, drove home for me how much she'd grown in the past two years. As I silently admired her newfound maturity, Eri was seemingly getting impatient for some reason and changed the subject.

"So, hey... Shouldn't you be getting ready?" she asked.

"Oh, right, yeah. Sorry, I'll get right on that... Er, ready for what, exactly?"

"...Wait. You didn't forget the wake is tonight, did you?"

"Wake? What wake? Did someone die?"

As soon as these words left my lips, she squinted at me yet again. Only this time, it wasn't a look of confusion but one of reproach.

"*Kanae.* You're kidding me, right?"

I decided to take her disrespectful tone on the chin this time and answer as honestly as I could.

"No, I seriously don't have any idea... It wasn't anyone close to me, was it?" I asked.

Eri hesitated a moment, then answered in a fragile, soft voice:

"...It was Akito. Akito Hoshina. How could you even forget that?"

It took my brain a solid few seconds to connect the dots between the name "Akito" and the word "dead." Once it did, my mind went straight into denial mode.

"Wh-whoa, whoa, whoa. Hold on. Are you pulling my leg? I saw him down at the ferry dock earlier today."

"*Huh?*"

"Wait, I see what's going on here. This is all just one big April Fools' joke, isn't it? Very funny, you guys. But it's really not cool to lie about people dying, y'know. Feel free to give it a rest now."

"...Kanae, what are you *talking* about?"

Her expression was graver than I'd ever seen it before. She was looking at me as though she genuinely thought I'd suffered some sort of brain damage. The next thing she said almost made *me* start to consider that as an option, myself:

"It's not April Fools' Day anymore, Kanae—it's the 5th. Akito died *four days ago.* I dunno if you're in denial or what, but you need to snap out of it. Now could you please move? I need to fix up my hair."

Eri gave me a side-eyed glance as she squeezed past me into the bathroom. I stood stock-still in the middle of the hall, unsure what to believe anymore.

Was Akito really dead? And not only that, he'd *been* dead for four days...? If that were the case, then who did I see down at the harbor when I got here this afternoon? A look-alike? Or his ghost? *As if.* Then I remembered something else Eri had said— that today was actually April 5th. Now, I knew I was on spring break, and thus could afford to lose track of the date a little bit, but there was no way I could be four whole days off. I pulled my cell phone out of my pocket in the hopes of vindicating myself, pressed a button, and the screen lit up. My phone's screen announced that it was indeed April 5th, exactly as Eri had said.

"...No way."

I ran into the living room, checking everything I could find that might display today's date—the TV, the newspaper, the electric table clock—but each and every one of them said the same thing: April 5th. Yet I still refused to believe it. Something definitely wasn't right here. This was going way too far, even for a very elaborate prank. I left the living room and went looking for my grandmother. I opened the sliding door to the Japanese-style sitting room, where I found her rummaging through some drawers.

"Hey, Grandma? Could I ask you something?"

"Oh, Kanae!" she exclaimed, turning around to face me. "I didn't know you'd come home. Good timing too. I was thinking that for the wake, you could wear—"

APRIL 5TH, 6 P.M.

"Grandma, what day is today?" I asked, cutting her off.

"Goodness. Where's this coming from?"

"Just tell me, please."

"Well, let's see... It's Thursday, so I suppose that'd make it the 5th."

"And that's the truth? You're one hundred percent sure of this?"

"Assuming I haven't gone senile yet! But yes, I'm sure. I can swear it on your late granddad's grave, if that'll convince you."

Okay. I knew my grandmother would never lie on her dead husband's name, so I guess that meant it really *was* April 5th, without a doubt. I couldn't find any hard evidence to the contrary, and both my sister and grandmother seemed pretty adamant about it. Maybe I really *was* the crazy one here.

"Man, what the hell is happening to me...?" I whispered.

It felt like the whole world was collapsing in on me. *First I pass out and wake up somewhere completely different, then I find out Akito's dead, and then they tell me I've got the date wrong by several days...?* This was starting to feel less like an elaborate prank and more like a nonsensical nightmare. While I stood there, clutching my head in my hands, my grandmother pulled a set of black clothes out of the drawer and held them out to me.

"Here, you should change into these."

My grandmother explained to me that proper funeral attire for kids my age was to simply wear our normal school uniforms. I, however, had run away from home, so I didn't have my own uniform with me. She graciously offered me my dad's old uniform

WAIT FOR ME YESTERDAY IN SPRING

from his days at Sodeshima High to wear instead. It was a traditional all-black affair with a stand-up collar, and it happened to
fit me perfectly, much to my chagrin. Once we were all changed
and ready, my grandmother, Eri, and I started walking over to the
Sodeshima Community Center where the wake was being held.
The chilly night air was the perfect temperature to cool off my
overheated brain, and the travel time gave me a chance to try to
put some of my disparate thoughts in order.

I did some logical deduction while we walked and eventually
managed to convince myself of two objective facts. Number one:
today was not April 1st but April 5th. That was what all the evidence pointed to, including two separate testimonies, so I had
no choice but to accept it as true. Number two: I had absolutely
no memory of the four-day period from 6 p.m. on April 1st to
6 p.m. on April 5th. Or in terms of actual events, there was a
huge gap in my memories between me touching that rock at the
shrine in the abandoned park and sitting on the seawall talking
to the island patrolman earlier. The only reason I knew both
events happened at almost exactly 6 p.m. was because in both
instances, I could hear the island's six o'clock chime ringing out
in the background.

This meant that there was a ninety-six-hour period for which
my memory was completely blank. The first, and perhaps most
rational, explanation I could come up with was that I'd suffered
some sort of brain injury or neural malfunction. An amnesic
episode, or a case of early-onset dementia. Granted, I didn't
know how rare it was for kids my age to come down with the

latter, but the former was extremely possible—it happened to kids who got concussions all the time. I'd read so many books with amnesic protagonists that I considered it a bit of a boring plot device, but now that I was faced with the possibility of it happening to me in real life? It was *damn* scary. The thought of having potentially serious brain damage at such a young age was not an appealing one.

The only other explanation I could think of was that it was somehow related to that stone in the little forgotten shrine, only because it legitimately felt like my mind and body were warped to a different place and time the moment I laid my fingers on it. Perhaps by simply touching the rock, I'd angered whatever god or spirit was enshrined therein and fallen under some sort of curse. It sounded pretty ridiculous, which may have been why I preferred it to the possibility of major brain damage. Regardless of what caused my memory loss, though, I needed to find out what happened in that four-day interim—and the best way to do that was to ask around. I jogged ahead a little bit to catch up with my sister and matched her pace.

"Hey, Eri, can I ask you something?"

"...What do you want?"

"So I know this is gonna sound like a weird question, but have I been spending a lot of time at home lately?"

"Huh?" she balked. "What kind of question is that? You'd know better than me."

"No, no, I know. I, uh, wanted to know if *you* felt like I was spending enough time at home or not. If that makes sense."

WAIT FOR ME YESTERDAY IN SPRING

She looked at me suspiciously, clearly not buying this explanation at all. I myself was fully aware that it sounded like a pretty flimsy pretext, but I didn't want to come right out and admit that there was a four-day gap in my memory and risk her potentially forcing me to go see a doctor. For now, all I could do was chain one lame excuse into the next. Eventually, Eri answered, though not before turning face forward again and breaking eye contact.

"You've actually been going out a lot the past few days. One or two nights, you didn't even come home. Or at least, not until after I was already asleep..."

This was valuable information. The fact that she noted I was gone "one or two nights" told me that I *had* spent at least half of the nights in my own bed, so it wasn't as if I was leading a totally different lifestyle. That still left a few unanswered questions, so I needed more information.

"Do you know where I've been going?" I pressed further. "Or if I was staying somewhere else on those one or two nights I didn't come home?"

"...Is there something in the water over there in Tokyo? Some sort of brain-eating bacteria or something?"

"Huh? What the hell's that supposed to mean?"

"I'm saying you've been acting weird ever since you got here," Eri said, turning to look me straight in the eye once more. "Normal people don't ask questions like that. No joke, I really think you should go to the hospital."

"Oh, come on. Now you're overexaggerating..."

"No, I'm not. Something is *definitely* wrong with you. It's *obvious*, Kanae."

I averted my eyes from her piercing stare, fumbling for some sort of excuse. This was exactly what I was hoping to avoid—but now that she was already suspicious, maybe I should come clean and tell her the whole truth: that I'd skipped ahead four days in time. The problem was that if I did that, there was a very real chance she'd drag me to the hospital, or tell someone that could, and I didn't want to make my grandmother worry...as much as maybe I really *did* need to go get checked out.

"Quiet, you two," my grandmother cut in. "We're almost there. Be respectful."

Phew. Saved by the bell, I thought to myself as we approached the community center where the wake was being held. It was a fairly large open building, about the size of a small gymnasium. A line of adults in mourning attire had formed in the building's usually vacant courtyard. I could tell that Eri still had plenty more she wanted to say to me, but she obediently let it go the moment we got in line.

After signing the guestbook, we headed inside. Once we entered the spacious main hall, I spotted Akari wearing her Sodeshima High uniform out of the corner of my eye. I knew that she went to high school there, obviously, but this was the first time I'd actually seen her in her uniform. She looked much more ladylike and refined compared to when I saw her down on the seawall. I thought about going over and saying hi, but she was talking to a group of adults dressed all in black; it really didn't seem like the right time. I sat down next to Eri and my grandmother in one of the many rows of metal folding chairs, then looked up at the altar. Seeing Akito's face up there in the picture frame drove the harsh reality of his death home for me in a way I hadn't yet fully come to grips with. This was my childhood hero, after all—he even came rushing to my rescue, once upon a time.

I was in the third grade, getting picked on by a group of delinquent junior high schoolers. I was scared and surrounded, when Akito happened to walk by. Despite being younger and smaller than the bullies, he jumped fearlessly to my defense, throwing punches left and right until the older kids ran off like scared rabbits. I could still remember the little exchange I had with him immediately after that:

"Next time, I don't wanna see you standing there shaking in your boots like that," he scolded me. "Pisses me off. You know you didn't do anything wrong, and so do they, so don't you dare let 'em get to you. Keep your head held high."

"What if that makes them angrier, and they start hitting me...?" I replied.

"Then you just grab a big ol' rock, chuck it right at their heads, and run like hell."

At the time, I couldn't believe the audacity of what he was suggesting, but as time went on, those words became something of a personal mantra for me. Whenever I felt uneasy or afraid, I'd tell myself that if it really came down to it, I could always throw rocks at their heads and run like hell. It was oddly reassuring to me. Obviously, I knew it wasn't really commendable advice, nor had I ever actually resorted to that, but it still gave a scrawny little kid like me the confidence he needed in order to not be afraid of other people. I didn't know how Akito felt about me or if he even remembered that little interaction...but I still felt his loss pretty deeply and wished he were still here with us.

After the incense lighting and sutra chanting was all said and done, Akito's mother took a stand before the altar to say a few words to the congregation. Even from afar, I could see that her face was haggard and emaciated. Her hair had lost its luster; her eyes looked somewhat vacant. She looked as though she might collapse at any moment, but Akari stood by her side to offer support while she gave her remarks. The ceremony was officially over after she finished her speech, so we all stood up from our seats and began filing back out toward the entrance hall. Apparently, the immediate family had prepared small thank-you gifts for attendees, so the three of us got in line and slowly advanced toward the reception desk. We were waiting for our turn to come when I overheard the two people who got in line directly behind us having a fairly blunt exchange.

"Looks like they're not gonna feed us, huh? No refreshments or anything..."

"I mean, what did you expect? That poor woman's got enough on her plate right now, especially as the lone breadwinner in the family. Anyway, did you hear what the cause of death was?"

"Yeah, acute alcohol poisoning, right? Heard they got the autopsy back yesterday..."

Alcohol poisoning, huh. In other words, he drank too much. Though actually, I remembered learning in health class that in most cases, it wasn't actually the alcohol in the victim's bloodstream that killed them. It was choking on their own vomit. I didn't even want to consider that in further detail; the image of Sodeshima's star athlete spending his final moments like that was too much to bear.

As the line moved forward, it eventually came to be our turn. Akari and her mother were handing out the thank-you gifts personally, so we gave them our condolences, and then I politely accepted the small gift bag from Akari.

"Wow, look at you," she whispered softly, scanning me up and down as she handed over the little paper bag. "Wait, where'd you get a Sodeshima High uniform...?"

"What, this? It's my dad's old one. Can't wait to get home and take it off, honestly. It's super tight around the neck."

"Ohhh, gotcha. Looks good on you, though... Really."

As she emphasized that last word, her eyes suddenly began to water. I wasn't sure if I was reminding her of Akito in *his* uniform or what—but I scrambled to pull out my handkerchief and offer it to her. It was a good thing my grandmother had convinced me to bring one along.

"Listen, uh... I know we haven't really talked for a couple of years, but if you need someone to talk to, you know I'm here for you," I said, cringing internally at how canned and predictable my words must have come across. Akari seemed to take it as a genuine offer of solace, as she gave a weak little nod while dabbing the corners of her eyes with the handkerchief.

There were still other people waiting in line behind us, so we said our goodbyes and made our way out of the building. Outside, the night sky was crystal clear, and the air was cold enough that it felt like winter still hadn't left us completely. My grandmother suggested that we start heading home, and so the three of us quickly got to walking. We'd hardly even made it a block from the facility when I heard footsteps running up on us from behind. I turned around—it was Akari.

"Hey, what's up?" I asked. "Oh, you don't have to give me back the handkerchief right now, it's okay."

"No, it's not that," she said, catching her breath. "Listen, um... There's something I need to tell you, Kanae-kun."

"There is?"

"Yeah. About what's been happening with you the last four days... Or what's *going* to happen, I guess I should say."

At first, I didn't have the slightest clue what she was trying to tell me. A moment later, the implications of her knowing something about "the last four days" hit me like a truck. I practically pounced on her, placing my hands on her shoulders.

"Wait, you know what's going on?!" I demanded.

She squealed in surprise, but I paid it no mind. It wasn't until I felt her shoulders trembling that I realized how wildly inappropriate it was for me to grab her like that. Immediately regretting my actions, I tore my hands away.

"Oh, s-sorry. I don't know what came over me. I just...don't know what's going on, and..." I tried to explain.

"No, it's okay... I get it. I can't explain everything to you right here and now, so..." she trailed off, then brought her lips in close to whisper in my ear: "Meet me in the old abandoned park tomorrow at five in the afternoon. I'll tell you everything you want to know."

She pulled her head back, said a quick "Okay, see you tomorrow," then turned around and started trotting back over toward the community center. I watched her round the corner, already sensing Eri's suspicious glare burning a hole in the back of my head.

"What was *that* about?" she demanded, right on cue.

"...Couldn't tell you even if I wanted to," I replied. Hey, it was the truth. Under my breath, I added: "Hopefully I'll find out tomorrow."

When I awoke the next morning, the first thing I saw was my cell phone lying next to my head. I snatched it up and checked the date and time. It was April 6th, at 8 a.m. I buried my face in my pillow. Time hadn't magically returned to normal overnight. It was starting to seem like this really wasn't a dream, much to my dismay.

After we made it home from the wake last night, I quickly took care of my nightly routine, then holed up in my bedroom. I didn't try to get any more information from Eri or my grandmother about the last four days; I didn't want to raise any red flags, but my main reason was that I had a glimmer of hope to cling on to at last, thanks to Akari.

"I'll tell you everything you want to know."

If she could shed some light on this bizarre and terrifying phenomenon that was happening to me, I'd be forever in her debt. That said, I had no idea how on earth she could know about the four-day gap in my memories, since I hadn't told anyone about it—and that wasn't the only mystery, either. There were several other gigantic question marks, like why she told me to meet her at the old, abandoned park—a place that I didn't even know existed until I stumbled upon it *after* the last time I talked to her on April 1st. It was possible she'd discovered it on her own, of course, but then, how could she be so confident that *I* would know where it was?

Things weren't adding up, and it was starting to give me a headache. Given that I'd been working my brain virtually non-stop since yesterday, though, that wasn't a surprise. Perhaps the brain could get strained or pulled from overuse, like any other muscle? It was as good a reason as any to go back to sleep for a while, so my brain could get some much-needed rest.

I awoke again sometime around noon and ate a light lunch with my grandmother. She told me that Eri had gone off to the mainland with a friend for the day, which came as a bit of a relief. She'd been blatantly suspicious of me ever since last night, and I didn't want to get trapped in another interrogation scenario with her. I did recognize, though, that all her prying was because she was concerned about me. I was the one who gave her cause to worry in the first place.

When we finished eating, my grandmother asked if I could help her with something.

"I've been meaning to reorganize the attic," she explained, "but there's so much clutter and so many heavy boxes that I've been putting it off. A strong young man like you would be just the helper I need."

I still had plenty of time before I was supposed to meet up with Akari, so I agreed to help. I used the little ladder we had in storage to climb up into the attic. Thanks to the illumination provided by a single undressed light bulb, I saw that there were a bunch of cardboard boxes strewn around the musty storage space, and each one looked pretty darn heavy. I began hauling down the individual boxes my grandmother requested one by one. It didn't take long before I was sweating like a pig; after a while I even accidentally knocked an entire box over and spilled its contents out all over the attic floor. It had been filled with textbooks and other reference materials.

"Must've been Dad's," I said to myself when I saw that they were all IT-related. My father worked as a programmer in Tokyo, and based on the amount of margin notes he'd taken, I assumed they were probably from his college days. I picked up a composition notebook at my feet and leafed through it. Each and every page was packed from top to bottom with methodical yet hastily scribbled notes in his trademark angular handwriting. Attempting to read it hurt my eyes. I was about to close the notebook and put it back in the box, when a single word circled in red pen caught my eye. It appeared to be a technical computing term, for which he'd written the definition underneath.

ROLLBACK

The process of restoring a database or program back to a previously defined state, usually in response to some sort of critical error. Helpful for salvaging data and preferences that have been lost or corrupted due to user mistakes or system failure.

"Rollback, huh..." I said, letting the word linger on my lips for a while. It had a pretty cool ring to it—though unless I decided to go into IT, I had a hunch that I'd never get a real chance to use it. I closed the notebook and put it back in the box.

By the time I was running through the abandoned part of town, I only had a handful of minutes before five o'clock. Helping my grandmother reorganize had taken way longer than I anticipated, and now I was at risk of being late to my meetup with Akari. I ran as fast as I could through the mazelike district, occasionally tripping on potholes and uneven ground. The exit to the narrow alleyway came into view shortly after 5 p.m. Finally slowing my pace to a jog, I tried to catch my breath as I entered the park perimeter.

Standing there beneath the cherry blossom tree was a young girl in a Sodeshima High uniform, squinting her eyes as she looked up at the rain of falling petals fluttering to the ground—almost like she was showering in them. I knew at once that she was Akari Hoshina, the girl I'd promised to meet here, and yet I couldn't bring myself to call out to her. It was such a breathtaking sight that I forgot my purpose altogether, only able to stand there captivated by its beauty. So when Akari noticed my presence at last, and we made eye contact, I floundered.

"Hey! How long have you been standing there?! Let me know you're here, why don'tcha!" she said, laughing awkwardly.

"Y-yeah, sorry about that. I was just having fun looking at—"

I barely stopped myself before saying the word "you." No way could I pull off a cheesy one-liner like that without sounding like a creep.

"Sorry, what was that? You were having fun looking at what, now?" she asked, urging me to finish my thought as she cocked her head in a cutesy, teasing manner. I had to come up with some sort of way to salvage this, and fast. *I was looking at, uh... Uh...*

"Oh, no, I...I was having fun looking at old photo albums with my grandma and lost track of the time. Hence why I'm a little late... Sorry."

Congratulations, Kanae. That was the lamest save in the history of mankind.

"...Oh. Gotcha. Nah, don't worry about it. I mean, you're only a couple of minutes late, if that," Akari said with a warm smile—yet I could hear the slightest hint of disappointment in her voice. Maybe she'd actually been *hoping* that I would say I was having fun looking at her...? *Pfft, yeah right. I've gotta be overthinking it.*

Akari suggested that we sit down, so I took a seat up against the trunk of the tree. Holding her skirt taut, Akari sat down right beside me, close enough that our knees were practically touching. I was getting a little flustered by now. Needing to regain my composure, and fast, I cleared my throat and got right down to brass tacks.

"So, last night you were saying you could tell me everything I want to know? You wanna elaborate on that?" I asked.

"Yeah, so basically, like... Ugh, where do I even begin? Maybe it would be easier if you asked *me* some questions first?" she suggested.

"You want *me* to do the asking? A-all right, um..."

I had a million questions I wanted to ask her. Yet now that she was putting me on the spot, I couldn't seem to come up with a single one. I *did* still want to ask her why she chose this park as our meetup spot, and about the past four days in general, but what other questions did I have for her? *Let's see, um...*

"How come you're wearing your uniform again today?"

"Ahaha... Seriously? *That's* the most pressing question on your mind right now? Gosh, you must really love these things, huh?" she teased, popping the collar of her jacket to show it off.

"N-no, stupid. I, er, y'know...wanted to get the easy questions out of the way first..."

This girl was really throwing me for a loop today, and I knew exactly why. It was her mannerisms—they were all so much more

WAIT FOR ME YESTERDAY IN SPRING

feminine, and far flirtier than I was used to her being. It was like every little thing she did tugged at my heartstrings in one way or another. Akari flashed an amused smile, then casually offered a real answer to my question.

"I'm wearing it again today because I just got back from the funeral. And unlike the wake last night, we actually had to go over to the mainland for this one. I didn't really have time to get changed after we got back to the house, so I came here in the same clothes."

"Ah. Makes sense..."

If I'd been in a more rational state of mind, I could have guessed that. It was pretty normal to have the memorial service the day after the wake. I rebuked myself internally for not think-ing twice before asking stupid questions and then moved on to the next one on my docket.

"Okay, that explains that. Moving on, then: Why did you think that I would know about this park?"

"Well, because you were the one who showed it to me in the first place."

"What? When was this? I don't remember that at all."

"Yeah, of course you don't. Because for you, it hasn't happened yet. But it will."

"...What's that supposed to mean?" I asked, totally unable to see what she was getting at. Her face turned deathly serious.

"You've heard the phrase 'quantum leap' before, right?"

Now *this* took me by surprise. She'd dropped a bit of termi-nology straight out of one of my favorite sci-fi novels.

"Yeah, it's like...a form of time travel, right?"

"Right."

"Okay. So...what about it?"

Akari looked me straight in the eye and told me point-blank:

"That's what's happening to you, Kanae-kun. You've leapt through time."

"...Huh?"

I couldn't wrap my head around it at first. Not that anyone in my position would have been able to hear "Hey, you've just traveled through time" and immediately go "Oh, *that* explains it!" However, I could at least tell that Akari wasn't pulling my leg here. The thought of her dragging me out to a deserted park right after her only brother passed away—for the sake of feeding me a big fat lie—was even more unthinkable than it being true.

"I know, it sounds crazy," she went on. "I totally get that. It was a hard pill for me to swallow too. But right now, I need you to hear me out."

A hard pill for her *to swallow?* Had she been time traveling too? I was getting more and more confused by the minute, but I needed all the information I could get. It wouldn't hurt to at least listen to what she had to say.

"...All right. Let's hear it," I agreed. Her grave expression finally softened a bit.

"Okay, cool. Warning you in advance, though: This is gonna get pretty convoluted. I'll try my best to make it as straight-forward as I can."

"Got it. Thanks."

"All right, so to make sure we're on the same page here, the main thing you want to know right now is why you don't have any recollection of the time period from 6 p.m. on April 1st to 6 p.m. on April 5th, right?"

"Y-yeah, that's exactly it!"

I wanted to ask her how the hell she knew that, but it seemed like she still had plenty more to say, so I mentally shelved my questions for later.

"Well, the reason for that," she explained, "is that your consciousness made a quantum leap between those two points in time. Still with me?"

"My...consciousness? Not my whole body?"

"Correct. This isn't like one of those old cartoons. You didn't accidentally step into a time machine and get physically sent forward or anything like that. Only your mind made the jump...or at least, that's what I was told."

I could feel a migraine coming on. That's what she was "told"? How was I supposed to believe her if she was reciting something secondhand?

"Sorry, who 'told' you this, again?" I asked dubiously.

"Yeah, so like I was saying before... Actually, no. Let's circle back to that later. For now, I should probably try to stay on track and explain things in order."

Something didn't sit right with me about how she seemed to be dancing around certain subjects, but I decided to keep my mouth shut and let her continue.

"So, I explained how you got into your current predicament.

Now I'll explain what's gonna happen to you going forward. This part's really important, so listen carefully," she emphasized, and I nodded. "Okay, so here's how this is gonna play out: You're about to relive the past four days, one by one, in reverse order."

"Um. How does that work?"

"Think of it like this: After every 24 hours, you're going to be sent back in time 48 hours. Kinda like one step forward, two steps back. Oh, and it'll always happen at 6 p.m. on the dot. You'll repeat this process until you've filled in the entire four-day gap in your memories."

"...Sorry, I think you've lost me. This is a lot to keep up with, is all..."

"Yeah, it's pretty hard to explain in words... Here, gimme one sec."

Akari picked up a thin branch from the ground and cleared off a large patch of dirt. Then, using the branch like a writing utensil, she wrote **4/1 (6PM)** and drew a long arrow pointing down from it. At its terminus, she wrote **4/5 (6PM)** and then used the branch to point at the arrow as she explained:

"So let's say this represents the initial quantum leap you made, right? You shot forward from six o'clock on the 1st to six o'clock on the 5th. With me so far?"

"Yeah, and that's why I don't have any memory of the last four days... Go on."

From there, Akari drew an arrow to the right, where she wrote **4/6 (6PM)**, then set the branch down and pulled out her cell phone.

"Okay, so it's April 6th now, and in about thirty minutes, it'll be six o'clock...and from there, you're gonna get sent back to six o'clock on April 4th."

Akari picked the branch back up and drew an arrow diagonally down and to the left, where she wrote **4/4 (6PM)**. According to the diagram, once I reached the end of the 24-hour period from the evening of the 5th to the 6th, I'd be sent back 48 hours to the evening of the 4th. I could see now why Akari had explained it as "one step forward, two steps back." Thanks to the visual aid, it felt like I was finally starting to grasp the bigger picture here.

"And then from there," Akari went on, "you'll have another 24 hours until you make it back to six o'clock on the 5th, at which point..."

"I'll be sent back to six o'clock on the 3rd...?"

"Yeah, exactly. See, you're getting it!"

Akari proceeded to sketch out the rest of the diagram—repeating the one day forward, two days back pattern a few more times—until she'd made it all the way back to six o'clock on April 1st, then finished off with one last horizontal line from **4/1 (6PM)** to **4/2 (6PM)**.

4/1 (6PM)

↓

4/5 (6PM) ⟹ 4/6 (6PM)

4/4 (6PM) ⟹ 4/5 (6PM)

4/3 (6PM) ⟹ 4/4 (6PM)

4/2 (6PM) ⟹ 4/3 (6PM)

4/1 (6PM) ⟹ 4/2 (6PM)

"So, yeah," Akari said, setting the branch back down on the ground. "This is what I meant when I said you'll be reliving the past four days in reverse order. We've been calling it the 'Rollback' phenomenon."

"...Wait. Rollback?"

I had a fairly good grasp of the process at this stage, at least in concept, but the more I heard Akari explain, the harder it became to believe. Every question she answered only raised two or three more in my head.

"So, uh. Obviously, I have a lot of questions," I began. "But I guess for starters: Why six o'clock? No, more importantly, how'd I get wrapped up in this weird 'phenomenon' to begin with?"

"I can't say for sure...but I was told it might've had something to do with you touching the stone inside that shrine. It just so happened to be at six o'clock—there's no special significance to the time, I don't think."

"Oh... Right, the shrine..."

I'd totally forgotten about that, to be honest. I stood up and went to take another peek inside the little shrine on the other side of the big cherry blossom tree. The hefty rock with the crevice in the middle was still there, exactly where I remembered it being. It hadn't moved.

"But I don't get it," I said. "How could touching a stupid rock cause all this supernatural stuff to start happening? I mean, even if it *did* have some sort of 'magical powers,' let's say...this reliving each day in reverse stuff is way too specific. It doesn't add up."

"...Well, this is my own personal theory," Akari said, having walked over to stand beside me, "but do you remember that time in elementary school when they took us on a field trip up to the big shrine on the island to learn more about Sodeshima's history?"

"Oh yeah... I think I do remember that."

It was sometime in fourth or fifth grade. They brought the entire class out to the Sodeshima Shrine and let the resident Shinto priest teach us for the day. I could still vividly remember how cold the wood floors they made us sit on were.

"Okay, so call me crazy, but didn't they mention something about how Buddhist monks used to make pilgrimages out to Sodeshima in the olden days to undergo some sort of trial...?"

"I don't remember that at all, personally, but... Are you saying you think I might have accidentally brought some sort of ancient 'trial' upon myself?"

"I mean, it's no crazier than any other explanation we've come up with, is it...?"

All right, now this is getting ridiculous.

"And what the hell am I being tested on, huh? By who? It doesn't make any sense. For another thing... How do you know all of this, Akari? About the Rollback, and me touching the stone in the shrine... I never told anyone about that, so how could *you* know?"

I could feel my tone getting more and more impatient as the questions kept piling up one after another. In the face of my frustration, Akari simply looked at me—gently, with a hint of genuine sympathy in her eyes—as if *I* were the one in need of condolences here.

"I heard it from you, Kanae-kun," she said.

"From *me*?" I balked.

"That's right. Everything I've told you here today, you explained to me yourself. In a past you haven't experienced yet."

Her words came out measured and slow, as if to make sure each and every syllable hit home. I closed my eyes, pinched the bridge of my nose, and let out a long, lingering sigh.

"Sorry, I need some time to think about all of this..."

After all those exhausting mental gymnastics, I felt like I needed a cigarette—and I'd never smoked before in my life. I tried my best to fully digest everything that Akari had told me. All of it was still hard to swallow, but I would need to take it one bite at a time.

The "Rollback" phenomenon, huh?

I was familiar with the term, of course, since I'd learned it earlier today from one of my dad's old notebooks. It was obviously a computing term, but it felt oddly apt for the concept of being sent backwards to previous points in time. Akari claimed that I was the one that explained all of this to her, which presumably meant that I came up with the name for the phenomenon. There were still a lot of aspects to this that I couldn't completely wrap my head around, but now I finally felt like I'd done enough mental organizing to free up some of my brain's processing power.

"Sorry," I said, "but I've gotta be honest: I'm having a lot of trouble coming to terms with the whole quantum leap idea and you claiming it was me who told you this stuff. On the other hand, I know you'd never lie about something like this, so I'm gonna try my best to take you at your word."

"Thanks. I really appreciate it," she smiled. Her warm expression reassured me.

"...Man, talk about bad timing, though, am I right? The one week I'm back in town, and we get sucked into some otherworldly bullcrap. Not to mention, you must be busy enough as it is, what with your brother's funeral and everyth—"

I trailed off, because at that exact moment, the final piece clicked into place inside my head.

The Rollback phenomenon.

Akito's death.

Think about it, Kanae—if you're already gonna be going back in time, then...

"...Hey, uh, Akari?" I asked. "Remind me, when exactly did Akito pass away?"

"Sometime between midnight and two o'clock in the morning on April 2nd," she said matter-of-factly, as though she'd been anticipating that question. "That's what the autopsy said, at least."

Okay, sometime between 12 a.m. and 2 a.m. on the 2nd. Got it.

Akari claimed I was going to relive everything from 6 p.m. on the 1st through 6 p.m. on the 5th—and Akito's death fell well within that period. Assuming Akari wasn't wrong about any of this, that presented a very interesting possibility.

"Does that mean we could prevent Akito's death from ever happening...?" I asked.

"...Sure does," she replied. Then she looked down at her feet for a moment, scrunching her face up pensively before looking back up to stare directly into my eyes. "Kanae-kun, I...I want you to save my brother."

Her words were so crystal clear in their conviction that they knocked me off guard, and it put me in a bit of an awkward spot. Keep in mind that I was still only half convinced that all this Rollback stuff was even possible... Hell, maybe not even twenty percent convinced. It was hard to jump up right away and say "Sure, I'll save your brother's life for you!" when I still had so many unanswered questions. But then, I couldn't bring myself to say no, either. Whether any of this was true or not, I couldn't leave Akari in the lurch during her time of need. I had to believe in the sincerity I saw in her face.

"...All right. I'll do whatever I can," I said at last. Akari nodded emphatically.

"Okay, so I told you the approximate time of death—between midnight and 2 a.m. on the 2nd. He died of alcohol poisoning, and his body was found in the empty lot behind the old tobacco shop."

There was only one tobacco shop in all of Sodeshima. It was a small, seedy place down a narrow side street, and I knew exactly where it was.

"What was Akito doing there? Do you know?" I asked.

"The police thought he might have been, um, 'relieving himself' in the empty lot. They found some traces in the vicinity that supported that theory, I guess..."

Welp, that must have been an uncomfortable question for her to have to answer. I felt kind of bad for asking. Still, if she was right about all this Rollback stuff, then saving Akito's life shouldn't be very hard at all. All I'd need to do was make sure he didn't drink any alcohol that day. Hey, even if I couldn't do that, I knew exactly where he would be and when. Now that I thought about it, I'd never actually repaid the favor to him for saving me from those bullies back in the day...which made this the perfect opportunity to do so. Right now, I was the only one who could save Akito's life.

"Okay, Kanae-kun. It's almost time," Akari said as she looked down at her phone. I followed suit and checked my own. It was 5:57; if Akari was right, the next Rollback would occur in three short minutes.

"Let's see... So you said I'm gonna be sent back to six o'clock on April 4th next?"

"Yeah. Pretty sure."

"*Pretty* sure?!"

"I dunno what you want me to say, Kanae-kun. I don't have any proof of this stuff. I only know what you've told me yourself, like I said."

"Right... Well, fair enough," I relented. I could tell that hounding her about it wouldn't do either of us any good.

"...I can tell you right now, though, that the Rollbacks *do* occur. Or at least, you've given me more than enough reason to believe they do," Akari said. Her voice was as earnest as could be.

Just then, the wind picked up. A few anxious moments later, it sent a cloud of cherry blossom petals spiraling through the sky like a kaleidoscope of tiny butterflies. The swirling pattern of pastel-pink blossoms shone beautifully against the amber evening skies. There was no doubt about it—these had to be the most gorgeous blossoms on the entire island. I stood there for a while, gazing up at them in a state of zen, until I heard what sounded like sobbing beside me. I turned to look and saw Akari covering her face with her hands, her shoulders quivering. The sound of soft weeping leaked out from between her fingers. It didn't *sound* like she was crying—she *was* crying. And this time, it was plainly evident that these were no pollen allergy tears.

"A-Akari? You all right? Is something wrong?"

"Hic... N-No, I...I j-just..."

"Wh-what's gotten into you all of a sudden...?"

And yet, before I had the chance to learn the reason for her tears, we were interrupted by the six o'clock chime. The sorrowful starting notes of *Greensleeves* announced to us both that the time had come and my anxiety accelerated.

"...Listen, Kanae-kun..." Akari said, practically choking the words out as she lifted her disheveled, tear-drenched face to look unflinchingly into mine. "I trust your judgment. So please... Take care of past me, okay? The rest is up to—"

INTERLUDE II

ALL MY MEMORIES of Kanae from our elementary school days were still vivid in my mind, so vivid that every time I looked back on them, it was like flipping through the pages of a beautifully illustrated children's book. Like, for example, this one interaction we had back in the third grade on our way home from school. It was a cool July afternoon, and we were sitting on the seawall like we always did, whiling away the hours. We would often sit there talking until the sun went down, usually about utterly trivial things: a stray cat someone found near the shrine, a classmate of ours who snuck his handheld game console into class, a book that one of us had borrowed from the library. On that particular day, though, I specifically remembered Kanae gushing to me about something of actual import.

"Hey, so guess what?" he grinned. "A bunch of junior high kids tried to gang up on me the other day, but then your brother came outta nowhere and scared 'em off."

"Whoa, really?"

"Yep. He was so cool, I'm tellin' ya. Can't believe he knows how to fight, *and* he's good at baseball... Wish I could be like him someday."

"You do, huh...?"

I never liked my older brother very much, mainly because he was always picking on me, but even I had to admit that what Kanae claimed he did was pretty cool. In fact, I was genuinely quite proud of him for sticking up for the defenseless like that.

"Man, if only I had something *I* was the best at..." Kanae mused.

"...I think you're fine the way you are, Kanae-kun."

"What, seriously? I feel like I should at *least* find some kind of sport or special talent I can show off to people. But *what*...?" he said, thinking aloud to himself before turning to face me. "You're so lucky, Akari. I mean, you're already a really good swimmer."

"I'm not *that* good at swimming..."

"Sure you are. Heck, didn't you get the fastest time out of our entire class the other day? That takes talent, right? Give yourself a little more credit."

"Yeah, maybe..."

It was true that I was a pretty good swimmer—but I never liked pool days all that much, since they meant showing more of my unconventionally pigmented skin than I had to already. But hearing Kanae speak so highly of my skills made me really happy, and it was at that point that I decided I was going to start taking swimming more seriously.

Summer vacation rolled around, and I opted to sign up for a more advanced swim class that the school pool offered. The lessons were a lot harder than I expected going in, but they made an obvious improvement to my lap times. On the last day of summer vacation, my swim instructor came up to me and suggested I consider enrolling in more formal swimming lessons at a big aquatic center over on the mainland. He was adamant about the amount of potential he saw in me and insisted that I should at least talk to my family about it.

Mind you, I'd always fantasized about being able to take lessons at a huge indoor facility like that. Such a huge pool felt almost mandatory if you wanted enough space to swim your heart out, and I was sure that lying on your back in the middle of a vast pool of crystal-clear water felt sublime. But I'd pretty much given up on the idea, figuring it was impossible given our means. I already knew, even at that young age, that my family's finances were pretty abysmal.

My mother supported my brother and I on her own, ever since my father died in a car crash when I was five. During the day, she worked the register at the supermarket, and at night, she mixed drinks at a local hostess bar. When I was really little, I pretty much convinced myself that my mother was some sort of superhuman that had evolved beyond the need for sleep—*that* was how hard she worked, day in and day out. To this day, I had no idea how or when she snuck in enough time to sleep. Needless to say, I didn't want to put even more stress on my mom's plate, so I opted not to ask her about the whole formal swimming lessons proposition at all—or that *was* the plan, anyway, until my instructor brought it up on parent-teacher conference night.

"I really think your daughter's got talent, ma'am," he said. "I think it'd be a travesty not to enroll her in more formal training."

My mother was a polite person who was quick to cave under pressure, so she immediately agreed to his proposal, and before long, I was enrolled in legit swimming lessons. Could I have still pumped the brakes at this point? Absolutely. All I had to do was say I was getting sick and tired of swimming or that I wasn't comfortable taking the ferry over to the mainland by myself. But I didn't, which says a lot about how much I really cared about not overburdening my mother—as soon as it looked like it might actually happen, I shut up real quick.

To be fair to myself, I worked myself to the bone when my lessons began, training as hard as I possibly could so as not to let the tuition fees and ferry ticket costs go to waste. As a result of this, I became such a good swimmer that by sixth grade I came in first place at the big annual district swim meet. I was honored for this achievement at the next school assembly, and it was at that point that the other kids in my grade started paying a lot more attention to me, with some even wanting to be my friends. Since athletic ability is pretty much the only thing that determines a kid's popularity in elementary school, I soon became the most popular kid in class. No one dared make fun of me for my appearance anymore.

This felt so good that I completely forgot the guilt I once felt for putting additional financial strain on my mom, and I started living my life to the fullest without a care in the world. Everywhere I went, people showered me with praise—but the words that meant the most, and gave me the strength to keep pushing myself even harder, came from Kanae.

"Man, Akari. You're on fire lately," he said on our way home from school one day. "See, I always knew you had it in you. I could tell you were destined for greatness *way* before anyone else realized what a good swimmer you are!"

"Oh yeah? You knew it all along, huh?" I teased.

"Yep! Guess I've just got an eye for these things, heh-heh!" he boasted.

"Wowie. You should be a talent scout or something."

"Hey! Don't be sarcastic with me!"

I giggled to myself; he'd caught me red-handed. In all seriousness, though, I really was grateful to Kanae. If he hadn't spoken so highly of my abilities that day in third grade, I might not have ever started taking swimming seriously like this.

"Thanks for everything, Kanae-kun," I said in a meek and quiet voice.

"The heck? Where'd that come from?"

"You always paid attention to me, even when no one else would. It really means a lot."

At this, Kanae dropped the braggadocious act and started downplaying it—saying things like "Nah, I didn't have anything to do with it" as his face went beet red. In that moment, I really felt like I was the happiest girl alive. If I could have sold my soul to make sure those days would never end, I would have done so in a heartbeat.

CHAPTER 3
April 4th, 6 p.m.

M Y CONSCIOUSNESS SNAPPED BACK to a different point in time in an instant. When I lifted my head, I saw a large crowd of people spread out all around me. I took in my first breath, and an aromatic mixture of sweet and salty scents wafted into my nostrils. And then came the sounds—the incessant crowd noises and, somewhere off in the distance, the crooning melody of *Greensleeves*.

Akari, who'd been standing beside me prior to the jump, was nowhere to be found. It was just like when I was instantly transported from the abandoned park down to the seawall—as if the projector for the world around me had switched over to a different slide in the span of a single blink. I was prepared for it this time, at least, thanks to Akari's explanation, but that didn't make it any less jarring to experience.

"You can't be serious..." I muttered in disbelief.

Despite my astonishment, I couldn't shake the residual image of Akari's tear-drenched face from my mind. *What was she so broken up about in that moment? Was she thinking back on her brother's death? Could I have unwittingly said something in poor taste? Or was there some other reason…?* I knew it would keep eating away at me, but for now I decided to forget about it and focus on regaining my bearings. If Akari was right, the Rollback should have sent me back to six o'clock on April 4th.

Just as I was about to pull out my phone and check the time, however, a man I didn't recognize suddenly shot into my field of vision. He was red in the face, and he looked to be middle-aged. It was the abruptness that startled me more than anything else; he hadn't dashed in from the side or behind me. It was more like he sprung up from below—like he'd been sitting directly at my feet, then shot straight up to get right in my face.

"Hey! Whaddya think yer doin', kid?!" he spat, his eyes glaring up from beneath the bulging veins on his furrowed brow. He was pissed off at me about something or other, that much was evident—but I had no clue who he was. I'd never seen him before in my life.

"Er… Sorry, can I help you with something?" I asked sheepishly.

"Huh?!" the man barked. I immediately knew that he was drunk; his breath *reeked* of alcohol. "You want me to beat yer ass, punk?! Don't you play dumb with me!"

"Wh-whoa, hang on a minute!" I sputtered, taking a few steps back as the man closed in. "Listen, I really don't know what's going on here…"

The man repeated my words in an exaggerated, mocking voice. Something told me he wasn't about to listen to reason. *Ugh, what did I do to deserve this?* First I was caught off guard by Akari crying, then my mind got sent back into the middle of a big crowd of people, and now I was being harassed by a man I didn't even know. This was way too much for me to handle all at once—I felt at serious risk of losing my mind.

First and foremost, I needed to think of a way to get myself out of this sticky situation. I knew my assailant had to be quite drunk and thus probably wouldn't be able to keep up with me if I made a clean break for it. At the same time, I knew that running away before I even figured out what I'd supposedly done to this man wouldn't sit well with me. It didn't seem like he was going to calm down enough to have a rational discussion with me anytime soon, though—rather, it looked like he was gearing up to slug me in the face. I didn't have time to stand around weighing my options at length. I took a few more steps back. The second before I turned to make a run for it, a young woman with blonde hair jumped in between me and the drunkard.

"Okay, that's enough! Break it up! What seems to be the problem here?" she demanded.

She quickly set about trying to calm the man down and deescalate the situation, letting him know very politely how disruptive he was being, that everyone was watching, and that he should probably drink some water. She was clearly a pro. As I stood there marveling at how she didn't let him get even a word in edgewise, she shot a glance over at me.

"I'll handle it from here," she said. "You run along home, okay?"

"Huh? Wait, but I..."

"Seriously, it's fine. Think of it as my way of thanking you for all your help."

It was becoming increasingly clear that hanging around here any longer was only going to make things harder for her. Total stranger or not, I didn't want to put her out any more than I already had, and since I was already planning to make a run for it anyway, I decided to take her up on her generous offer.

"All right, fair enough," I said. "Thank you."

I bowed my head to her slightly and then took off at an easy sprint. Weaving my way through the crowd helped me to finally realize where I was and subsequently why there were so many people here. These were the temple grounds of the Sodeshima Shrine. Judging from the massive crowd, as well as the various food and entertainment stalls lining the main path leading up to the shrine, I'd apparently been sent back in time directly into the thick of Sodeshima's biggest annual event: the Ocean's Bounty Festival. This didn't help explain why I'd come there in the first place, though. I was extremely uncomfortable in large crowds, so I generally avoided the festival like the plague.

Who was that blonde-haired woman, anyway? I felt like I might have recognized her from somewhere, had I not been too preoccupied with the belligerent drunkard to get a good look at her face. Still, she said that it was her way of thanking me "for all my help," so I must have assisted her with *something* over the past couple of days. I was finding more questions than answers, as usual, and it was starting to get really annoying. I felt like a new hire that was being brought into a highly complicated position as a replacement for someone else, only to find that my predecessor had quit on mysterious terms without leaving any notes or guidance for me—except in this case, that predecessor was myself.

I figured I should at least check the time. I reached into my right-hand pocket where I usually kept my phone and was pleased to discover that it was actually there this time around. I pressed a button, and the screen turned on—it was April 4th, 6:05 p.m. Akari was right, then—I had indeed been sent back 48 hours in time from the evening of the 6th. *Guess the Rollback is real, then,* I thought to myself. This time, it was surprisingly easy for me to accept—though maybe it was just that my brain had gotten numb to all the crazy things happening to me. Hey, it was a fair bit better than feeling insane. I slid my cell phone back into my pocket and headed off for home.

By the time I made it back to the house, I'd already decided what my first priority there would be—gathering as much intel as I could. When I entered the living room, I found Eri doing her schoolwork at the table like the good student she was. It was the perfect opportunity to ask her a few questions.

"Hey, Eri? Mind if I ask you a thing or two?" I asked.

She shot me a quick glance, then turned back to her notes.

"Sure, whatever. Make it quick," she said.

"Awesome, thanks. I'll get right down to it, then: Where do you think I went today?"

Eri looked back up at me, one eyebrow raised in curiosity.

"What is this, some sort of trick question?"

"No, just answer honestly."

"...I mean, you went to the festival, didn't you?"

"Ding ding ding. Atta girl. Okay, next question: Do you know *why* I went to the festival?"

"You were gonna help out at one of the booths, right? That's what you said yesterday, anyway..."

Aha. So I'd been helping them set up or something. That would explain why that blonde-haired lady felt indebted to me— she must have been on the planning committee or something. As for why I agreed to help out, that remained a mystery, but at least now I knew why I was there to begin with. I was scared she'd get too suspicious if I asked her point-blank, so I decided to frame it like a cute quiz show. It had paid off, apparently. Eri didn't seem to suspect a thing.

"Congratulations, young lady! You got every answer right! ...Okay, so there were only two questions, but still. Thanks for your participation, and we'll see you next time!"

As I made my dramatic exit from the living room, I heard Eri mutter a single word under her breath: "Weirdo."

Back in my own bedroom, I sat down at my desk and pulled out a pen and a notebook from the drawer. Flipping open to a blank page, I tried as best I could to recreate the diagram Akari had drawn in the dirt when she was explaining the Rollback to me. The incident over at the festival grounds left me a little out of sorts, so I wanted to refresh my memory and make sure I hadn't lost any of what she told me. I drew the dates and arrows one by one as she had, moving ahead one day, then two days back. When I drew the last arrow to April 2nd, I set the pen down. *Okay, yeah. I've still got it down pat. We're good.*

"...Hey, wait a minute."

As I looked down at the diagram, an old question resurfaced in my mind. It was one that I'd tried to ask Eri about the night we were walking to Akito's wake.

What was I *physically* doing between 6 p.m. on the 1st and 6 p.m. on the 5th?

If the only part of me that made the quantum leap was my mind, then that would imply that my physical self still experienced those four days in their natural order. In other words, the *body* I was in right now had already experienced all of the events that I was about to "relive," but my *mind* couldn't remember them because mentally, I was going through them in reverse order.

I grabbed my cell phone, thinking there might be something recorded within it that could give me some hints as to how I'd spent the previous few days. I figured it might be a bit of a long shot, but when I tapped the Memos app, it opened up to a set of notes I didn't remember taking:

- 4/2: Found Akito's body @ 6:30 PM in empty lot behind tobacco shop & called police.
- Est. time of death between midnight and 2 AM that morning.
- Was drinking heavily earlier that night @ the Asuka Tavern, ~9 PM to midnight.

"The *hell*?" I muttered incredulously.

It was all specifics related to Akito's death. The second bullet point I'd already heard from Akari, but the other two were completely new information to me. I scrunched up my forehead and carefully reread each word, and then suddenly it clicked.

"Oh, duh!" I exclaimed as the light bulb flashed on in my head.

I must have typed these notes out sometime between six o'clock on April 1st and six o'clock on April 4th. To put it plainly, this was information that my *future* self had left for me in the *past*. That explained why there were details here that I hadn't learned yet. But with that being the case, I couldn't help but wonder how accurate this intel really was...aside from the stuff Akari already told me, of course.

For example, the first bullet point seemed to imply that *I* had initially found Akito's body in the empty lot behind the tobacco shop and reported it to the authorities. Akari told me the body was found in that exact location, to be sure, but she didn't say anything about *who* found it. It seemed like a relevant detail to include if it was me. Still, the fact that it was written here in my own cell phone made me inclined to believe it was true. In which case, there probably would be a record of me calling the emergency hotline around that time. Upon realizing this, I hastily opened up my recent call history.

RECENT CALLS

Akari Hoshina	Yesterday	7:56 PM
Akari Hoshina	Yesterday	6:35 PM
Akari Hoshina	Yesterday	5:32 PM
Dad	Monday	10:24 PM
Home	Monday	7:15 PM
119	Monday	6:30 PM
Home	Monday	11:07 PM
Akari Hoshina	Sunday	9:06 PM
Akari Hoshina	Sunday	9:05 PM
Home	Sunday	6:29 PM

WAIT FOR ME YESTERDAY IN SPRING

Sure enough, there it was: a record of me calling 119 at exactly 6:30 p.m. on Monday, April 2nd. It matched up perfectly with the time listed in my notes, and since you couldn't really forge your call history, I had no choice but to accept the notes in my phone as the real deal. However, I did find it somewhat peculiar that I had logged so many phone calls with Akari over the past few days—especially "yesterday," when we'd apparently had three calls within a matter of hours. *Let's see... Yesterday would have been the 3rd, so... Maybe we made plans to meet up or something?*

In any case, I now had a much better grasp on the intricacies of Akito's death. All that remained now was to establish what I'd been doing for the past several days, but I could probably figure that out pretty easily with some carefully worded questions to Eri or my grandmother. As though she'd read my mind, Eri yelled up at me from downstairs that very moment to let me know that dinner was ready. When I stood up from my chair, I heard something crinkle in my left pocket. I reached inside to discover a mysterious, folded-up thousand-yen bill. Maybe I'd been planning to use it to buy a snack over at the festival or something. I unfolded the bill and slid it into my wallet, then headed downstairs.

"Hey, Grandma, can I ask you something?" I asked after we were done eating and she was washing dishes in the kitchen.

"What is it, dear?" she replied without even turning around as she kept scrubbing away at the plate she was currently washing.

"Do you remember how I've been spending my time since I came back to Sodeshima?"

I was planning to talk to Eri at first, but then figured she'd probably get suspicious as to why I was asking and decided to ask my grandmother instead. My grandmother wasn't a very skeptical person in general, and she'd typically answer just about any question in a straightforward manner without questioning the asker's intent. Unfortunately, it seemed I made a bit of a miscalculation this time.

"I beg your pardon?" she said in puzzled surprise as she turned to face me. "Goodness, that's an awfully broad question."

She was totally right. I should have narrowed it down a bit.

"Er, yeah, sorry. Here, why don't we start with the day I got here? April 1st. What sticks out most in your mind about me from that day?"

"That was several days ago now, Kanae... Well, you got in a bit of a fight with your sister," she recalled, but that was something I already knew. What I really wanted to know was what I did *after* six o'clock that night.

"Right, Eri and I got into an argument, and I stormed out of the house. What did I do after that, though?" I pressed her.

"Sweetie, why are you asking me these strange questions? Shouldn't you already know the answer to that?"

"Sure, of course I do... I was curious how much *you* knew or remembered."

"How would I know what you did after that? You didn't come home that night."

"I didn't?"

"No, don't you remember? You called back here to say you

WAIT FOR ME YESTERDAY IN SPRING

were spending the night at a friend's house. Really, dear—how is *my* memory better than yours?"

Aha. That explained the record in my phone history of me calling home that night. To be clear, I still had my grandmother's house registered as "Home" in my address book, even after moving to Tokyo, because my father didn't have a landline. But what was this about me spending the night at a friend's house? I had no friends here in Sodeshima who would offer to let me stay at their place—or in Tokyo, for that matter. Sure, there was Akari, who I was fairly close with, but there was no way I'd spent the night at a girl's house. So where *did* I sleep that night?

"Whose house was it, anyway?" my grandmother asked before I even had the chance. "Eri was wondering about it too."

"Oh, yeah, um... Sorry, I'll have to tell you later."

"I beg your pardon? Don't tell me you stayed the night at the house of some ne'er-do-well your father and I wouldn't approve of."

"No, no! It's nothing like that... I don't think."

"You don't sound very sure of yourself. You haven't gotten involved in any shady business, have you? If you're in danger, you need to tell us about it. If not me, then your father, at least..."

"Er, yeah. No, I get that. But I mean it—I'll tell you as soon as I can, okay? Bye."

"The bathwater's ready, so feel free to wash up!" she called after me as I beat a hasty retreat from the kitchen. As I made my way toward the bathroom, I felt a sudden haze of anxiety roll over my mind like ominous black storm clouds.

After a quick hop in the bath, I returned to my bedroom. I spent my entire time in the tub trying to figure out where I could have possibly spent the night of the 1st but still couldn't come up with anything. I'd never spent the night at a friend's house in my entire life, as sad as that sounded—so for me to do so while I was already running away from home seemed almost unthinkable. There had to have been a very compelling reason why I couldn't go back to my grandmother's house that night, and the fact that the 1st was *also* the night Akito died made me wonder if perhaps the two things were related.

No, that couldn't be right. Not if the body wasn't found until the next evening. Still, I needed to find some answers as to where I was staying that night. I didn't want to leave any questions un-answered before I made it back to the 1st, since then I could give saving Akito's life my undivided attention. Not that I had any solid proof that the Rollback was going to take me back that far, I guess, but I wanted to be ready in the event that it did. I'd need to do some footwork around town once tomorrow hit.

I was about to jump in bed when I spied the notebook I'd left laying out on my desk. I flipped it open on a whim and took another look at the Rollback diagram I'd drawn in it earlier. Then a thought occurred to me: When exactly was the Rollback supposed to end? Akari's diagram had finished off at 6 p.m. on April 2nd—and yes,

WAIT FOR ME YESTERDAY IN SPRING

that would be when I finished filling in the four-day gap in my memories—but what would happen after that?

I decided I probably shouldn't think too hard about it, though; I wasn't going to find any answers that way. For now, I needed some rest. My whole body felt extremely sore—maybe from helping out at the festival, if what Eri said was true. Obviously my mind didn't remember doing any heavy labor, but my body sure did. I shut the notebook and snuggled up under the covers. In a matter of minutes, I was out like a light.

I was awakened by the sound of my cell phone vibrating. I reached for it with one hand, rubbing the sleep out of my eyes with the other. After my vision had time to adjust, I looked down at the screen and saw the name "Akari Hoshina."

"Akari...?" I grumbled drowsily, then answered the phone. "Hello?"

"Oh, you did pick up! Hey, Kanae-kun! Sorry for calling you at this hour. You were probably asleep already, huh?"

"Yeah, I was... What time is it right now?"

"Oh, it's about one o'clock. One o'clock in the morning."

No wonder I still felt so sleepy.

"Why are you calling so late?" I asked, stifling a yawn. "Do you need something?"

"I mean, I wouldn't say I need anything. I was just wondering if maybe, I dunno..." she mumbled, her voice growing quieter and quieter. I pressed the speaker right up against my ear, but even then it was too soft to discern.

"Sorry? I didn't quite catch that..."

"Um... I was wondering if maybe we could meet up for a little bit?"

"What, you want to hang out? Like, right now...? At one in the morning?"

"Mm-hmm..." she answered in a weak little voice. I could practically see the pleading puppy-dog eyes on the other end of the line. This, too, was very unusual; the Akari I knew would never call someone up this late at night, let alone ask to hang out. The fact that she was doing it now led me to believe that *something* must have been up. Concerned for her, I agreed right away.

"All right, sure thing. Just tell me where to go."

"Wait, really? You mean it? ...Okay, meet me at Central Park in, like, twenty minutes."

"Central Park. Got it. Guess I'll see you there, then."

"Yeah, see you in a little bit."

Central Park was a small but popular park that sat a little bit further inland. Generally, when someone from Sodeshima said "meet me at the park," that was the one they meant. I assumed Akari had only specified so that I knew she wasn't referring to the old, abandoned park I discovered the other day.

After hanging up the phone, I hopped out of bed and changed out of my pajamas into some sweatpants and a hoodie. I knew it would only take me about ten minutes to get there, but I decided to head out early anyway. Creeping down the stairs so as not to wake the rest of the family, I snuck out the back door and closed it quietly behind me. As the frigid night air caressed my cheeks, any semblance of drowsiness I may still have felt shot right out the window. Icy wind swept through the empty neighborhood streets, chilling me to my core.

I set off at a light jog in an attempt to conserve my body heat. Sodeshima's neighborhoods had a lot of steep hills, so I normally never tried to run through them unless I was in a real hurry. I didn't have many other options at this point—they got rid of my bike when I moved to Tokyo, so unless I felt like borrowing Eri's, it was either run, or walk and turn into a human popsicle.

The scuffing of my sneakers against the pavement echoed loudly through the streets in a staccato rhythm. Sodeshima was awfully quiet at night this time of year. Whereas in Tokyo you could never escape the constant hum of car engines whirring past, here, the whole world seemingly came to a halt as soon as the sun went down. Sure, you'd have the occasional obnoxious jerkwad zooming loudly by on a motorbike, but those guys were the same no matter where you went.

I was at the park before I knew it, though Akari was nowhere to be found. I took a look at the tall street clock, its face lit up by the nearby lamplight, and saw that I'd arrived almost ten minutes early. I sat down to wait on a park bench, and the icy metal quickly set about draining all of the heat I'd built up in my flushed skin during the jog over here.

"...Brrr," I shivered, belatedly realizing that I should have worn another layer or two.

Nothing set the imagination running wild quite like the anticipation of waiting for someone else to arrive. If I'd known I'd get here this early, then it might have been a good idea to swing by Akari's place and pick her up along the way. Even if we did live out here in the boonies, it was still dangerous for a young girl like her to go walking around by herself at night. You never knew what kinds of creepers were lurking in the shadows, and the lack of light made it harder to see where you were going. I'd never had a late-night meetup with a girl like this before, though, so I guess I forgot to consider that aspect of it. Maybe it'd be a good idea to call her and offer to come meet her somewhere closer, even if she'd probably already left. Just as I was about to pull out my cell phone, I noticed a shadowy figure standing at the entrance to the park, and I could tell immediately from the silhouette that it was Akari. I shot up to my feet and called her name. She came trotting over the second she identified where I was.

"Hey, sorry," she huffed. "Didn't keep you waiting too long, I hope?"

"Nah, you're good. I just got here myself."

Now standing under the lamplight, I could actually see what Akari looked like. She wore a loose-fitting heavy cardigan, her fingers poking out from the overlong sleeves and gripping the thick fabric tightly. I felt a funny feeling well up inside my chest—there was something exhilarating about meeting up in the dead of night, especially since we'd never done anything remotely like this before.

"Oh, okay. Anyway, sorry for dragging you out here so late," she said.

"Don't worry about it. So tell me..."

I was about to ask her why she called me to meet up, when all of a sudden, the image of her crying beneath the cherry blossom tree at the abandoned park came shooting back into my mind so that her tear-drenched face overlapped perfectly with the one in front of me right now. I couldn't get the sound out of my head: her softly weeping as *Greensleeves* began to play while a flurry of petals soared through the sky. I still wanted to know the reason behind those tears, so I decided to pivot to a different question.

"Why were you crying the other day?" I asked.

"Huh...? Crying? When was this?" she replied, staring back at me in bewilderment.

"Don't you remember? Right before the last Rollback, you—"

Then it hit me. We met in the abandoned park on the 6th, and right now, it was only the 5th. Of course this Akari wouldn't know what I was referring to.

"Er, n-never mind. Forget I said anything. Sorry, I guess I'm still getting used to the whole Rollback thing..."

"Ohhh, gotcha... Yeah, it's pretty hard to wrap your head around."

"No kidding. If you hadn't explained it all to me, I'd probably be curled up in the fetal position somewhere right about now."

"Wait. When did I explain anything to you?" she asked, tilting her head to one side.

"Oh, right. That was yesterday too... Er, I mean, tomorrow. April 6th. You gave me the rundown at the abandoned park."

"I did...? Huh. Weird," she said, her face clearly indicating that she was still confused but had given up on trying to decipher my

APRIL 4TH, 6 P.M.

lunatic rantings. I could hardly blame her, really—imagine being told about something you'd done on a day that hadn't even happened yet. After the past couple days, I could relate to the feeling.

"Anyway, why did you want to meet up so bad? Did something happen?" I asked.

"No, nothing happened... I couldn't sleep, is all."

"Oh, seriously...? How come?"

"I dunno," she said, lowering her gaze. She brought a clenched fist up to her sternum. "Just, whenever I closed my eyes, I kept having these really dark intrusive thoughts... Like, of someone I really cared about going somewhere far away or of them one day deciding they didn't like me anymore...stuff like that. I couldn't take it."

These sounded like pretty vague, abstract anxieties, especially for Akari. Still, I didn't feel comfortable prying at what seemed to be a pretty uncomfortable subject for her, judging from her vulnerable expression. I didn't know if this was all the same "someone" she was envisioning in each of these episodes, like maybe her brother, or some faceless entity standing in for the world around her. Regardless, it was clear that Akito's death had really done a number on her mental state. And even if I didn't have all the details, she was clearly shaken up enough that she couldn't sleep and resorted to calling me in the middle of the night so she'd have someone to keep her company. I felt I at least owed her that much, as her longtime friend.

"All right. Then let's talk for a while, why don't we?" I smiled, and Akari's expression immediately softened into one of relief.

"...Thanks, Kanae-kun."

"Don't mention it. It's fun to get outta the house sometimes," I said and then pivoted immediately into casual small talk. "So what have you been up to today?"

"Today...? I didn't really do all that much, to be honest. My mom was on the phone pretty much nonstop making calls about my brother, though."

"What kinds of calls?"

"I *think* she was calling a bunch of different doctors from some university hospital? Trying to get more information about my brother, I guess."

"Huh... That's interesting," I replied, not knowing what else to say.

If Akito was already long dead by the time I found him, then there was no way they transferred him there for treatment. Meaning...they were probably doing his autopsy. I bit my lip, realizing that I may have unintentionally reminded her of even more unpleasant thoughts. Then, as I was scrambling to think of something more uplifting we could talk about, an ice-cold gust of wind came whooshing by. Now officially freezing, I rubbed my upper arms in a futile attempt to make some heat via friction.

"Man, it's cold out here," I said. "Can we go somewhere else?"

Back in Tokyo, there were 24-hour diners and fast-food restaurants all over the damn place, but there was nothing of the sort here in Sodeshima. The only business establishments that would still be open at this hour were a handful of small bars and pubs—and unfortunately, we were both still minors.

"...Well, it's not heated, but I know one place where we can escape from the cold," said Akari.

"Oh yeah? Where's that?" I asked.

She looked me in the eye and said, without a hint of sarcasm: "Sodeshima High."

After successfully scaling the front gate, the two of us hopped down and made a beeline across the center of the vacant athletic field. Ahead of me, Akari was walking with a confident skip in her step, not even making the slightest effort to be sneaky about it.

"H-hey!" I whispered harshly. "Are you *sure* we're not gonna get in trouble for this?"

"We'll be fiiine," she said, shrugging me off. "Our *one* security guard goes home at ten o'clock. There's literally no chance of anyone catching us. Trust me."

"Wait, for real? Do they just not care about people breaking in, or...? Y'know what, never mind. But even if we don't get caught, this is still super illegal, right?"

Akari stopped in her tracks and turned around to look up at me.

"Don't think of it as illegal, think of it as an adventure! Don't you wanna go on an adventure with me, Kanae-kun...?" she whimpered.

No, not the puppy-dog eyes... Anything but that...

"Fine, fine... You win," I said, giving up. "At least we're not hurting anyone."

"Yaaay! C'mon, let's go!"

Akari's face beamed with delight as she spun on her heels and headed for the school building. It was no use—I'd have to go along with this. Having crossed the field, we began circling the perimeter of the main building. When we'd made it about half-way around, Akari came to an abrupt stop in front of a frosted sliding glass window. How she was planning to get in, I didn't dare imagine, but she quickly grabbed the window by the edges and started rattling it around in its frame.

"Um, what exactly are you trying to do?" I asked.

"Hey, don't give me that look," she pouted. "When you think about it, it's kinda their own fault for never fixing the lock."

"Wow. So you can open it from this side, just like that?"

"Uh, yeah? Didn't you already know this?"

I was officially confused. *How could I possibly know that? I never went to school here.*

"Oh, wait," Akari exclaimed, slapping her forehead as if struck by an epiphany. "Sorry, I'm stupid—of course you wouldn't know about that yet. Duh."

For a moment, a huge question mark popped up over my head, but then I quickly figured it out. Judging from her tone, there'd been some moment over the past few days in which she'd told me about the broken window lock, but it was one that I hadn't person-ally experienced yet. In which case, it made sense why she thought she'd already told me, but I had no clue what she was talking about. Upon realizing her blunder, Akari proceeded to explain.

"Yeah, so basically, all these windows have sash locks, but this one's kinda janky, so the handle won't turn all the way, and the latch doesn't engage. So if you kinda wiggle it around like this and apply a little bit of horizontal pressure..." she said, then proceeded to demonstrate. Sure enough, the window popped right open, and she looked back at me with a smug grin. "Aaand presto! See? Piece o' cake."

"Well, well! Color me impressed. You sure do know all the ins and outs of this place."

"Yeah, I mean, I would hope so! Been goin' here for two whole years now."

Akari hoisted herself up onto the windowsill and jumped inside. This still felt a little too close to breaking and entering for my liking, but I followed after her anyway. Once inside, I realized that we were in the girls' bathroom. It was completely empty, but I still felt like a bit of a trespasser in there, so I quickly shuffled out into the main hallway.

"Whoa... Now *this* is pretty cool," I marveled quietly to myself—though even that was enough to echo loudly through the empty corridor. The soft moonlight pouring in through the windows did offer some illumination, but it was still very dark inside the school. I looked down toward the other end of the hallway, where the only thing I could see was the eerie spectral glow of the fire alarm's big red bulb. As someone who had no problem wandering through the abandoned part of town, even I had to admit this was pretty spooky. On the other hand, it was also kind of exhilarating—this was the first time I'd ever snuck into a school at night. I hesitantly started to make my way down the hall, but then a stressful thought hit me.

"Aw, crap. I didn't take my shoes off."

"Don't worry about it," said Akari, coming out of the girls' bathroom just as I was kneeling down to unlace my sneakers. "They let us wear our street shoes here, it's no biggie."

"Oh, for real? I had no idea. Never even set foot in Sodeshima High before."

"Then allow me to give you the grand tour!"

Akari strode off down the hall, and I followed after her. There wasn't a hint of trepidation in her step—on the contrary, she seemed almost comfortable here.

"Sheesh, Akari. Slow down," I said, strolling up alongside her. "I mean, aren't you scared at all?"

"Oh, please. This is a cakewalk compared to yesterday. Plus, I've got you here with me, don't I? What do I have to be afraid of?"

"W-well, if you say so."

I didn't really know what to say to that. I wished she would stop saying things that could be misinterpreted as flirting, though, because I never knew how to react. What was this about yesterday, anyway? Had we really gone out and done something even spookier than breaking into the school at night? I couldn't even fathom what that entailed.

"Why, are *you* scared, Kanae-kun?"

"Who, me? Psh, as if. I'm just shakin' in my boots a little bit, that's all."

"So you're terrified. Got it," she snarked, then slowed to a stop before a pair of mysterious double doors. "Oh hey, here's the library. You wanna check it out?"

"I mean, can we even get inside?"

"Let's find out," she said, then grabbed both door handles and pulled hard, but they didn't budge. "Well, shoot. It's locked."

"Yeah, not surprised," I said with a wry smirk as Akari scratched her cheek and laughed sheepishly. We proceeded past the library and soon arrived at the main stairwell.

"You used to spend a bunch of time in the library, didn't you, Kanae-kun? Do you still read a lot of books?" she asked as we were walking up the stairs.

"Not so much lately... Studying kinda eats up all of my free time."

"Dang, it's that brutal over there, huh?"

"I'm struggling just to keep up, yeah. If I'm not careful, I might get held back this year."

"Seriously? That's really surprising to me. You always had such good grades in junior high."

"Yeah, by Sodeshima standards, maybe," I sighed as we reached the second-floor landing. I continued ranting as I followed Akari into the main hall: "I mean, don't get me wrong, I thought I was a pretty bright kid back then too. But once I got to Tokyo, it was like all bets were off. So much competition there, y'know? You've really gotta go above and beyond to stand out. It's...stifling, honestly."

It wasn't until after I finished talking that I realized I was basically venting at this point. I felt bad. Akari wasn't my therapist, and it couldn't be much fun for her to hear me complaining like this.

"Sorry. Didn't mean to be a downer or anything," I apologized.

"No, no, it's fine. Everyone's got their own problems they're dealing with. Glad to know I'm not the only one... Oh, hey. Here we are," she said, coming to a stop in front of a classroom with a big SECOND YEAR nameplate above the door. "Yep, that's where I was sitting up until a month ago! Pretty crazy stuff."

She proudly pushed her pointer finger against the window, while I pressed my forehead up to the glass and tried to get a better look. For how big of a classroom it was, there weren't that many desks inside—maybe thirty at most.

"Wanna go inside?" she asked mischievously.

"If they locked the library, then I'm sure they lock up the classrooms too."

"You're not wrong. But whaddya know—they left the window *above* the door hanging wiiide open for us."

"...This school really needs to tighten up its security."

As I shook my head in disbelief, I heard a spry "Hup!" and looked over to find that Akari had already stepped up onto the neighboring windowsill, where she was now trying to hoist herself up and through the small open window above the door. Right when she was almost halfway through, she gave a sudden yowl of pain.

"Hey, are you all right?" I asked as she lowered herself back down into the hallway.

"Yeah, sorry..." she winced as she rubbed one side of her lower back and waist. "Thought I'd be all healed up by now, but it still kinda hurts from time to time."

"Healed up? Did you get injured recently or something?"

"Oh, uh... Yeah, sort of. But I'm like ninety-nine percent good now, so don't worry about it. It's really not a big deal."

"You sure...?"

Akari nodded, albeit with a rather melancholy expression. Whatever had happened, it was obvious that she didn't want to talk about it, so I let it go and changed the subject.

"Okay, then why don't I go in first and unlock the door for you from the inside?" I offered.

"That'd be great, thanks."

I climbed up on the neighboring windowsill, just like Akari had, then wriggled my way up and into the classroom through the higher window over the door. Inside, it felt even more spacious than it had looked from the hallway. The smell of wood and fresh wax flowed into my lungs as I scanned the neat rows of empty desks. The pale blue moonlight leaking in through the windowpanes bathed the tabletops in a faint, luminous glow. I unlocked the door to let Akari in, and she stepped past me into the classroom. After giving it a good, long once-over, she headed over to a desk by the window and sat down.

"Yep, this was my spot. Have a seat, Kanae-kun," she said, indicating the desk in front of her as she ran her other hand over the smooth wooden surface. I felt a little awkward treating myself to a random stranger's seat, but I reluctantly obliged. "Gosh, this sure brings back memories, huh?"

"Yeah, no kidding," I agreed. "It's like we're back in junior high."

"I'd rather go back to elementary school, personally."

"Really? ...I mean, I guess I can understand that."

Now that she mentioned it, I couldn't summon up many fond memories from my junior high years whatsoever. I was always being treated like an outcast by my other classmates, and getting picked on, and then backstabbed by the few kids who pretended they were on my side... It was awful. But even so, I still cherished all of the time I got to spend with Akari back then.

"If you could go back to elementary school, what would you do differently?" Akari asked, propping one elbow up on her desk.

"Good question," I answered. "Probably study real hard from day one and try to get into Tokyo U."

"What, that's it? Bor-riiing."

"Yeah? Well, what about you, huh?"

"Me? Mmm..." she pondered, folding her arms as she mulled it over. I didn't intend for it to be such an introspective question, but I waited patiently for her answer, until finally, she had a sudden flash of inspiration. "I'd wanna go on more field trips!"

It was such an anticlimactic answer after all that buildup. I couldn't help laughing.

"You *do* realize those aren't exclusive to elementary school, right?"

"Well, yeah—but we were supposed to go on a whole lot more back then, remember? They'd always get canceled due to rain or something."

"Oh yeah, I *do* remember that. It was like the weather had a vendetta against our class or something—always waited until the morning of to turn nasty on us."

"What's that called, again? Murphy's Law?" Akari muttered.

"Pretty sure, yeah," I nodded.

"Hey, Kanae-kun… Do you remember that one field trip we went on in fifth grade?"

"Fifth grade? You're not talking about the one where you fell face-first into that giant mud puddle, are you?"

"That's the one!"

Now *that* brought me back. I lapsed into reminiscing about that fateful day. As I remembered it, the entire class had gone out on an excursion to hike up a small mountain over on the mainland. It was our first field trip in a long time, so we were all having a blast, Akari included—that is, until she slipped and fell deep into the muck. I would never forget the total 180 her expression made in that instant—from giddy elation to abject horror.

"But then you went and fell in right after me, Kanae-kun, remember? How'd *that* happen?" Akari asked, and I realized I'd totally forgotten about that part. After Akari slipped and fell, I practically dove into the mud puddle right alongside her.

"Oh, yeah… I think I just tripped on a rock or something."

"You *think*?" Akari pressed, her eyes skeptical.

In actuality, I'd tripped and fallen over on purpose. Not wanting to stand there and watch while everyone else in class pointed and laughed at Akari's mud-covered distress, I decided to join her down there and hopefully take some of the negative attention off of her in the process. That plan ultimately backfired, though, since all it did was make everyone laugh even harder at the both of us. Still, after all these years, I didn't quite feel comfortable revealing the actual reason to her, so I tried to paper over it with a lame excuse instead.

"Well, I mean, it was a long time ago. Hard to remember exactly," I said.

"Oh, reeeally... Well, okay. Hey, that reminds me—speaking of field trips..."

Akari and I carried on waxing nostalgic like this for a good, long time. Here I was, sitting alone in an empty classroom at night with the very girl I once had intense—though unrequited—feelings for. One might assume that I would feel pretty nervous and antsy in this situation, but right now, I was simply having too much fun talking with her to care. It wasn't until the little wall clock over the blackboard struck 3 a.m. that a great big yawn escaped from my mouth.

"Getting sleepy?" she asked.

"Nah... Not really," I lied, determined to stay here and talk with her for just a little longer. The truth was that I felt extremely tired, and our conversation was kind of dying down—so I racked my brain for other potential topics to bring up before she had a chance to suggest that maybe we should call it a night. "Oh, yeah! There's something I wanted to ask you about."

"Oh, really? What's that?"

"It's about the night that Akito died. Do you have any idea what I was doing, or where I was that night after I said goodbye to you down at the seawall?"

As soon as the question had left my lips, Akari's eyes shot open as though I'd just caught her in a compromising position.

She seemed to be in genuine shock; her mouth hung open the slightest crack, but no words came out. All I could hear was a long, shallow breath. Concerned, I called her name again, and this time she snapped out of it. Then, her expression warped into a smile that was blatantly insincere.

"S-sorry, sorry. You're talking about April 1st, right?"

"Yeah. My grandma told me I spent the night at a friend's house that evening, but I couldn't think of a single friend who'd post me up like that. Wondered if maybe you knew anything about that."

"Er... No, sorry. I only saw you that one time at the seawall that day, so I wouldn't know what you did after that..."

"Gotcha... Well, thanks anyway."

Well, that was fruitless. If Akari didn't know, then I hadn't the first clue who else I could ask. Neither Eri nor my grandmother seemed to know either. I was trying to brainstorm other avenues I could investigate when I heard Akari let out a tiny gasp beside me. I turned to look at her and saw that she was covering her mouth with one hand, meaning that I couldn't quite make out her expression.

"What's wrong?" I asked, and she turned, slowly and fearfully, to face me. Her brow was furrowed as if she'd realized some grave mistake. After a few moments of silence, she lowered her hand and flashed a weak smile in an attempt to reassure me.

"It's nothing, sorry," she said. "I had this sinking feeling because I couldn't remember if I'd locked the door on my way out or not."

"Oh, gotcha... Yeah, that happens to me all the time," I commiserated, even if I still thought that was a bit of overreaction. I reiterated: "So you're sure everything's all right?"

"Yeah. I thought about it some more, and now I'm like ninety-nine percent sure that I *did* lock the door, actually. So we're cool."

She shot me a carefree grin which finally convinced me that it really hadn't been anything more than that, even if I still found her initial reaction a bit odd. I was probably overthinking it, though. Akari stood up from her chair and stretched her arms out.

"All right, it's getting pretty late. Or early, I guess. You ready to head home?"

"...Probably a good idea."

Though I still didn't want to have to say goodbye, I knew we couldn't stay here forever. I rose from my own chair as well. I let Akari leave the room first so that I could lock the door from the inside, then I exited through the tall window the same way I'd come in.

"Well, guess that's the end of the grand tour, huh?" I joked as we made our way down the hall.

"Yeah, not too much else to see," Akari nodded. "Plus, all the other classrooms are gonna be locked... Oh, but actually, there *is* one more place I'd like to show you before we go. C'mere for a sec."

I followed Akari as she led the way up the stairs, past the third floor, all the way to the roof-access landing. The only things I could see up there were some stacks of student desks that weren't currently in use and the door leading out onto the roof, which was secured with an ordinary padlock—meaning we couldn't get outside.

"*This* is what you wanted to show me?" I asked.

"Heck no. Gimme a little more credit, wouldja? It's on the other side of this door."

Akari pulled two small lengths of wire from the inside of a nearby desk. They looked like hairpins which had been yanked on until they were relatively straightened out. Before I could even register the implications of what she was about to do, she'd already jammed the wires into the padlock and begun rattling them around inside. In a matter of seconds, the lock was picked.

"There we go!" she exclaimed. "Well? Pretty sweet, huh?"

"Like hell it is! Where the heck did you learn to do that?"

"I used to come up here a lot whenever I needed some alone time. And, well... I always saw the padlock here, and eventually I started to wonder how hard these things *really* are to break, y'know? So I started practicing on it out of sheer boredom, basically, but then I ended up figuring it out in no time flat."

"You've got waaay too much time on your hands, kiddo."

"What can I say? I'm a simple woman. I see a door, I wanna open it."

Akari did just that, and a bone-chilling gust of wind immediately blew inside from the newly opened door. I stepped through the doorway before taking a necessary moment to catch my breath. A gleaming full moon hung in the cloudless night sky. Beneath that were the sporadic dots of light from the fishing boats out on the ocean and, far off on the horizon, the distant lights of the mainland. The view was stunningly gorgeous. I felt like we were standing at the center of a panoramic impressionist painting.

"Damn... Now *that's* pretty," I said in awe.

"Yeah, wow... It's my first time being here at night, but even I didn't expect it to look *this* cool," Akari agreed. Then, still gazing up at the night sky, she began slowly tottering over toward the edge of the roof. The protective fence around the perimeter only came up to about waist height, so it didn't completely allay my uneasiness. The high school stood at such an elevated point on the island that there was nothing around it to block the strong winds. Yet Akari didn't seem to care. She grabbed the railing with her hands and leaned her upper body out over the edge.

"Hey, be careful over there," I warned.

"Oh, I'll be *fiiine*. Hey, come on over here, Kanae-kun," she implored me, but I was already well on my way. I took my place next to her along the railing; my eyes soaked in the nightscape sprawled out before us. Beautiful as it was, I faltered whenever I looked down from this height. It was so dark out, I couldn't even see the ground below us. All I saw was a deep, black abyss. I shivered.

"What, are you afraid of heights?" Akari inquired.

"N-no," I scoffed. "I'm a tiny bit cold, that's all."

"Oh, reeeally..." she said, eyeing me suspiciously. A moment later, she made a mischievous grin, as though she'd devised a fun new way to troll me. Without another word, she leaned in close and pressed her shoulder right up against mine. For a split second, I was extremely flustered by this. Then I decided to roll with it and act like it didn't faze me at all. I was determined not to let her win. The fragrance of her shampoo drifted in the air between us, tickling my nose.

"You know, this is my favorite spot in all of Sodeshima," she whispered in my ear. "It's pretty during the day too. You can see the ocean, and the whole island, and even all the way over to the mainland."

"Wow, yeah... That sounds really nice."

"Doesn't it, though? ...Hey, look. There's the Big Dipper," she said, pointing up toward the sky and tracing the contours with her fingertip.

"Dang. The constellations are so easy to see from out here."

"Can you not see many stars over in Tokyo?"

"You might be surprised, actually. The light pollution doesn't affect it as much as people tend to think."

"Really?"

"Yeah. And the nightscape's really beautiful too, of course. In a way, it's kinda like the starry skies and city lights all come together to create one big, seamless gradient."

"Huh... It sounds really cool when you put it like that," she said, then lowered her gaze back down to stare across the ocean. She reached out a hand toward the distant mainland and whispered to herself: "I'd love to live there someday."

"Then do it."

"I'm not sure I could make it in the big city like you."

"Sure you could. You've just gotta put yourself out there," I said. "Heck, even if it *didn't* work out, you could always come and live with me, y'know."

Akari looked over at me, her eyes wide. I couldn't blame her—even I couldn't believe the words that had just come out of my mouth. I might as well have proposed to her. It took a solid few seconds for the full implications to truly set in, but my entire face flushed red in the instant that they did. I tried to backpedal a little bit.

"Er, sorry. I didn't mean that in a weird way or anything..."

My mind was like a spinning whirlpool of emotions made up in equal measure of embarrassment and regret. I was so mortified, I wanted to die. But before I had a chance to consider hopping over the railing and putting myself out of my misery, something happened.

Akari wrapped her arms around me, suddenly and without warning. I was so startled by this that I completely froze in place, unable to even hug her back. With her hands clutching the back of my hoodie, she rested her head on my shoulder. The one-two punch of her soft touch and sweet fragrance must have blown a fuse in my brain, because for a minute, I forgot to even breathe. I stood there, thoughts empty, letting myself be embraced by Akari—unable to even freak out and ruin the moment. Then, eventually, I felt her warm breath seeping through the fabric of my hoodie. She was trying to say something.

"Please don't ever hate me," she begged.

Her voice was fragile and scared, like a lost child who'd been left behind by their parents. I couldn't tell what the significance of these words was, or if there were any hidden undertones she was trying to convey, but I knew there was only one way I could respond.

"Of course not," I said. "How could I ever hate you?"

I managed at long last to wrap my trembling hands around Akari's back. Tension continued to lock every inch of my body into place, but somehow I managed to will my arms around her. I knew it was the right thing to do. We stood there like that for anywhere from a few seconds to a few minutes, until eventually, Akari gently tugged herself away. Now, her faintly flushed cheeks were mere inches from my face, so I could watch her bleary eyes twinkle in the soft moonlight.

"Let's go home," she said softly.

The two of us continued making small talk on the walk back to Akari's place, almost as if the embrace we shared up on the rooftop had been nothing more than a fever dream. We were talking as candidly as we had been in the classroom an hour or so ago, each of us taking turns recounting memories that we could both laugh at or be astonished by. It felt so natural that it honestly made me start to wonder if the rooftop incident really *had* been nothing more than a figment of my imagination.

Still, I couldn't stop myself from speculating as to why she'd been so assertive in embracing me like that. Obviously, that was intended as a show of affection of some sort—what I couldn't grasp was what *kind* of affection. For all I knew, that could have been anything from a simple expression of momentary gratitude to a confession of love. Without knowing where on that spectrum it fell, I had no way of knowing the proper level of affection to reciprocate with.

"Hey, Kanae-kun," she said, breaking the silence.

"Wh-what's up?" I replied. My voice cracked.

"Thanks for hanging out with me tonight. Something tells me I'll be able to get a good night's sleep now."

"Sure thing... Glad to hear it. Yeah, feel free to hit me up whenever you need a friend to talk to."

"Nice. I think I'll take you up on that."

Akari smiled at me—and that alone was enough to send a euphoric rush coursing through my veins. That in turn made me realize that it didn't matter if I couldn't tell where her head was at; I was grateful to earn affection from her in any form. I decided, then and there, to stop overanalyzing her emotions. From now on I'd bask in the glory of whatever affection she felt I deserved. For tonight, though, the end of our dreamlike encounter was drawing near. Akari's apartment complex soon came into view.

"You wanna meet up tomorrow too?" I offered, half out of concern for her, half out of my own desire to get as much quality time together as possible.

"Sorry, I don't think I'll have time. What with getting ready for the wake, and all."

"The wake...? But that was... Oh, right."

Akito's wake was held on the night of the 5th. I was going through the days in reverse, so I'd already experienced it, but it hadn't happened for Akari yet.

"Yeah, sorry. We've been running ourselves ragged the past couple of days, trying to get things ready for the funeral... And I can't leave my mom to handle it all herself, y'know?"

"Hey, no need to apologize. You've got a lot on your plate right now, I get it."

"Thanks for understanding..."

Her expression turned glum, and she hung her head a little. I ground my teeth together, wishing I hadn't ruined the mood by asking about tomorrow. Determined to salvage the conversation so we could end off on a high note, I forced a chipper inflection and tried to reassure her.

"Hey, don't get too down on yourself about it! I'm gonna go back and save Akito anyway, remember? Then everything will go back to normal."

"...Yeah, I know."

"I know I can pull it off, just you wait. All I've gotta do is make sure he doesn't go out drinking that night."

"...Right."

This didn't seem to do much to raise Akari's spirits—if anything, she seemed even *more* crestfallen now. Somehow, my attempts to cheer her up had backfired, and I started panicking internally. Her one and only brother died a few days ago. I should have avoided bringing him up in conversation at all costs. I was reprimanding myself for this critical judgment error when Akari surprised me by deliberately continuing the conversation about him.

"What was *your* impression of my brother, Kanae-kun?" she

asked, still looking down at the ground. "Do you still look up to him, even now?"

"Man, that's a tough question... Obviously, he was my hero growing up, but nowadays? I wouldn't say I 'idolize' him anymore, per se. Not that I don't still have a ton of respect for the guy! I mean, how could I not, after he saved me from those bullies back in elementary school?"

"Oh yeah... I totally forgot about that."

"As for my impression of him, well...he always struck me as a bit clumsy when it came to expressing his emotions and stuff like that."

"How do you mean?" Akari asked.

"Well, I remember this one time in third grade, I think it was... He came up to me at the little candy store in town, and he was like, 'Hey, you're friends with Akari, right? Do me a favor, will ya?' or something similar."

"What was the favor?"

"He basically just asked me to look out for you, and be a really good friend to you, and stuff like that. Because he felt like he wasn't really being a very good older brother and like the only thing he was any good at was baseball."

Akari stopped dead in her tracks and turned to face me.

"Hang on. He really said all that?"

"I mean, maybe in slightly less eloquent terms, but yeah. I specifically remember him asking me to keep an eye on your footing, 'cause he said you used to lose your balance and trip over things a lot. He definitely cared about you in his own way, that's for sure."

I remembered the encounter quite well, actually. Akito was already renowned for his baseball skills by that point—he was practicing with the junior-high team despite still being in elementary school, and even played pinch-hitter for the island's amateur adult team. A local legend like him approaching me out of the blue to ask that kind of favor was a memorable surprise.

"But I guess that's how older brothers are, y'know? Always looking out for their younger siblings, but they're too proud to admit it, heh. Me and Eri are the same way. Sometimes it feels like all we ever do is bicker at each other! Hell, we got into a big argument within minutes of me coming home the other day," I said, chuckling at my own pettiness. Then something struck me. Akari wasn't laughing along. Her expression was, if anything, soberingly serious.

"My brother really said that about me...?" she asked, her voice shaky. Something was clearly not right here, but before I had a chance to ask what the problem was, she ran off toward the apartment complex as fast as she could.

"H-hey, wait! Where are you going?!" I yelled, frantically chasing after her. I managed to catch up right before she reached the stairs, grabbed her by the arm, and twisted her around to face me. "What the hell, Akari?! Why'd you run off like that all of a..."

My words caught in my throat when I saw that she was sobbing profusely.

"I'm sorry... I'm so sorry," she whimpered.

A chill ran through my entire body, and I let go of her arm without a second's delay. She dashed off up the stairs and into her apartment with animal speed, as though she was terrified of being seen like this and desperately wanted to escape from my gaze. Even after I heard the door slam above me, I stood there at the base of the stairs for a time, frozen in place.

After letting myself in through the back door, I crept up the stairs and slipped soundlessly into my bedroom, where I collapsed into bed without even changing out of my heavy clothes. I pulled the covers up all the way over my head to shut out the world. I should have been more than ready to turn in by this point, but sleep still eluded me. The image of Akari's tear-soaked face was burning a hole in the back of my mind; I couldn't shake it, no matter how hard I tried.

I had my guesses as to why she'd broken down like that, of course. We'd been talking at length about her newly deceased brother, and I'd just revealed to her an anecdote that showed a compassionate side of him she probably didn't get to see very often. It made sense for her to get a little teary-eyed about that— and she probably only ran away from me because she didn't want me to see her crying. So I knew, rationally, that it probably had nothing to do with anything I said or did...but it still *felt* like I'd hurt her feelings.

"Man, I'm a dumbass..."

I really shouldn't have let Akito's name come up in any capacity. Akari may have doubled down on the subject, but I was in the wrong for bringing him up in the first place. I decided to make a point of calling her tomorrow to apologize. Finished sorting through the last of my thoughts, exhaustion crept up on me like a thief in the night. I closed my eyes and drifted off into a deep and wakeless sleep.

I slept soundly all the way until noon. After dragging myself out of bed, I went downstairs and had lunch with Eri and my grandmother, then headed back up to my room. According to my alarm clock, it was past 1 p.m., and the date still read "April 5th" as expected. I sat down on my bed, pulled my cell phone out of my pocket, and gave Akari a call like I'd promised myself I would the night before. After redialing twice, then thrice, she finally picked up on my fourth attempt.

"*Yes, hello?*"

"Hey, it's me. You got a minute?"

"*Uhhh... Sure, what's up? I can't talk for very long, though. We're running around getting things set up for the wake tonight.*"

"Yeah, no worries. I'll make it quick," I assured her, then paused for a moment to gather my nerves. "So, I just wanted to say sorry about last night. I, uh...know I said some things that were probably pretty thoughtless, given what you're already going through."

"*What? No, no—you didn't do anything wrong, Kanae-kun. If anyone should be apologizing here, it's me... Reminiscing about my brother like that was a little...too much for me to handle last night, that's all.*"

So my theory was right, then.

"Yeah, I getcha. It's cool. How are you holding up today?"

"Oh, I feel way better after sleeping it off. It's just..."

"Just what?"

I heard the sound of Akari swallowing her saliva on the other end.

"Sometimes, it just feels like my heart can't take much more... That's all."

I was at a loss for words—it was like I could feel the depths of Akari's depression permeating through the speaker from the other end of the line. None of the shallow condolences I could think to offer would do anything more than feed the void. I had to think of something more personal, more meaningful than empty words—but before I could do that, Akari rushed out an excuse to end the call and cover up her sorrow.

"Sorry, I need to get back to work. I'll talk to you later, okay?"

"H-hang on a second!" I blurted without even thinking of what words might come next; I couldn't bear to leave her in such low spirits. After a moment's hesitation, I mustered up the steadiest voice I could manage and said: "Don't worry yourself sick over this, okay? I promise I'll figure something out. I'll find a way to use the Rollback so that you never have to go through all this heartache. Leave it to me...and try to hang in there for now. All right?"

Despite my best efforts, the words came out as little more than empty reassurances. They were all I could offer her right now, though. All I wanted was to give her some sort of hope to cling to, some light at the end of the tunnel. I didn't know whether that sentiment made it through to her or not, but after a while, I heard what sounded like a tiny, halfhearted chuckle from the other end of the line, muffled and slightly nasal.

"...*Thanks, Kanae-kun. I'll talk to you later.*"

She hung up. I fell backwards onto the bed. Whether or not that was actually laughter I heard remained up for debate, but I may have succeeded at raising Akari's spirits the tiniest bit after all. Not that I expected the effect to last very long; she was still lost and alone in a void of depression, the true depths of which I couldn't possibly discern.

I wanted to, though. I wanted to know how deep her sorrow went, so that I could dive in and rescue her from it—no matter what it might take. So then, what was I to do? It went without saying: I would delve deeper into the past and save Akito's life.

All I had to do was undo the source of all her pain, and she'd go right back to being her old happy self again. Or more specifically, she would never even have to go through the pain of her brother's loss to begin with. All of a sudden, I could feel a warm and bubbling sensation building within my chest—a sense of duty, a driving purpose. I now had a fire of motivation burning within me, spurring me onward to save her brother no matter the cost.

"...I'll do it, Akari. You wait and see."

I stood up from my bed and began ruminating over what my first steps to that end should be. *Right, I still need to do some good old-fashioned investigating.* I hadn't figured out where I was and what I was doing on the night of April 1st when Akito died—last night had wiped away all memories of my plan to look into that today. But how was I supposed to go about finding that information? I'd already asked my grandmother and Akari, but neither of them knew anything. Eri was a potential option, but judging from what my grandmother told me, she wasn't likely to know anything either. I couldn't think of a single other person who might be able to tell me—my social circle was admittedly quite small.

Maybe a change of scenery would help me think of something. I headed downstairs and slipped my shoes on, but before I could walk out the door, my grandmother accosted me.

"Where are you going, Kanae?"

"Just out for a quick walk."

"Well, don't forget that the Hoshina boy's wake is tonight. Make sure to be home by suppertime, won't you?"

"Will do, Grandma," I replied, then shut the door behind me.

I knew walking around without a set goal in mind would be a waste of time, so my plan was to take a look at two places I knew for a fact were related to Akito's death—both the bar he was drinking at beforehand and the empty lot behind the tobacco shop where his body was found. I knew exactly where both places were, so I figured the next logical step would be to take a look at each of them with my own two eyes. I headed down the route toward the harbor, until eventually, I arrived at the Asuka Tavern—only to find that there was a sign posted on the sliding entrance door that announced they were "CLOSED TODAY."

Thinking there might still be someone working (doing inventory or cleaning, for example), it seemed like a good idea to at least check inside; that way I could see if there was anyone I could ask about that night. Sadly, the door was locked, so I was apparently out of luck on that front. I looked at the sign posted next to the door and saw that Thursdays were the only days they were closed completely—they opened up at 5 p.m. on all other days. I would just have to try again tomorrow. Giving up on this lead, I left the bar behind and headed over to the empty lot where Akito's body was discovered.

It took me about fifteen minutes to reach the empty lot. Flowers and other offerings had been laid out in tribute to the deceased: a couple of bouquets, a few bottles of fruit juice. There was no doubt about it now—this was the scene of Akito's death. I had to say, these were some pretty paltry offerings for a man who'd once been the most famous person on the entire island.

The lot itself was so overgrown with weeds that you could scarcely even see the ground. If you ventured a bit further in, though, you could see a spot where a clearing had been made in the overgrowth, which was presumably where the body had lain. No, forget presumably. It must have been the exact spot where Akito fell over due to alcohol poisoning and met his end. I imagined what his last moments must have been like—his heart stopping, all the color draining from his skin—and the thought gave me chills.

I found myself wondering for a moment if I should go buy something to leave as an offering for him too but rejected that notion as soon as I thought it up. That would be akin to accepting his death, and I had no intention of doing anything of the sort. As such, I decided it would be a bad omen to do so, not to mention a waste of my time. What I needed to focus on now was gathering more information on the night of April 1st. I left the empty lot behind.

I spent about another hour roaming around the island but ultimately wasn't able to gather anything of value. And no wonder, considering I hadn't tried to ask any of the people I'd passed on the street about it. Could you really blame me? I mean, imagine a random stranger out in public approaches you, trying to ask if you knew their location from four nights ago—anyone would think they were a crazy person. So instead I putzed around the island for a little while, trying in vain to devise a way of investigating this that didn't involve cold-calling total strangers, but ultimately failing and giving up. I sat down on the seawall and gazed out over the ocean as I contemplated what to do next. The evening sky was already painted in streaks of deep vermilion.

"Well, let's see. If today's the 5th...then that means I've only got three Rollbacks left before I reach April 1st again, right?"

This meant I only had two more days to gather information before I'd have to relive the night of Akito's death, and I needed to make them count. I listlessly watched the sun sink down below the horizon, trying to think of how to make the best use of the time remaining to me—when all of a sudden, I had a thought.

"...Hang on a second."

Granted, it had nothing to do with preventing Akito's death, but it was an interesting prospect nonetheless—a way to take advantage of the Rollback phenomenon that seemed so obvious, I couldn't believe I hadn't thought of it sooner. If I was moving back into the past, then I could bring all sorts of information back with me—I could even "predict" the future, in a sense. And what might I be able to use that information *for*?

Well, I could make a whole lot of money, for one thing.

It was one of the first answers most people would give when you asked them what they'd do if they had the chance to go back in time. They'd bet all their money on horse races or buy a ton of a valuable stock before the company ever made it big. There were plenty of high-stakes gambling opportunities like that. The only problem was, I had no idea how to go about buying stocks or placing bets. There was really only one realistically lucrative option for a kid my age: the lottery.

I did know how to play the lottery, at least, since I'd bought a couple of tickets before. The Rollback would make it simple as pie for me to hit the jackpot: all I had to do was look up the most recent winning numbers now, then place a bet using those same numbers after another Rollback or two. Bingo, instant piles of riches.

...Holy crap. This might actually work.

I gulped down a mouthful of saliva. The thought alone was enough to make my heart race. I decided to check the different lotteries that were available on my phone, just for reference. I needed to find one where the sales cutoff date *and* the date when the winning numbers were announced fell within the Rollback period, or else the strategy wouldn't work. Luckily, I found one that announced the winning numbers today—and it looked like the cutoff date was only three days ago, just within range. It was one where all you had to do was pick five different numbers, and if you got them all right you'd win a payout of three million yen. That was enough to buy a pretty nice car, and certainly enough for a student like me to live off of for a few years. I scrolled down the page eagerly to find the winning digits. I just had to memorize five little numbers, and then I could secure a small fortune for myself. It was more money than I could really even visualize; my hands shook as I read the numbers aloud to myself several times, trying as hard as I could to commit them to memory. Then I stopped.

Should I really be doing this?

Feelings of shame and guilt began to bubble up inside of me. I knew deep down that what I was thinking about doing wasn't ethical. Sure, it *would* be an easy way to get rich quick—but was it even appropriate for me to think about my own personal gain right now, when Akito's life was on the line? Something told me it wasn't. Unless...maybe that was a matter of moral perspective. After all, I never *asked* to get dragged into this crazy supernatural phenomenon. I might as well try to get *something* out of it... right?

I glanced down at the winning numbers again, but the guilt was strong enough now that they didn't even register in my brain. At that exact moment, as my basest human desires were duking it out with my moral barometer, I heard a voice call out to me from behind. Despite the fact that I wasn't doing anything technically illegal, this still rattled me pretty good, and I nearly dropped my cell phone into the ocean. I whirled around—it was the island's patrol officer.

"Wow, that was quite the overreaction, kid. Don't suppose you were watchin' naughty videos on that phone of yours just now, were ya?" he teased, lowering the kickstand on his bike before hopping off and walking over to me.

"God, you scared the hell out of me," I said, twisting around so that my legs were back on solid ground facing the island. "What's the big idea?"

"Hahaha... Sorry, kid. Didn't mean to spook ya or anything. Saw you sittin' there and wanted to chat for a little bit, that's all."

I clicked my tongue in frustration. How could someone have such perfectly bad timing? It was honestly kind of impressive.

"Aren't you supposed to be on the clock?" I asked.

"Aw, c'mon. Checkin' in with the islanders to see how y'all are doing falls well within my job description. You sure you're not bitter about the other day?"

"Not sure what you mean."

"You know—the way that detective from the mainland kept grillin' you like that. Couldn't help thinkin' it must've felt real bad for him to treat you like a suspect and whatnot. Would've liked to speak up in your defense, but you know how it is."

"...Sorry, when was this?"

"Whaddya mean...? It was the day you found the body, remember?"

Based on the notes I left for myself in my cell phone, that must have been...the night of the 2nd, right? So it was something I wouldn't experience for another couple of days—but I didn't want to raise suspicion, so I simply pretended that I knew what the officer was talking about and tried to pivot away from the subject.

"R-right, of course. Sorry, it's just been a hell of a week, y'know? It all kinda blends together," I laughed. This casual dismissal did raise one eyebrow's worth of suspicion from the officer, but then he accepted my excuse and nodded in agreement.

"Definitely. I'm sure that day especially must've been pretty traumatic for you, huh? What with finding his body like that and then gettin' raked over the coals about it," the officer recounted with a small sigh. "So hey, did you hear they got the autopsy results back?"

"Yeah. Acute alcohol poisoning, right?"

"Yep, you got it. So the lesson here, kid, is to always know your limits. You go getting blackout drunk and passing out in public this time of year, the cold'll kill ya even if the alcohol doesn't."

"Good thing I don't drink, then... I'm still a minor, in case you forgot," I quipped back and then casually looked down at my cell phone. It was rapidly approaching six o'clock. I needed to wrap this conversation up so I could prepare myself for the next Rollback.

"Oh yeah, and somethin' else I was meaning to tell you, kid: Do me a favor and don't go meeting up with Akito's little sister after dark, all right? I let it slide this last time, but don't let me catch you two breaking curfew again. Capiche?"

Aw, crap. He must've seen me and Akari.

"Er, yeah, sorry about that. She really needed someone to talk to last night..."

"Hang on—you guys did it *again* last night? Gimme a break, kid. You're just *trying* to start a scandal now, I tell ya."

"Wait. What do you mean, 'again'?"

"You guys were hangin' out late on Sunday night too, weren'tcha?"

For a split second, I thought I must have misheard him.

"Sorry, did you say Sunday night? As in...April 1st?" I asked to confirm.

"Yeah. I saw you two together while I was out on patrol but looked the other way. Sometime around one in the morning, I think it was."

That didn't make any sense. Akari told me herself that she didn't see me at all that night after we said our goodbyes at the seawall.

"And you're *positive* it was me and Akari you saw?"

"I mean, it's not like I've got photo evidence to prove it or anything... Why, are you tryin' to tell me that wasn't you?"

He had to be mistaken. If I took his eyewitness testimony to be true, then that would mean Akari was lying to me, and I knew she would never do that. The officer's eyes must have been playing tricks on him, I concluded... Yet for whatever reason, I couldn't bring myself to say that to his face with a hundred percent confidence.

I remembered how I'd asked Akari last night if she knew what I was up to on the evening of the 1st and how she'd seemed visibly shaken by the question. Not that that was irrefutable evidence of her lying, mind you, but it did make me unsure of who to believe. Before I could make heads or tails of it, the six o'clock chime began to play. *Greensleeves.*

This was bad. I'd lost track of time and let the conversation drag on all the way up to six o'clock, and now I was about to hit a Rollback right in front of a live audience. Frantically, I tried to brace myself for what was about to occur—if today was the 5th, then I was about to get sent back to the evening of the 3rd, right?

"Hey, what's the matter, kid? Why so panicky all of a sudden?" the officer asked.

But it was too late.

INTERLUDE III

As soon as I graduated from elementary school, I stopped taking swimming lessons over on the mainland, because I knew once I entered Sodeshima Junior High, I could just join the school swim team...and that's exactly what I did. It didn't take any time at all for me to ingratiate myself with the other members of the team, possibly because most of them had already heard about the crazy lap times I was getting as an elementary schooler. It felt like all eyes were on me; the eighth and ninth graders all had high expectations of me, as did my advisers, and the other seventh graders all looked up to me as if I were invincible.

Being a part of a competitive team did more for my swimming skills than I ever could have hoped. The only major downside was that now, I had to stay late for swim practice every day, which meant significantly less time to hang out with Kanae after school. Heck, the only reason we got to spend *any* time together at all was because he would hang back in the library and wait for me to get done. As soon as practice was over, I was always the fastest to get changed out of my swimsuit and back into my school uniform so that I could dash out of the locker room to meet Kanae over in the library, at which point he and I would head home together. It was usually so late by then that we would head straight home, but every once in a while, we'd stop by the little candy store in town on our way.

I remembered how, on one such occasion, the two of us were sitting next to each other on the bench right outside of the candy store, drinking our respective bottles of Cheerio as the hot setting sun in the western sky cast its final rays warmly against my right cheek.

"Man, why does it feel like soda always tastes better in a glass bottle—y'know what I mean?" I casually pondered aloud when I was about halfway through my melon-flavored beverage.

"What, you never learned about this?" he asked. "It's because the carbonation dissolves some molecular component in the glass that activates your taste buds. Everyone knows that."

"Wait, seriously? So it's not even the soda I'm tasting, but the glass itself? That's nuts!"

"Wow, you're so gullible. I made that up."

"Huh...? Oh, you were messing with me. Gotcha," I said. My voice echoed in the bottle as I brought it back up to my lips for another swig. Then I looked over at Kanae, who was apparently unsatisfied with this response.

"You really don't get angry very often, do you, Akari?"

"I don't?"

"Like, hardly at all. Most people get at least a *little* upset when someone pulls their leg like that. I mean, when was the last time you got really angry about something? Do you even remember?"

I thought about it for a while but couldn't think of any recent instances. I could think of plenty of times when I probably *should* have gotten mad, but I was the sort of person who'd sooner mope and feel sorry for myself than lose my temper.

"Yeah, I'm not sure I ever get mad, really," I said. "I don't like being confrontational..."

"Well, you probably need to work on that. People aren't gonna take you seriously if you never lay down the law. You might be fine for right now, but once you're in eighth grade, you've gotta be able to exert your authority over the incoming seventh graders," Kanae declared, nodding as if in agreement with himself. "Hey, I know! Why don't you try getting angry at me, just for the hell of it?"

"What, like, yell at you and stuff? No way. I don't wanna do that."

"Aw, c'mon! Think of it as practice! Show me your worst," he said, turning his entire body to face me as he braced with anticipation. I still didn't feel comfortable with this at all, but I decided to give it a good college try and raised my voice at him.

"H—hey, you...!"

A moment passed, then Kanae snorted out an amused laugh.

"Sure, whatever. Guess that works," he snickered.

"Wow, rude. See if I ever do anything for *you* again..."

My face was flushed red from the embarrassment of trying something new—but I hadn't hated trying it out. And as long as Kanae was laughing, I knew that all was right with the world. That was part of the reason I cherished even casual little interactions like these. Like pictures in a photo album, I made sure to hold on to each and every memory I had with him.

After the first few months of junior high, I started to notice some changes in my class environment. For one thing, the students had divided themselves up into two distinct factions: those who were good at sports or socializing, and those who weren't. There was a massive divide between the two groups; whichever one you were a part of determined the people you were allowed to eat lunch with, as well as who you could talk to during passing periods.

Though I had nothing to offer outside of my swimming abilities, I was still inducted into the socialite faction through sheer peer pressure, and as a result I spent my passing periods with an entire posse of female classmates gathered around my desk. I vividly remembered feeling antsy all the time in that classroom—mainly because it left me with virtually zero chance to talk to Kanae, no matter how much I wanted to. He was a member of the "uncool" faction, after all. No matter how stupid and petty it sounded now, everything really did feel like a popularity contest at that age, so snubbing the "cool" kids to go talk to Kanae would be like committing social suicide.

I still walked home with him after practice each day, of course.

That much never changed. Obviously, I wanted much more than that, but I lacked the courage to break free from our socially designated roles, not to mention the status quo of our current relationship. Which, in retrospect, may have been the reason Kanae ended up going the direction he did. It was from this point on that a rift began to form between the two of us.

One day, in the fall of our eighth-grade year, I walked into the classroom and found that someone, or a group of people, had written horrible things about Kanae all over the blackboard. They'd written his name in big letters in the center of the board, surrounded by things like "Loser," "Everyone hates you," and even "Kill yourself."

"What the... Who did this...?" I muttered in disbelief, standing with my mouth agape at the front of the classroom. A moment later, Kanae came walking in behind me and, without a single word, began erasing all of the scribblings on the chalkboard. I scrambled to try to help him, but he practically shouted me down.

"It's *fine*. I'll do it myself," he said. His tone of voice conveyed the real message, which was "stay the hell away from me right now."

I was in shock. I wasn't sure he'd ever told me off like that before. Until that day, I had no idea that the male bullies in our class had set their sights on Kanae. I asked one of my friends about it later, and they told me it was because he'd stuck up for another kid that they were bullying. Now *that* sounded like the Kanae I knew.

Unfortunately, their harassment of him didn't stop with some mean words on the blackboard—they would often hide his shoes and textbooks, and even convinced a lot of our other classmates to ignore him completely. At first, Kanae was livid about all of this, but after a while, he gave up and simply took the harassment as it came. It was like something inside of him had died, or been extinguished. All I could do was watch from the sidelines. They were bound to make me their new target if I were to jump to his defense, just like they switched to Kanae after he stood up for the other kid. Besides...I didn't want to do anything that might accidentally damage his pride.

Frustrated as I was that I couldn't do anything to help, I did tell our homeroom teacher about the harassment at one point. I was assured that the school would do something about it—but of course they didn't. I was left helpless to do anything but pretend not to notice how my best friend was being bullied relentlessly—some "friend" I was. The one sorry way in which I could try to atone was by being as bright and peppy as possible for him when we walked home together. I wanted to give him at least *something* fun to look forward to each day.

Winter came around the bend soon enough, but nothing changed. My swim team still had practice during the winter too. We would go swimming at an indoor pool on the mainland once a week, while the rest of the time we did all sorts of other basic exercises and drills. They'd make us do laps until we were all run ragged, and by the time practice was over, it would already be dark outside. Kanae would wait for me in the library, undaunted by the late hour, and we would walk home together in the bitter cold. No matter how exhausted from practice I was, I always tried my hardest to be as chipper and talkative as possible for his sake.

"Oh, man—so I read this manga the other day, right? And it's, like, *unbelievably* good," I gushed.

"Uh-huh," he nodded.

"It's got this, like, understated sci-fi thing goin' on, all about this one girl on a journey through a post-apocalyptic world, but *boy*, lemme tell ya, I was *not* prepared for that gut-punch twist at the end."

I waited, but Kanae didn't say anything, so I kept going:

"Oh yeah, and in the afterword, the author says it was based on an amateur comic book she wrote back in high school. How crazy is *that*?! Imagine being so talented at such a young age. It's really cool to see female authors getting more and more—"

"Hey, Akari?" Kanae stopped in the middle of the sidewalk as he cut me off.

"Yeah? What's up?" I stopped walking as well so I could turn to face him.

"You sure you're not overdoing it lately? Seems like you're pushing yourself a little too hard."

It was like I'd taken a bullet to the chest. *Why would he say such a thing? Was it really so obvious that I was overexerting myself?* I choked back the urge to ask such questions and instead played it off like I had no idea what he was talking about. "What do you mean? I'm not pushing myself at all."

"...Well, okay. Sorry for jumping to conclusions. C'mon, let's go home," he said and started walking down the sidewalk again. I stood there for a moment in the dark, watching his lonely silhouette grow further and further away from me, before chasing after it at a brisk jog. I caught up to him in no time at all, yet from then on, I increasingly felt that there was no way for me to close the distance between our hearts. It was like the real Kanae had long since gone somewhere far, far away from me, some place that my hands could never reach.

A few weeks passed. One day during lunch hour, I was innocently eating my food when one of the girls who always sat around my desk asked a very leading question.

"So tell us, Akari—are you and Funami, like, a thing, or...?"

"Wh-what?! N-no, we're not *dating*!" I blurted out in adamant denial. It was only after the words had left my lips that I realized my mistake. Praying dearly that Kanae hadn't heard any of that, I shot a quick glance over to his desk, but he wasn't there. I scanned the rest of the classroom as nonchalantly as I could, but thankfully, he was nowhere to be found. I allowed myself to breathe a sigh of relief.

"Really? But you guys walk home from school together *every day*, don't you?"

"Well, yeah, but that doesn't automatically make him my boyfriend."

"I dunno... Seems pretty couplesy to me. I'll say this, though: you've sure got an interesting type, Akari. I mean, what do you even see in that guy?" she asked, grinning from ear to ear.

Even back then, I knew that there were many different types of smiles that people used for many different types of occasions. Smiles of elation, smiles of relief—sometimes people smiled simply to let the other person know they weren't a threat. This girl's smile was one that I recognized on sight; it was the wry smirk of someone who was mocking me for their own amusement.

"C'mon, tell us the truth," she urged. "Have you guys kissed yet? Or have you gone even further than that?"

My face went beet red as I pictured what she was suggesting in my head. And then I got angry. It wasn't that I hadn't *ever* imagined myself doing those kinds of things with Kanae before— but the fact that *she* had the gall to broach that subject so casually, as though he and I were puppets dancing for her entertainment, flooded me with fury. How *dare* she spit on our lifelong friendship like that? I kept my cool nonetheless, not wanting to make a big scene, and simply told her calmly but firmly:

"Read my lips: me and Kanae-kun? Not a chance. We're *just* friends. There are *zero* feelings there, believe me."

The second I finished laying down the law, I heard someone walking up behind me, the soles of their slip-ons squeaking against the linoleum floor. I turned around to see Kanae standing right behind me. I was too horrified to even speak. When had he come back into the classroom? Had he heard that entire exchange? He was clearly uncomfortable, judging from the way he immediately broke eye contact with me and turned to scratch the back of his head. Then he spoke up, and my worst fears were confirmed.

"Yeah, you heard her. We're just friends. Don't get the wrong idea," he said, then immediately went back to his own desk and sat down.

The girl who'd been prodding me said only one word: "Borriiing," then lost interest and went back to eating her food. I picked up my chopsticks again as well, but it was hard to keep eating. None of the things I put in my mouth had any flavor anymore.

When school got out that day, and I was done with practice, it finally came time to head home. Kanae and I made the same old casual small talk we always did as we walked back together, but our conversation that day was extremely vapid; far more so than usual. It was like I was merely stringing words together to fill the silence, and I assumed Kanae could see right through it. Still I kept on, frantically running my mouth.

I knew I needed to apologize for what I'd said during lunch and clear up that misunderstanding ASAP. The only thing keeping me from doing so was my fear of the potential implications, because telling him I didn't mean what I said in class would be akin to admitting I really *did* have feelings for him. I'd basically *have* to ask him out, right then and there, or lose my chance forever.

What if he said no, though? The thought alone made my heart feel like it might split in two. There would be no going back from that; even if I cleared up the misunderstanding, it would only cast an awkward shadow over our friendship forever if he said no. I couldn't bear that. *Ugh. What did I ever do to deserve this?* I found myself wishing we could go back to those carefree days in elementary school, before all of this stupid social drama. I was lost in my internal languishing when Kanae called my name.

"Akari, listen," he said. There was a weight to his words that told me things were about to get serious.

"Wh-what's up?" I asked, bracing myself for the worst.

"There's something I need to tell you."

My heart raced. What could it be? Was it about what happened at lunch? Wait. What if *he* was about to confess his feelings to *me*? Like, "I need to take back what I said earlier," or something like that. God, I would be over the *moon*! I'd probably kiss him right then and there. Granted, I knew I probably shouldn't get my hopes up—but when he did drop the bomb, it was far beyond anything I ever could have imagined.

"I'm thinking about moving to Tokyo," he said. "Not until the end of next year, of course, but I still wanted to give you a heads-up."

My mind immediately went blank. It went so blank that it took me a while to even register the word "Tokyo." That was...the capital city of Japan, right? Thinking back on it now, I was pretty sure the initial confusion was just a product of my mind dissociating itself from reality. I stood there, dumbfounded, while Kanae explained the rest.

"Long story short, my dad offered to let me come live with him over there a while back. And I mean, you know how much I always wanted to move back to the big city, right? So obviously

I said yes. Well, not that it's set in stone or anything yet. I still need to figure out what high school I'd be going to and whatnot..."

Then Kanae looked at me, as if to say, "What do you think I should do, Akari?" But did it even matter? If I told him I didn't want him to go, would he stay here with me in Sodeshima? Probably. Kanae was too nice to abandon someone like that. To be clear, I *didn't* want him to go; I wanted him to stay right here with me forever. I wanted us to be able to sit and talk and drink Cheerio and watch the sun go down together until we were both old and wrinkly. I knew that I couldn't ask him to abandon his dreams for my benefit, even in spite of all that, so I tried my best to fake a smile.

"If that's what you wanna do, then I say go for it. You've got my support, anyway."

"...You mean it?"

"Of course! Besides, a smart guy like you deserves to be in Tokyo. It'd be a real shame for you to be trapped here in Sodeshima your whole life."

"...Well, all right. If that's how you feel, then I guess I'll just have to study real hard," he said with a slightly apologetic smile.

I tried to build him up with a nonstop barrage of reassurances, like "C'mon, you'll be fiiine," and "I know you can do it," and "If there's any way I can help, say the word." But in truth, I was only saying these things because I knew I'd break down and cry the moment I stopped talking. Not long after we said our goodbyes, the six o'clock chime rang out over the island—the melancholy notes of *Greensleeves* reverberating in harmony with the sorrow I now felt inside my heart.

CHAPTER 4
April 3rd, 6 p.m.

*S*HOOT, *I'm all outta time,* I thought to myself—but the Rollback had already occurred, and the officer I'd been talking to a moment ago was nowhere to be seen. What I saw instead was a bunch of children at play, swinging on swing sets and building great big mounds in a large sandbox. This was clearly a park, and not the one in the abandoned part of town, but Central Park, where I'd met up with Akari the night before. I was sitting on a bench beside the main walkway. Behind my back, I could still hear *Greensleeves,* but the tune was a fair bit louder now than it had been before the Rollback. Assuming the phenomenon was still keeping to the same pattern, then this was Tuesday, April 3rd, at 6 p.m. I'd jumped back yet again, deeper into the past, but that one little sentence the officer said still lingered in my ears.

"You guys were hangin' out late on Sunday night too, weren'tcha?"

Sunday would have been April 1st, but I hadn't seen Akari that night—she told me so herself—which directly contradicted the officer's eyewitness testimony. Maybe his eyes were playing tricks on him that night, or maybe Akari was the one who got it wrong... I knew I had to get to the bottom of this mystery, but before I did anything else, I needed to regain my bearings. Having ascertained my location, I reached for my cell phone to check the time...

"Yeah, like I said, I really don't know what happened to him..."

...But then I noticed the lady sitting next to me. She was a slender young woman, maybe about twenty years old, with long hair that had been dyed blonde and a couple of different ear piercings. She had a dog leash in her hand, attached to the collar of a Shiba Inu sitting at the foot of the bench. She must have stopped for a breather while out on a walk with her dog. I recognized her from somewhere—she was the same lady who'd rescued me from that angry drunkard at the Ocean's Bounty Festival. The thing was, I felt like I knew her from someplace else long before that. Who was she? I thought about it some more as I stared intently at her profile, until *finally* I was able to put a name to the face.

"Wait a minute. Hayase?" I asked.

"Yeah? What is it?" she said, turning to face me.

Now that I got a good look at her face from straight-on, I was sure of it. She was Saki Hayase, Akito's high school girlfriend and student manager of the baseball team. I couldn't quite tell at first because she'd dyed her hair from its natural black color, but it was her, all right. Now the question was: Why on earth were she and I sitting on a park bench together? What had we been talking about? It wasn't like she and I had ever interacted before.

"...Um, hello? Did you want to ask me something, or...?" she asked impatiently, furrowing her brow.

"Oh, uh... No, sorry. Don't mind me."

"Why so skittish all of a sudden? If something's on your mind, just say it."

She was being awfully friendly—and I already knew from the way she came to my rescue at the festival that she was probably a very good person, even if she *did* look like a bit of a punk rocker now. Since I was getting a little sick of beating around the bush to try to avoid suspicion at this point, I decided to ask her point-blank:

"Sorry, could you remind me what we were just talking about?"

"Huh? Are you serious? *You* asked the question, and you weren't even listening to the answer? We were talking about Akito, remember?"

We were? Had she and I been recounting old stories about him or something? I found it hard to believe that I'd go out of my way to ask one of his old girlfriends about him, but I had no way of knowing what my intentions were. More than anything, though, I wanted to know whatever it was she had just told me.

"Right, right. And what were you telling me about him, exactly?" I asked innocently, not expecting it to be a major problem. It was a shock when this caused all of the emotion to drain from Hayase's face in an instant. Her eyes turned sharp as daggers.

"You're really gonna make me repeat all of that, huh?" she said, with a sort of soft-spoken anger to her voice. Her imposing demeanor won out over my curiosity, and I quickly backpedaled.

"N-no, it's okay. I think I got the gist. Sorry for being annoying..." I said, bowing my head in apology. Thankfully, Hayase's expression softened quite a bit after this, and she leaned back against the bench as heavily as if she'd finished running a marathon.

"It's just...not a very pleasant subject, you know?" she said. "I'd rather not talk about it more than we already have."

Okay, now I was *really* curious. Why did the Rollbacks always seem to happen right in the middle of important events and conversations? I wished my future self had left me a note or something saying I should try to be alone in a quiet place whenever six o'clock rolled around. Hopefully I could at least remember to do that next time.

"Mmnngh!" Hayase moaned, stretching her arms up over her head. "Okay, I think that's enough talking for one day. Now don't forget, you still have to hold up your end of the bargain! I'll be expecting you bright and early tomorrow!"

"Wait. Did we make a deal or something?" I asked, genuinely confused.

"Uh, yeah?" she nodded. It was obvious that she was starting to have concerns about my short-term memory, but she thankfully gave me a refresher anyway: "You offered to help out at the festival, remember? My family's liquor store runs a big booth there every year, from sunup to sundown. Only problem is, we're a little shorthanded this year...but you said you already knew that, which was why you offered to help us out in the first place. That's the only reason I'm here talking to you right now. There—did that refresh your memory?"

Wait a minute... Waaait a minute. Things were starting to come together. Eri mentioned that I was helping out with a booth at the festival during the last Rollback. This must have been what she was talking about. But *why* did I offer to help out at the festival? That seemed extremely uncharacteristic of me, especially when I was already wrapped up in a supernatural phenomenon.

"Sorry, just to clarify: *I* offered to help you guys?" I asked.

"Yeah? That's what I've been saying this whole time..." Hayase answered.

She seemed pretty suspicious of the way I was acting at this point, but it didn't sound to me like she was lying about anything she said. I could only assume that I had offered to help her out, which seemed like an awfully irresponsible thing for me to do when Akito's life was on the line...but I didn't have much of a choice now. Maybe I could even learn a thing or two about what we'd discussed here at the park today while I was helping her out tomorrow.

"Right, of course. I remember now. Guess I'll see you tomorrow, then."

"Okay, phew! Boy, for a minute there, I was starting to think you hit your head on something and forgot all about it! Ah ha ha!"

Hayase clapped me on the back as hard as she could, and I actually winced because of how much it hurt. The little dog at her feet barked, stood up, and started wagging its tail impatiently, ready to resume their walk. Hayase obliged and stood up from the bench, then turned to face me.

"Okay then! I'll see you on the temple grounds tomorrow morning at six o'clock sharp! Wear some clothes you don't mind getting dirty, and don't be late!"

Wait, did she say six in the morning?! Man, maybe I should've faked amnesia to get out of it after all...

After waving goodbye to Hayase, I headed back home and sat down on my bed upstairs. It was half past six—6:30 p.m. on April 3rd. I needed to hurry and figure out what went down on the night of April 1st. The officer claimed he'd seen me with Akari, while Akari claimed she had no idea where I'd been after we said our goodbyes down at the seawall. Obviously, these stories weren't consistent with one another, which meant either the officer or Akari wasn't telling the truth. It would be easier for me to assume the officer was simply mistaken if Akari hadn't also been acting a little strange when I first asked her about it, which sowed some seeds of doubt in my mind. At this point, I didn't know who to believe—and the only way to know for sure was to determine if Akari was telling the truth or not.

Easy enough to say, but how exactly was I supposed to do that? I couldn't ask her the same question again, because she would probably give me the same answer. Should I try to mislead her into revealing it another way? If I could smoothly pivot the conversation topic to that night, and Akari didn't contradict her previous alibi, then I could be relatively certain that the officer had simply seen two other teenagers who weren't us. I didn't like having to be conniving about this one thing, but it was probably the least confrontational option, so I decided to go with it.

Right as I made up my mind, I felt my cell phone vibrating in my pocket. It was Akari. *Perfect timing,* I thought to myself as I answered the call.

"Hello?"

"Oh, hey, Kanae-kun. Sorry, I was really busy and couldn't pick up the phone. What's up?"

"Huh? You called *me.*"

"What, no... You tried to call me, like, an hour ago, didn't you?"

"I did...?"

I had no memory of this, but then I thought about it and realized that an hour ago would have been around 5:30 p.m.—prior to where I ended up after the last Rollback, and therefore something I hadn't experienced yet. I didn't know *why* I had called, and there was really no way for me to find out, but that didn't matter too much right now, because this was the opportunity I was looking for.

"Oh yeah, so hey—there's something I wanted to talk to you about, Akari. Is this a good time?"

"For me? Yeah, of course. What did you want to talk about?"

"Okay, so here's the thing..."

It was then that I realized I still hadn't come up with a plan as to *how* I would segue into the subject of the night of April 1st. *Crap.*

"Kanae-kun? Are you still there?"

"Y-yeah, sorry. So listen, um..."

I needed to think of something, and fast.

"...Would you be interested in going on a picnic at all? I was thinking it'd be really nice, what with the cherry blossoms in full bloom and all."

"Huh? A picnic?"

I could practically see her puzzled expression from the other end of the line. Heck, I was pretty baffled by it, myself—why, oh why had *that* been the first thing my mind jumped to? Was I for real right now? *"Hey, Akari! I know your brother died, but do you wanna have a picnic?"* It was more than a little insensitive...not to mention stupid.

"S-sorry, I guess I didn't really think that through. Just pretend I never said anything."

"...No, I think that sounds kinda nice, actually. Let's do it."

"Wait. You mean it?"

I was genuinely shocked. I thought for sure she would politely decline the invite, especially since it came completely out of the blue. I wasn't prepared in the slightest for her to actually say yes, but I couldn't very well back out now, could I?

"All right, um... Sounds like a plan. Just gotta iron out a time, then. Let's see, I've got plans pretty much all day tomorrow, so..."

I trailed off, recalling that I'd agreed to meet up with Hayase at six in the morning. And since the festival usually went until late into the night, I was pretty sure they'd need my help all day. And I couldn't make it any later than that, because the next Rollback would occur, which meant I only really had one option.

"Does tonight work for you?"

"Ooh-hoo! A little late-night picnic, huh? Sure. Sounds fun."

"Awesome. Do you wanna pick a time? I'm free all evening."

"Hrmmm... Okay, how 'bout eight o'clock?"

"Works for me. I'll come pick you up at your place right around eight, then."

"Cool beans. See you then."

I hung up the phone. That certainly hadn't gone the way I expected it to, but hey, a picnic would be the perfect setting for us to have a laid-back conversation about things. I bet that the cherry blossoms would look awesome in the dark too. In my rush of excitement-slash-jitteriness, I practically jumped up to my feet—and my cell phone slipped out of my hand in the process.

"Whoops..."

I bent down to grab it but then noticed that the impact with the floor had caused the screen to turn on. When I picked it up properly, I was reminded that there was something I meant to check on my phone. I swiped over and opened the Memos app, where I found a note containing the same three bits of information regarding Akito's death that I'd seen previously.

- 4/2: Found Akito's body @ 6:30 PM in empty lot behind tobacco shop & called police.
- Est. time of death between midnight and 2 AM that morning.
- Was drinking heavily earlier that night @ the Asuka Tavern, ~9 PM to midnight.

The fact that the note was already here meant I must have left it for myself on either the next Rollback, or the one after that. I'd need to remember to do that at some point—who knew what might happen if I forgot. But before I had the chance to start stressing myself out about time paradoxes and whatnot, I heard my grandmother calling me from downstairs. It was probably dinnertime. I slid my cell phone back in my pocket and headed down to the living room. For now, I would try to keep the Memos thing in the back of my head.

I left the house shortly after finishing my meal. It was freezing cold outside, but after deeply regretting my lack of layers the night before, I remembered to wear an undershirt this time, so thankfully it wasn't as bad as it could have been. I already let my grandmother and Eri know where I was going to be tonight, as well as my plan to get up early and help out at the festival tomorrow morning. They both seemed awfully surprised by this—probably because I'd never gone out to meet up with friends at night in my entire life. Eri asked me who I was going on a picnic with, but the thought of revealing that much left me a bit too embarrassed. I just kinda dodged the question without answering it.

After making my way down the dusky streets for some time, I turned into Akari's apartment complex. I didn't feel quite brave enough to go up and ring her doorbell, so I opted to call her cell and let her know I was outside. In less than a minute, she emerged from her second-floor apartment and came scampering down the stairs with a large tote bag slung over her shoulder.

"Hey, Kanae-kun. Fancy seeing you here this evening," she said, greeting me with a giddy smile. It felt surreal to think that a single night before, she'd been standing right in that exact same place, but with tears streaming down her face. Though that wouldn't happen until tomorrow night from her perspective, so I supposed that contrast was to be expected. The bright-eyed girl standing before me right now had no way of knowing that in about thirty hours' time, she'd be breaking into the school with me, or embracing me on the rooftop, or breaking down and crying outside her apartment in front of me. So all I could really do was play it cool and try not to make the mistake of bringing up Akito again.

"Hey, good to see you too," I said. "Sorry again for inviting you out on such short notice."

"Nah, don't mention it. I've been wanting to get out of the house and see some cherry blossoms anyway. I really appreciated the invite," she smiled again—but I could somehow sense she was putting on a brave face. It had been a mere two days since her brother passed away, so there was no way she was already over the grieving process. She was either forcing herself to seem okay, or she was only coming along as a distraction to keep her mind off the pain. She probably wouldn't appreciate me prodding her about it in either case, so I chose to keep acting casual and treating her the same way I always did.

"Cool, glad to hear it," I said. "Well then—shall we?"

We set off toward the temple grounds. The backstreets of Sodeshima were in desperate need of more lampposts, yet despite the dim lighting and gloomy atmosphere, Akari was practically skipping through the neighborhood with a cheerful spring in her step.

"So, what's in the bag?" I asked, pointing to the large canvas tote over her shoulder.

"Oh, y'know. Just the basic stuff. A picnic blanket, a couple smaller blankets for if we get cold, and a little bit of food in case we get hungry."

If cringing had a sound, you could have heard my embarrassment from a mile away. I'd invited *her* out on a picnic, and yet I didn't even think to bring any of the necessary stuff and just showed up empty-handed on her doorstep. I should have at least brought *some* sort of food item to contribute. I guess I figured since it was already eight o'clock, she'd probably eaten beforehand.

"Aw, shoot, my bad!" I apologized. "I should've brought something too. Here, let's swing by the supermarket real quick."

"No, that's okay. I made enough for both of us."

Akari's kindness and consideration was a warm balm for my weary heart. I was eternally grateful to have such an angel for a lifelong friend.

"Thanks... You didn't go too overboard making food just for this, I hope?"

"Gosh, no. I clumped together some rice balls, that's all. Don't get your hopes up *too* high."

"Oh, they're already way up there, I'm afraid. Don't think I've ever gotten to try your home cooking before, have I?"

"Aw, stop it," she blushed, looking down at the ground. "Rice balls don't count as home cooking. You're making a big deal out of nothing."

We reached the temple grounds before long. I was surprised to see that there were actually quite a lot of people there, mostly middle-aged, drinking alcohol and making merry. This was not the quiet, secluded atmosphere I'd been hoping for.

"...Lot of people here, huh?" said Akari, clearly a little disappointed as well.

"Yeah, I guess they must be pregaming for the big festival tomorrow."

"Oh, right. I kinda forgot that was tomorrow... Oh well. We're here now, I guess," she shrugged. It was pretty obvious that all of her enthusiasm had just crawled into a hole and died. Desperate to salvage the situation, I mulled over our options for a minute before offering an alternate solution.

"Y'know, we could just go to the old, abandoned park instead," I suggested. "No one would bother us there."

"Wait... You mean the one in the run-down part of town? With the little wooden shrine that you said you thought might be the cause of the Rollback?"

"Yep, that's the one. Why do you say it like you haven't already been there?"

"Because I haven't... I've only heard about it from you."

"Huh? But you were the one who invited *me* there the other day when we—" I began but stopped myself short. I was confusing the order in which I experienced events with the actual, chronological timeline again. Akari wouldn't experience that for another several days—I really needed to get my head on straight with this stuff. "Sorry, now I'm with you. Of course you haven't been there yet. But hey, now's as good a time as any to take you there, right? C'mon, let's go."

I turned on my heels and headed off in the direction of the abandoned park, and Akari—though quite bewildered by my impulsiveness—followed close behind. As we made the long trek over there, I couldn't help but grumble internally about how convoluted this whole thing was. How was I supposed to explain the rules of the Rollback phenomenon to Akari one of these days (so she could turn around and explain it to me on the 6th) when it felt like *I* still didn't even have a very good handle on it? When *had* I explained it to her, for that matter? Judging by the fact that she already knew about it now, it had to have been sometime prior to 6 p.m. on April 3rd. *Maybe I should just ask her.*

"Hey, Akari?"

"Yeah?"

"You remember how I explained the Rollback phenomenon to you and all that jazz? When was that?" I asked, looking over at her through the corner of my eye.

"Uhhh, lemme think. That was…two nights ago, I think?" she recollected.

Okay, hold the phone. How could that make any sense? Two nights ago would have been April 1st—but Akari had previously told me that she and I didn't meet up that night in any capacity. Did she have the date wrong? Otherwise, I didn't see how I could've explained things to her on that particular night.

Wait, I've got it. This wasn't necessarily a contradiction; I could've explained it to her over the phone. My cell phone's call history *did* have a record of me calling her that night, if I remembered correctly. I covertly pulled out my phone just to double-check, and sure enough, there was her name: two calls, back-to-back, shortly after 9 p.m. on April 1st. That was one feasible way I could have explained the Rollback phenomenon to her, for sure. But was it *the* way?

I tapped on the two calls for more information, thinking perhaps I could discern something from the respective lengths of each call. As it turned out, one of the two calls hadn't gone through at all, while the other one only lasted three seconds. This pretty much nipped the phone theory in the bud. There was simply no way I could have explained all the intricacies of the Rollback phenomenon to her in a mere three seconds, and there was no evidence of me texting her either.

In other words, we were essentially back to square one. I really had to have explained things to her in person. Sure, it was theoretically possible that I'd used my grandmother's landline, or gotten someone else to convey the message to her, but those possibilities seemed so minuscule that I felt it was safe to rule them out. Besides, the fastest way to get confirmation was to simply ask the girl herself. I put my phone back in my pocket and took a deep breath.

"Two nights ago... That would've been April 1st, right?" I confirmed. "Did I explain it to you in person, or just over the phone?"

"No, no. It was in person," she answered without a second's hesitation.

I began to feel a little bit dizzy. There was no doubt about it now—she had unequivocally stated that she and I met up on the night of the 1st, directly contradicting what she told me before.

"...Okay, thanks," I said, practically choking the words out as my vision began to blur. Why would Akari lie to me about something like that...? Or rather, why would *future* Akari feel the need to lie about this one thing in particular? I had no idea, not the slightest inkling. What did she have to gain or lose? What was she hiding from me?

"Whoa!"

My manic thoughts were cut short by a sharp pain in my rear end. I'd accidentally gotten my foot caught in a sewer grate, it seemed, and had fallen backwards onto my ass as a result. It was so dark outside, I didn't even notice it. *Man, I'm such a klutz. Guess that's one way to take the edge off of a disturbing revelation, though.*

"A-are you all right, Kanae-kun?" Akari asked. "Do you need help standing up?"

"Nah, I got it, thanks," I assured her with a smile as I pushed myself back up to my feet. There was still a stinging pain in my backside, but I had a feeling that would go away pretty quickly. At least I hadn't broken anything. I wiped the dirt from my pants and was about to start walking again when Akari stopped me.

"Hang on," she said. "You've still got some gunk on you."

She squatted down beside me and started patting the dust off my pants—as if she were my mom or something. Feeling awkward, I told her not to worry about it and tried to step away, but

APRIL 3RD, 6 P.M.

she grabbed my pants by the hem and told me to hold still. There was no escape now that she'd seen me fall over, so now I had to live with the repercussions... I was so embarrassed, I could feel the sweat making my undershirt cling to my back.

"Okay, that ought to do it," Akari said, bouncing back up to her feet with a smile.

"Th-thanks," I said, then hurriedly shuffled off once more toward the abandoned part of town. The closer we got, the more I could feel my nails digging deeper into my palms. *Damn it, man.* I didn't want to have to suspect Akari of being a liar.

Breaking into the high school yesterday had been a fairly atmospheric experience in its own right, but walking through these abandoned streets at night blew it completely out of the water. Though there were plenty of streetlights lining the sidewalks, they were all unlit, meaning the entire area was draped beneath a veil of absolute darkness. There were no sounds either, aside from the occasional mewling of a stray cat off in the distance or the pitter-pattering of a small animal's footsteps scurrying away as we drew near. This almost suffocating silence only served to amplify the bone-chilling atmosphere.

We pressed on nevertheless, using the flashlight function on my cell phone as our only beacon through the darkness. I had to admit, I was scared out of my mind. Akari seemed to be in the same boat this time around. She'd handled our midnight venture into the school like a champ, but right now, she was clinging to my sleeve like her life depended on it.

"K-Kanae-kun? Are you *sure* this is the right way?" she asked.

"Pretty sure..." I replied, though it was so dark I couldn't be a hundred percent certain. If it was, we should have been nearing our destination any minute now...and sure enough, the exit to the narrow alleyway soon came into view. *That has to be it,* I thought, picking up the pace until we broke through out into the clearing. *Bingo.* Before us lay the abandoned park, its plentiful cherry blossoms blooming in splendor despite the complete and utter lack of light. The gentle breeze plucked petals from their branches and sent them flying through the beam of my cell phone camera light, illuminating each one to twinkle fleetingly against the night sky.

"Whoa..." Akari marveled softly in wonder. Her grip on my arm loosened as she walked toward the majestic tree in the center of the park, almost as if in a trance. The sheer beauty of it all had apparently overwritten her fear. "This is incredible, Kanae-kun... To think this was here all along, right in our own backyard..."

"I know, right? I only discovered it a few days ago myself, but I still can't believe it."

Leaving the flashlight on, I propped my cell phone up against the jungle gym. This way it lit up the entire tree while also brightening up the surrounding area enough to see by.

"See, what did I tell ya? Nobody's gonna interrupt our picnic here," I joked.

"Yeah... You weren't kidding..." Akari replied absentmindedly. She was still gazing up at the tree, spellbound by its glory. I decided to give her a moment to take it all in.

Circling around to the other side of the tree, I peeked inside the small wooden shrine and saw that the large, cracked rock was still sitting right where I'd left it. I caught myself wondering if perhaps something would change if I were to touch it again, and even began to reach out my hand, but then stopped myself, realizing that there was a good chance it would only make an already difficult situation even worse. *If I knew we'd be coming here, I might have brought a small offering to lay at the foot of the shrine,* I thought to myself as I walked back over to where Akari was standing. But then I saw her, and I stopped dead in my tracks.

She was holding her right hand out at about eye level, letting the petals fall right into her palm. Then, once she'd caught a few, she lowered her hand down a bit, pursed her lips, and blew them away with a single soft breath. As they fluttered down to the ground, her lips curled into a gentle but ever-so-slightly mischievous smile. It was an oddly captivating sight, both serene and adorable at the same time, and I found it so alluring that I decided to keep my distance for a while longer so as not to ruin the moment. I stood there, watching Akari from afar, until eventually she noticed me.

"...Kanae-kun? What's wrong?" she asked.

"O-oh, sorry," I said, snapping out of it. "I was just enjoying—"

Once again, I stopped myself short before admitting the truth.

"Just enjoying what?" she inquired, tilting her head curiously.

Man, talk about déjà vu. We had almost this exact exchange a couple of days ago. The last time, I pulled a lame excuse out of my ass and told her something about going through old photo albums with my grandmother—and I remembered Akari seemed strangely disappointed with that answer. Should I try to come up with another excuse to hide what I truly felt again? ...*No.* This time, I would try to be brave and own up to what I really wanted to say. It was the least I could do to repay her for the unwavering affection she'd shown me up on the rooftop last night.

"I was just...enjoying the beautiful view," I said, my tone unapologetic and clear.

It seemed I'd still chosen my words too ambiguously.

"I know, right?!" Akari gushed, her eyes aglow. "This tree is *gorgeous*, isn't it?! Yeah, it definitely takes a minute to soak it all in."

My shoulders slumped as I realized she thought I was talking specifically about the tree itself, not her. I couldn't back down now, though, or else I'd be a *real* coward. I mustered up my courage and took a single step forward.

"No, that's not what I meant," I said.

"Huh?" she blinked.

"I wasn't looking at the tree, Akari."

Yet even after tacking on this dead giveaway of a hint, Akari still seemed confused at first. It took her a moment or two to catch my meaning. When the gears finally did start to turn, her face grew redder and redder by the second. She slouched over a little, fiddling with her bangs as she looked off to the side.

"Oh... W-well, uh... Th-thanks, I guess?"

"S-sure thing."

This was ten times more embarrassing than I was ready for. I immediately started beating myself up internally. *Way to go, dumbass. Think you might've laid it on a liiittle too thick there. How are you gonna follow* that *up, wise guy?* We simply stood there in silence for a while, Akari refusing to make eye contact while I plumbed the trenches of my mind in desperation for anything remotely decent to say. An ice-cold breeze tickled the back of my neck, sending an electric chill down my spine and breaking the moment at last.

"L-Let's lay the blanket down, why don't we?" I blurted out after far too long. "It's not much of a picnic if we're standing up the whole time."

"R-right, good idea," Akari agreed. "My legs could use a rest anyway."

Akari pulled the picnic blanket out from her bulky tote bag, and together we laid it out at the foot of the tree. We both took our shoes off and sat down side by side. It wasn't the largest blanket in the world, however, so our knees were practically touching.

"Okay, so are you ready to try one of these rice balls or what?" she asked.

"Oh, hell yeah," I said. "Let's pull those babies out."

Since I'd just had dinner a couple of hours ago, I wasn't actually very hungry, but I wasn't about to voice that when she'd gone to the trouble of making food for us. She pulled a small plastic container out of the tote bag, set it on her lap, and removed the lid, revealing two neatly packed rows of triangular rice balls—about ten in total.

"Wow, you really went all out!" I said.

"Ah ha ha, thanks... Yeah, I hadn't made them in a while, but once I got started, I just couldn't stop."

"Well, I guess we'd better check out how they taste!"

I plucked a single rice ball from the litter. It was beautifully shaped and still a little bit warm. I bit into it and was pleased to discover some juicy bits of salmon inside. I wasn't sure whether she actually remembered salmon was one of my favorite foods or it was a sheer coincidence, but it made me pretty happy regardless.

"Oh yeah," I nodded. "That's really good."

"You mean it?!" she beamed. "Phew, thank goodness. Feel free to have as many as you like, okay?"

I proceeded to thoroughly stuff my face, though I made sure to chew each bite thoroughly and with my mouth closed. I didn't want to let the love and care she poured into them go to waste. Akari simply watched me chow down with a giddy smile on her face.

"You're not hungry?" I asked between bites.

"Oh, I'll be having some. Don't you worry," she said—then grabbed a rice ball, took a polite little nibble, chewed, and swallowed. By the time she finished her first one, I was already reaching for my third.

"Kinda reminds you of eating cafeteria food back in elementary school, huh?" I asked.

"Mmyeah, I guessh sho," Akari said with her mouth full.

"You were always the last one to finish your lunch, I remember. Heh-heh."

Akari gulped down her current mouthful before responding.

"I mean, I was a shrimpy kid back then, with a tiny stomach to match, y'know? It was honestly an ordeal just trying to cram everything in there each day. Had to take lots of breaks."

"Yeah, but it's not like anyone was *forcing* you to eat it all, either. I remember being really worried about you hurting yourself back then—half the time, you looked like a chubby-cheeked chipmunk choking to death. It's not worth cleaning your plate if it means having literal tears in your eyes by the end of it."

"Hey, you know I don't like wasting food! Though there *was* that one time I puked it all up. Now *that* was a nightmare."

"Oh yeah, I forgot all about that..."

"Wow, really? That surprises me, considering you stayed behind to help me clean up afterwards."

"...Wait, I did? Heh. Nice job, little me."

We carried on like this, reminiscing about old times as we munched on rice balls. After about another thirty minutes, the container was empty. I was thoroughly stuffed by that point and rubbed my bloated waistline with both hands.

"Phee-yew!" I said, exhaling hard. "That was really good. Don't think I could eat another bite, though."

"Yeah, me neither. Want some tea?" Akari offered.

"Oh, absolutely."

Akari pulled out her thermos and poured some tea into a little cup; I could see that it had been kept steaming hot. I thanked her and reached out to take the cup—and our fingers touched for just a split second.

"Gosh, your hands are *freezing*, Kanae-kun."

"Really? Pretty sure this is my normal body temperature."

I glugged down the tea and handed the cup back to Akari. She put it down, then reached out her own hands and wiggled her fingers in a "gimme" gesture.

"Here," she insisted. "Let me see."

"What, are you gonna read my palm or something?" I quipped but held out my right hand regardless. Akari grabbed it firmly with both of hers and pulled it in close, mere inches from her face. The softness of her skin and the rolling, massage-like movements of her fingers were more than enough to make my heart beat double time.

"Yeah, you're pretty cold, all right," she said.

"W-well, you know what they say. Cold hands, warm heart."

"Oh, is that how that works? Gotcha."

I'd given a canned response on my part, but she took it as genuine. Meanwhile, I was stuck in limbo, my eyes darting from side to side without ever looking directly at her—I knew no matter how uncomfortable I felt about this, wresting my hand away from her would only make things ten times more awkward. I knew one thing for sure, though. This method of hers was making my face heat up way faster than it was warming up my hands.

Something I'd noticed but hadn't really dwelled upon over the past couple of days was how assertive Akari was being with me, to the point that it would be very easy for someone to read it the wrong way—especially after what happened last night on the school roof. Perhaps something had happened between us in the time period I hadn't experienced yet which helped bring us closer together. Though it must have been pretty abrupt, if so, because there were only two days of Rollback left at this point.

"Hey, Kanae-kun. Do you still remember that time back in second grade when you came to my rescue?" Akari asked, snapping me out of my reverie.

"Huh? In second grade?" I replied. "Could you be a little more specific?"

"You know, the time everyone was making fun of my skin. You came up, grabbed me by the hand, and dragged me out of the classroom."

"Oh, riiight... I feel like I vaguely recall doing something along those lines..."

"Yeah? How 'bout the part where you tried to cheer me up by sucking on my fingers?"

All of a sudden, the contours of the faint memory I'd been reaching for at the back of my mind became crystal clear—and the thick layer of embarrassment and regret it had been buried under came rushing to the surface.

"Oh my god, why did you have to remind me of that?" I groaned. "And here I tried so hard to block that awful memory out of my mind..."

"Awful?! What?! I mean, yeah, it was a little cringeworthy... But it meant so much to me at the time!"

"A *little*?! You don't just shove other people's fingers in your mouth, Akari. Even a second grader should know better than that..."

"Oh, please. It's not *that* weird."

Akari stared down at my hand for a moment, fixated, then brought it in even closer to her face. Then, she opened her mouth, and my heart raced. Was she really about to do the same thing to me, just to prove it wasn't anything to be ashamed of? For a split second, I panicked, but no. All she did was purse her lips and blow out a few slow puffs of hot air, so that her humid breath enveloped my hand in a blanket of warmth.

"There. Did that warm you up?" Akari asked with a playful grin.

"...Yep. I'm officially nice and toasty," I surrendered.

"Heh-heh... Good."

I had to resist the urge to let out a long and wistful sigh. I was thoroughly content in this moment. Being together with Akari like this felt so comfortable, so natural, that I nearly forgot the reason I'd brought her here—to find out whether or not she was hiding something from me. If I allowed myself to let that little tidbit slip from my mind, I could fully immerse myself in the happiness I was feeling right now. Too bad that it wasn't an option. I needed to clear up as many remaining uncertainties as I could if I was going to prevent Akito's death. There was no excuse for me to leave any stone unturned when someone's life was on the line.

"Kanae-kun? What's wrong?" Akari asked as I sat there lost in thought, her voice tinged with concern. Her eyes looked so pure and innocent, clear as a winter morning's sky. After hemming and hawing about it for much too long, I finally said screw it and asked her point-blank:

"Akari, I really hope you don't take this the wrong way, but..."

"Mm? What's up?"

"You're not hiding something from me, are you?"

"...Hiding something? Like what?" she asked, narrowing her eyes.

"Like...what happened on the night of April 1st, for example?"

I could almost hear Akari's heart skipping a beat. Or at least, that was how it felt to me. Judging from the way her hands were trembling, my question had obviously come as a huge shock to the system. She slowly pulled her hands away from mine, and I watched the vivacity drain from her face as she did so. This time, it wasn't just my right hand that felt exposed to the cold night air. My heart did too.

"Kanae-kun, I..." she began, her voice a fragile whisper. She didn't finish her sentence, and so I waited. I was prepared to wait as long as it took for her to complete that thought. After what felt like an entire minute, she delivered, in a soft yet heart-wrenching voice: "I can't talk about that."

I could hardly believe my ears.

"What do you mean, you can't talk about it...? Are you kidding me right now?" I pressed impatiently, not wanting to accept that she'd been hiding things from me all along. "Great, now you're making me even more worried. I mean, if something that unspeakable happened, don't you think I deserve to know about it in advance?"

"Please, just..."

"No, you need to tell me. Or do you just not trust me? Is that it?"

"O-of course I trust you!" she pleaded, raising her voice. "Look, you'll find out soon enough, all right? Believe me, it's nothing you need to know right now. So please, don't say things like that..."

Her voice was cracked and trembling, and her face looked utterly heartbroken. It made me feel downright horrible, and a wave of guilt crashed over me, as though I were a cruel pet owner who kicked a helpless puppy out of the car and drove off.

"...Fine. Sorry I brought it up," I said. It was a question that needed to be asked, but I conceded that I should have found a better way to go about it. Akari looked down at the ground and shook her head weakly.

"No... I'm the one who should be apologizing."

"...I said it's fine."

I picked my cell phone up off the ground and checked the time. It was already after ten o'clock; we were officially out past curfew.

"C'mon, let's go home," I suggested.

Akari reluctantly nodded, her eyes still downcast.

We hardly spoke a word to each other on the way back, and the few brief exchanges we did have were so superficial that I completely forgot what we talked about by the time we said goodbye outside her apartment complex.

Immediately after I made it back to my place, I hopped in the bathtub, submerged myself up to my shoulders in hot water, and let out a weary sigh. I was officially exhausted. Maybe if I hadn't made an ass of myself by accusing Akari like that, I would still be riding the emotional high of our otherwise incredible evening, but that ship had long since sailed. This icky, grimy sensation I was feeling deep inside could have been completely avoided. I knew that no amount of scrubbing could wash the guilt away.

At least I managed to glean a few new tidbits of information from this unfortunate experience: namely, that Akari was indeed hiding something from me but that it was probably nothing *too* earth-shattering or dire. She probably felt like she had good reason to withhold that information from me for the time being, although I couldn't even start to imagine what that reason might be. I resolved to stop being suspicious of Akari and believe in her promise that I would find out soon enough. Obviously, I was still highly curious about what she and I were up to on the night of Akito's death, but I knew forcing the issue any further would only hurt our relationship.

I pushed myself up and out of the bathwater. Tomorrow, I'd promised I would help Hayase out with her family's festival booth. I'd need to wake up early so I could head over to the temple grounds by six in the morning, so I decided it would be best to turn in for the night. Time to rest up for what would probably be a pretty physically demanding day.

At about 5:30 a.m. the next morning, Wednesday, April 4th, I stepped out of the house and made my way over toward the big festival, still rubbing the sleep out of my eyes. It was dark enough at this hour to see the stars out, though the sun was just beginning to peek its head up over the eastern horizon.

I made good time, arriving at the temple grounds slightly earlier than six o'clock. There were already quite a few people there getting things set up, along with a couple of apparent event organizers darting around in traditional festival garb. I stood at the entrance to the grounds for a minute, trying to take it all in, when I heard a voice call out to me. I turned to see that the voice belonged to Hayase, who was standing in the middle of a group huddle with adults twice her age. I jogged over to meet her.

"Morning, Funami," she waved. "Sorry to make you roll outta bed so early."

"Nah, it's fine. But, uh..." I trailed off, glancing around at the adults surrounding Hayase. There were four men and women, a couple of whom might pass for being in their late twenties, while the others were clearly in their forties.

"Oh, them? They're the other helpers you'll be assisting," she explained.

"Right, okay."

For a single booth, this seemed like a lot of people. Was my help really *that* necessary? I was dubious but introduced myself to the other workers as Hayase instructed anyway. When I finished, they proceeded to give their own introductions to me.

"Okay, now that you're all acquainted, you can help us start raising the canopy tents. Here, put these on," Hayase said. She was already walking away as soon as she passed a pair of work gloves to me, so I slipped them on as quickly as I could while trying to keep pace with her.

She brought us into a large storage shed on the temple grounds, from which we hauled out the long metal framework pieces that would form the skeleton of the booth. It took several trips back and forth to get all of the hardware to where it needed to be, but less than an hour later, we had three canopies set up side by side, complete with triangular white polyester tent covers. From there, we started unloading folding tables, cookware, and signage from a van parked nearby. By about half past seven, the booth was more or less finished. I walked out a short distance to marvel at our handiwork from afar.

"Man, this thing's huge..."

It looked less like what you tended to envision when picturing a festival food stand and more like it could serve as the central HQ for the entire event. Hayase apparently heard me gawking and walked over to where I was standing.

"Yeah, my family goes big every year. Didn't you know that?" she asked.

"Not really," I admitted. "I don't usually take part in the festival, to be honest..."

"What?! Well, you should! I expect to see you here every year from now on, bub! But for today, I need you to work your butt off!"

She clapped me hard on the back and walked off. I was beginning to feel like I might have gotten myself in a little over my head. Hayase soon called another group huddle where she doled out tasks to each of us helpers: Some would be doing food prep, while others would be taking orders and running the cash register. I was assigned to work the back, where I would ensure ingredients were well stocked, handle plating and packaging, and tend to other odd jobs like that. This was, admittedly, not how I imagined I'd be spending my precious spring break...especially not when I should have been focused on saving Akito.

At around nine o'clock, the customers had started rolling in, and things gradually got much more hectic. Now it was almost noon, and the temple grounds were packed to capacity. The Ocean's Bounty Festival was Sodeshima's biggest annual event, to the point that even people from outside the island knew about it, and so a huge influx of mainlanders would take the ferry over each year to take part in the festivities. The festival's main attraction was the grand cavalcade of boats, which would leave port in the early afternoon and circle the waters surrounding Sodeshima. At the center of the procession was a magnificent replica of a mythical treasure ship that was said to be piloted from the heavens down into the human world by the Seven Gods of Good Fortune. It offered its symbolic blessings unto the sea and prayers of bountiful harvests and safe journeys for the local fishermen. It never seemed all that cool to me, personally, but there was obviously *some* sort of novelty appeal to the many festivalgoers.

More than anything, though, I wanted to be done with this massive "favor" I'd signed myself up for. Ideally, I'd at least like to be home before six, so that the next Rollback wouldn't happen in the middle of a bunch of confusing action again... *Wait a minute.*

I recalled the previous Rollback, when I found myself here at the festival and realized that was exactly what was going to happen. That drunkard was going to try to pick a fight with me, and then Hayase would swoop in to the rescue. I still had no idea *why* that guy got so angry at me, but I assumed I'd probably find out soon enough. I never thought of myself as the type to go pissing off random strangers, but...

"...Hang on."

A new hypothesis floated its way into my brain. What if I made a point of being somewhere far, far away from the festival when the next Rollback occurred? There was no way I could get accosted by that balding drunkard if I wasn't even there in the first place. Then again, that would change the future, and thus everything I'd already experienced in the previous Rollbacks. It would essentially create a time paradox.

Was that something I wanted to attempt, though? There were plenty of books and cartoons in which people went around changing the past all willy-nilly without a care in the world, but the rules of fictional universes like that didn't always apply to the real world. In a certain sense, that was already what I was trying to do here. My aim was to alter the past to prevent Akito's death, thereby creating a future in which there was never a necessity for me to go back and try to prevent it, thereby creating a world in which I *didn't* prevent it, and so on, and so forth. This cyclical pattern of contradictions was the very definition of a time paradox, but I was in too deep now to get cold feet. I would have to give my best effort and hope that was enough. I decided I'd give my hypothesis a try and see what happened if I left the festival grounds prior to six o'clock. Until then, I had work to do.

By 5:30 p.m. I could hardly even feel my legs. I was officially beat. The multiple breaks they'd given us hadn't made much difference; this was much harder than I was prepared to work. I wasn't sure if I was getting paid for this or not yet, but it was definitely the sort of extended manual labor that I *should* have gotten paid for doing. I went searching for Hayase, hoping to ask her if I could be let off the hook a few minutes before six o'clock, when out of nowhere, I felt something warm and metal pressed up against my cheek. It was Hayase, surprising me with a can of hot coffee.

"Good hustle out there," she said. "Here, take this. You've earned it."

"Thanks," I said, accepting the warm beverage. "So listen, um... I'm really sorry to bail on you like this, but I should probably be heading home soon..."

"Sure, no problem. I was just about to tell you you're free to go, actually. But come around back with me for a few minutes and drink that coffee first, will ya? I wanted to give you a little token of my gratitude before you leave."

A token of gratitude, eh? What might that be?

I was pretty intrigued, so I followed Hayase around to the back of the booth, where I immediately plopped down on the ground to give my weary legs a rest. I cracked open the coffee can and poured the warm liquid down my throat. It had the perfect amount of sweetener, and to my parched throat it tasted like the nectar of the gods themselves. After I'd downed almost half the can in one gulp, Hayase hunkered down and took a seat beside me.

"You really came in clutch today, Funami," she said. "You hardly made any mistakes at all, and you're a damn quick learner, besides. You wouldn't happen to be interested in working at my family's liquor store after you graduate, wouldja?"

"Err... Maybe? Let me get back to you on that one."

"Heh. Now there's a 'no' if I've ever heard one. Don't sweat it, though, I was mostly joking." Hayase pulled a pack of cigarettes from her coat pocket, popped one in her mouth, and puffed it to life with the help of a long-necked barbecue lighter. "Whew... Looks like we had another successful year, huh? Hard to feel that excited about it when all the proceeds are going straight to the shrine, though... Oh, wait. You don't mind me smoking, do you?"

"Nah, you're fine," I said.

"Okay, phew," she exhaled, allowing herself to release the smoke she'd been holding inside her lungs. There was an awkward pause in the conversation after that, so I decided to take another sip of my coffee. As I did, I glanced over at her out of the corner of my eye. Now that I got a good look at her, I realized Hayase was actually quite traditionally attractive in spite of her punk rock exterior. I could see how a girl with her natural beauty could have been Akito's high school girlfriend, though being the student manager of the baseball team likely didn't hurt her chances either. I was wondering what their relationship dynamic might have been like when Hayase turned to look at me again.

"Well, thanks for all your help today," she said. "You really did me a solid, and you sure did a great job filling Akito's shoes."

"Hey, don't mention it... Wait, what was that about Akito?"

"Oh, did I not bring that up already? Yeah, he was originally gonna be helping us run the booth again this year, but then he wasn't able to for obvious reasons... We were gonna be a little shorthanded until you showed up and offered to help."

"Wow, that's... Yeah, I had no idea..." I admitted. This revelation filled me with a lot of complex emotions. "You two must've stayed pretty close through the years, huh?"

"Nah, not really. Nothing like how inseparable we were in high school, at least."

"What was he like back then?" I asked, genuinely curious.

"Oh, man. He was the coolest kid in school. Like, pretty much celebrity status. Everyone looked up to him, whether they admitted it or not."

"Yeah, for sure... I definitely remember that," I nodded. Even I knew all about him back then, and I was the biggest loser in my junior high class.

"Oh, sorry, were you asking more about what he was like behind closed doors? Yeah, I mean, he was pretty much your standard teenage egotist, I guess. Very full of himself, extremely competitive and a sore loser at the same time. He did walk the walk, to be fair. Not sure I've ever known a harder worker than him."

"Huh. Interesting..."

"Well, until his shoulder injury, that is."

"...Sorry?" I blinked, turning to face her.

"Huh? How come you're acting like you've never heard about this before?"

"I'm serious. I'm not sure that I have..."

"Man, you're a weird one. We literally talked about it yesterday. *You* brought it up."

Whatever she was referring to, it must have been something I hadn't experienced yet. I waited for her to finish disposing of her cigarette butt in her portable ashtray before probing further.

"So how'd he hurt his shoulder?" I asked.

"Again, I already explained all of that to you. And like I told you yesterday, this stuff really isn't fun for me to talk about, so I'd prefer not to have to repeat myself," she said. Then she stood up, pulled a thousand-yen bill out of her wallet, and passed it down to me. "Here. I know it's not much, but think of it as a small token of my gratitude. Don't spend it all in one place, now."

"M-much obliged," I said. *A thousand yen for a full day's work? Seriously...? That's hardly enough to buy myself dinner.* I resisted the urge to let out a heavy sigh and simply folded the bill in half and slipped it into my pants pocket.

"Anyway, thanks again for all your help today. You really saved my ass. We'd be happy to have you back, if you wanted to help us out again next year."

With that, Hayase waltzed off and let herself back inside of the booth. I had absolutely zero intention of doing the same amount of work again next year without proper compensation, but I *did* appreciate the few new tidbits of Akito-related intel.

I'd never heard anything about a major shoulder injury. When did *that* happen? Sometime after I moved to Tokyo? For a pitcher like Akito, a serious shoulder injury could be enough to end his entire athletic career. What really piqued my interest, though, was the *way* in which Hayase had brought it up.

"Not sure I've ever known a harder worker than him... Well, until his shoulder injury, that is."

This, to me, made it almost sound like his entire personality changed after the injury. I remained there on the ground for a while, groaning as I tried to make sense of it all. Then it hit me— I'd been sitting here far longer than I intended to. I checked my cell phone, and sure enough, only five minutes remained until the next Rollback. This was bad; I had to hurry up and get away from the festival grounds if I was going to test my hypothesis.

I shot up to my feet and guzzled down the rest of my coffee in one gulp, tossed the empty can in a nearby waste bin, and made a beeline for the exit, being extra careful not to bump into anybody as I ran. I was nearly there, and with plenty of time to spare, when I heard a voice say the name "Akito" mere inches from my ear. I stopped dead in my tracks. I knew I needed to get going, but my curiosity was too strong to bear. I turned around and saw two young men standing in line for yakitori skewers who seemed to be discussing Akito. I could afford to spare a minute or two, so I inconspicuously got in line behind them and eavesdropped on their conversation.

"Yeah, he still owed me a pretty big chunk of change too," said one of the guys. "Guess I won't be seeing *that* money ever again."

"Aw, seriously? He swindled you too?" said the other. "I mean, I knew he'd run up some ungodly tabs at a number of bars, but... damn."

"Wait, are you kidding me? *That's* what he used my money for? Goddammit, Akito."

"Well, I dunno, actually. Word on the street is, he got himself involved in some pretty shady organizations over on the mainland, if you catch my drift. Wouldn't be surprised if he was in some serious debt or even getting extorted."

"Holy crap, man. How does a guy like that go from hero to zero in no time flat? Yikes."

I couldn't believe my ears. Akito, in debt to and involved with the mob? No way. The Akito I knew would never stoop to being such a lowlife. I found myself rooted to the spot, unable to stop listening despite how ludicrous it sounded. If what they were claiming *was* true, then I couldn't help but wonder if it might be related to how he broke his shoulder. I decided to stick around and listen in on their conversation a little bit longer, but at that exact moment, I heard the six o'clock chime begin to play.

Uh-oh. Time's up.

Hoping in vain that I could still make it out of the festival grounds somehow, I took a few steps back so that I could turn around—only to accidentally trip over the leg of another customer who'd just gotten in line behind me. We both went falling backwards in spectacular fashion. Immediately, I stood back up, turned around, and tried to apologize.

"S-sorry, I wasn't paying atten—"

My breath caught in my throat. I realized then that I recognized the bright red, intoxicated face of the man on the ground in front of me. He was the very same middle-aged drunkard who'd tried to pick a fight with me right after the second Rollback. He growled in pain, then glared up at me from where his butt had hit the ground. This wasn't looking good for me; at this rate, we would get into the same exact fight all over again. I needed to hurry up and apologize before—

INTERLUDE IV

IT WAS THE FALL of our second year of junior high. I walked home with heavy, plodding footsteps that evening, following the gut-wrenching revelation that Kanae would leave Sodeshima for Tokyo at the end of ninth grade. Trudging up the stairs, I unlocked the door to our family's apartment and let myself in. My brother was still at baseball practice, and my mom was working her night job at the hostess bar, so I was home alone at this hour, as per usual. I slipped out of my shoes and walked down the dimly lit hallway, the floorboards creaking beneath my feet. I dumped my book bag on the ground in the living room, then hobbled over to the bathroom so I could look in the mirror. My face was haggard and pale, and I could even see some slight wrinkles on my forehead. I was suddenly very grateful that it was so dark outside. I would *not* have wanted Kanae to see me like this.

"Ha ha..."

My face looked so ridiculous, I couldn't help but laugh at myself. And as I did, all of the tears that I'd been holding back finally broke free and began trickling down my cheeks. My laughter slowly shifted into weeping, and then I fell to my knees, right there in the bathroom. I couldn't take it anymore. When at last there were no tears left to shed, I got up, walked over to my bedroom, and collapsed face-first onto the bed. I couldn't even be bothered to change out of my school uniform.

"Tokyo, huh..."

I pulled out my cell phone and searched "cost of living tokyo transfer student." Some cursory article browsing suggested that living expenses would run me several tens of thousands of yen per month at the very least, plus a couple hundred thousand for the initial move, not to mention potential enrollment, textbook, and tuition fees. I tried to add it all up in my head, but it quickly began to feel pointless. It was futile for me to think I could ever afford to live in Tokyo, and trying to work out the logistics would only give me a migraine. I would simply have to come to terms with the fact that after we graduated from junior high, I might never see Kanae again—and yet the mere thought was enough to make me start crying all over again, even when I thought my tear ducts had already run dry. What in the world was I supposed to do?

The inevitability of losing my best friend loomed over me all through the winter, and when spring came, Kanae and I began our final year at Sodeshima Junior High. Our relationship remained in a sort of stasis where all we really did was continue walking home together, growing neither closer nor further apart. Then spring turned to summer, and about halfway through the hottest months of the year, I retired from the swim team, so I had a lot more time on my hands that I could spend with Kanae.

Our junior high careers were rapidly drawing to a close by this point. So naturally, I started trying to think of ways in which I could stretch out my remaining time with him as much as possible. Obviously, the easiest way to have all the time I wanted with him would be to simply ask him not to move to Tokyo, but I could never do that, not after telling him I would support his decision. It wasn't like I was his girlfriend, let alone a family member, so what right did I have to complain about the educational path he'd already chosen? All I could really do was sit there in anguish as Kanae told me about all the arrangements he was making for the big move.

"So hey, I finally picked what high school I'm gonna try to aim for," he told me on the way home after class got out one day. "You know the U of I, right? Well, I've decided to take the test for their official feeder school. Their watermark for acceptance is a little high, but if I make it in, I'll be able to just ride the escalator system and coast all the way into college."

Feeder school. Escalator system. These were both terms that I was familiar with, of course, but they were concepts that were so far removed from my lower-class means and unambitious educational goals that they never registered in my brain whenever

I heard people talking about them—they would go straight in one ear and out the other. All I could really offer him were vapid encouragements like "Wow, good for you!" or "Don't worry, you've got this," and it made me feel like a pathetic excuse for a friend.

When I got home that night, I looked up the high school he was trying to test into. Kanae had mentioned that the barrier to entry was "a little high," but even that was selling it short. What made my jaw drop even more than the acceptance threshold, however, were the tuition costs. I could never, ever afford to go there on my family's income. The inescapable reality that I would never be able to live in Tokyo with him was becoming so overwhelmingly evident that it was like walls were closing in around me, eager to crush what little hope I had left.

And yet still I cheered Kanae on, staying as supportive as possible on the outside while in a state of constant suffering on the inside. No matter how much time went by, this was one pill that proved too hard for me to swallow, and before I knew it, it was fall again. It was under those overcast autumn skies, right as the winds began to grow colder, that my older brother broke his shoulder.

I didn't know how it happened. I was sitting alone at home one evening when all of a sudden, my mom and brother came in the front door together—a rarity in and of itself. My brother's face was white as a sheet. My mother looked downright heartbroken. It wasn't until later that I learned he'd had some sort of flare-up of inflammation in his shoulder that was causing him an awful lot of pain.

"It's sounding like he'll need to undergo surgery for it," my mother explained. "He might never be able to play baseball again. He's taking it really hard, so please try not to bring it up, okay?"

I nodded. She didn't have to tell me twice; I knew better than to kick the hornets' nest on a touchy subject like that. My brother had approached me earlier himself and warned me not to tell anyone about his injury under any circumstances. The whole thing didn't really faze me all that much at the time anyway, as my mind was much too preoccupied with Kanae's imminent departure to spare more than a passing thought for my brother. That is, until one particular night when I was sitting at my desk doing homework, and I heard him cursing angrily through my bedroom wall.

"Damn it... God *damn* it! What did I ever do to deserve this?! This is such bullcrap! I worked harder than anyone, goddammit...! Baseball was the one thing I had left... The only thing Dad ever said I was any good at... Ugh, why me...?"

This shook me up significantly. I couldn't help but feel sorry for my brother after that. I wasn't at all surprised to hear that he based his entire sense of self-worth on his baseball skills, what with baseball being the only thing he ever truly loved and worked hard at. I wasn't only talking about the time spent during his school career, either. I could remember him and my dad playing catch outside our apartment each and every day back before he was even in kindergarten.

I never liked my older brother very much. Ever since we were little, he'd done nothing but pick on me. He also loved to boss me around and would take his anger out on me anytime his feelings got hurt in the slightest. I'd always tried to put as much distance between me and him as possible for this reason, both physically and emotionally. In that moment, though, I felt nothing but sympathy for him. Unfortunately, that same moment marked the beginning of my brother's slow but steady decline. It was from this point on that he started letting his entire life veer way off course.

In the end, I wasn't able to stop Kanae from moving to Tokyo. He passed his entrance exam and got into the U of I feeder high school, and arrangements were made for him to move in with his father in the big city that upcoming spring. I, on the other hand, couldn't care less what high school I went to if I couldn't go to the same one as Kanae, so I settled on Sodeshima High since it was the cheapest and closest option. When they announced the results of our entrance exams, I was neither overjoyed nor devastated. I felt nothing. Next came the day of our graduation ceremony, and with it, the last day I would ever get to walk home from school with Kanae.

"You sure you don't want to go to the end-of-the-year party?" he asked me as we walked back from the ceremony. "I'm sure your classmates and fellow swim team members were really hoping to see you there."

"Eh. I'm not into big parties like that." I shrugged. "Anyway, I figured it'd be nice to have at least *one* last chance to talk to you before you go."

"We go home together pretty much every day, though."

"I mean, yeah. So what?"

"...All right, then whaddya say we have a little year-end shindig of our own?"

We stopped by the candy store for the first time in months, only to make an unfortunate discovery: the old vending machine that had been parked out front—the one with the glass-bottled Cheerio we always loved so much—had been taken away and replaced with a newer, state-of-the-art model. This made me feel a sort of profound, yearning sadness, though I couldn't quite put my finger on why. Maybe because I might never have the chance to enjoy the flavor of dissolved glass molecules again.

"...You okay, Akari?" Kanae asked.

"Huh? What do you m—" I started to ask, but then I figured it out. My voice was nasal and cracked; I'd started to cry without even realizing it. "O-oh, sorry. I tried my best not to cry during the ceremony, but I guess I couldn't hold it back any longer...or something..."

My lacrimal glands were getting awfully weak lately; I found myself crying over the tiniest, most trivial of things. And once I got started, it was nearly impossible to stop.

"Sorry," I said, snot dripping from my nose. "I'm really sorry..."

"Here, use these," said Kanae, handing me a pack of pocket tissues. I graciously accepted them and sat down on the nearby bench to dry my eyes and blow my nose. Kanae took a seat next to me, but he didn't say a word. He sat there and waited patiently for me to stop crying. *Some year-end shindig this turned out to be,* I thought to myself. *More like a funeral.*

We sat there for some period of time—I didn't know how long—whiling away the early afternoon together. The skies overhead were clear and blue, the wind through my hair cool and crisp, and as we sat together my eardrums were tenderly caressed by the lulling sound of rolling waves off in the distance. The moment was perfect, and I knew this might be the last opportunity I'd get.

Don't leave me.

I just couldn't bring myself to say the words.

CHAPTER 5

April 2nd, 6 p.m.

"R EALLY SORRY ABOUT THAT!" I apologized in a flustered voice, but it was too late.

The Rollback had already occurred, and now the rosy-faced drunkard I knocked down seconds ago was nowhere to be seen. My consciousness had been sent far away from the festival grounds in the blink of an eye. I looked around and soon discovered that I was someplace very familiar—standing near the window in my own bedroom. I could just about make out the sound of *Greensleeves* on the other side of the glass. I reached down and pulled my cell phone out of my pocket to check the date, almost by reflex at this point. The screen flashed on to tell me that it was Monday, April 2nd, at 6 p.m. Feeling somewhat defeated, I sat down on my bed and pinched the bridge of my nose between my fingertips.

"Well, that didn't work..."

In the end, I didn't manage to apologize to the middle-aged man after knocking him over, let alone remove myself from the festival grounds. Unfortunately, I knew exactly what was going to happen after that: he would try to start a fight with me, only to be talked down by Hayase, meaning I was unable to test my hypothesis about disconnecting the past from the future I'd already experienced. I should have been a lot more careful. I needed to not let myself get sidetracked by eavesdropping on some random guys' conversation and get the hell out of the festival like I was supposed to. It really shouldn't have been that hard. I could only blame my own poor judgment.

The other possibility was that time paradoxes just didn't exist in the real world. The past was already set in stone, in other words. Maybe our entire lives were predetermined, and there was nothing I could do to escape from whatever fate had decided for me. Though if that were the case, I could kiss any hope of saving Akito's life goodbye.

"...No way. Screw that noise."

I clenched my fists as if to choke the life out of any potential misgivings before they had a chance to take root. I didn't have the time nor mental acuity to sit around contemplating the true nature of time and destiny. All I knew was that the timing of the Rollback phenomenon aligned almost perfectly with Akito's death, and that couldn't be just a coincidence. There had to be a reason I was being sent back. I refused to believe that any higher power could be cruel enough to send me back in time like this without giving me a chance to change things. I alone had the power to prevent Akito's death. I needed to firmly believe that, or else I'd lose the will to keep going like this.

I did, however, have some misgivings related to the conversation I'd overheard back at the festival. All that stuff about Akito being severely in debt or getting himself involved with criminal organizations. I didn't want to think he would stoop that low, but those two guys sure didn't seem like they were joking around. I wasn't sure what to believe anymore.

"...Not that it really matters."

Whether he was into some shady stuff or not, I still needed to do whatever I could to save his life. I could find out if there was any truth to those accusations *after* the job was done, by confronting Akito himself about it.

I stood up from my bed to close the curtains, and my stomach let out a sudden, burbling growl. *Wow, I really need to eat something,* I thought to myself. Then I realized that these went way beyond usual hunger pangs; I was absolutely starving. How had I let myself go so long without eating? *Strange,* I thought as I closed the curtains and turned on the lights. Only a moment later, there was a knock on my door.

"Come in!" I yelled, and Eri walked in the room. "What's up?"

"Um... Just wanted to tell you it's almost time for dinner," she said skittishly.

"Oh, okay. Thanks for letting me know," I said, standing up from my bed to go downstairs. Eri made no indication of wanting to leave and instead remained firmly rooted to the spot. "Sorry, was there something else you needed?"

She looked pensively up at me for a moment, then gathered the nerve to ask what was on her mind.

"...So you're not still mad at me?"

"What? Why would I be?"

"Well, I dunno... You kinda stormed out of the house after that fight we had yesterday... And then you didn't come back home until this morning, and even then, you just holed up in your room. I thought maybe you were still angry..."

Stormed out of the house? What the heck is she... Oh, right! She must have been referring to the argument we had when I got here on April 1st. I put together a rough chronological sequence of events in my head: Shortly after disembarking from the ferry, I went back to my grandmother's house, immediately got in a spat with Eri, then left the house and stayed at someone else's place that night. Then, I apparently came home sometime on the morning of April 2nd but stayed cooped up in my room until right now, when Eri came to check up on me. *Yep, that seems about right.*

"H-hello...? See, I knew it. You *are* still upset, aren't you?" Eri said nervously.

"Nah, you're overthinking it. Relax. I wanted to apologize to you, actually. Really wasn't cool for me to blow up on you like that."

The tension visibly drained from Eri's shoulders as she breathed a sigh of relief.

"Well, okay then. That's all I wanted to say," she said, then turned to walk out the door.

"Hey, wait up a sec," I cut in, grabbing her by the arm. "I had a question for you, actually: do you know where I was staying last night?"

"No? Why would I?" Eri replied, one eyebrow raised with suspicion.

"...Yeah, okay. Never mind, then. Sorry for the weird question."

On that note, we both stepped out into the hallway, and Eri went on ahead of me. But just as I was about to walk down to the living room behind her, I was hit by a sudden wave of anxiety. It felt like I was forgetting something important. *But what?* I pulled out my cell phone and checked today's date again. It was Monday, April 2nd, and the time was 6:20 p.m...

"Oh, crap!"

I ran down the stairs like a bat out of hell and put on my shoes as fast as I could.

"Hey, what's with the big rush?" Eri asked, poking her head out from the living room.

"Sorry, can't talk! And I need to borrow your bike!" I shouted back as I slammed the door behind me. Straddling Eri's bicycle—which I already knew she didn't usually keep a bike lock on—I took off at full speed toward the old tobacco shop. With everything that had transpired over the past couple days, I nearly forgot about the note I left myself regarding how I was supposed to find Akito's body in the empty lot there tonight. Obviously, he would already be dead, since the autopsy estimated he passed shortly after midnight, but I wasn't about to let his body rot out there in the elements even if I couldn't actually save him until the next Rollback. Plus, the authorities needed to know.

After about a ten-minute bike ride, I rolled up to the front of the empty lot. It was overgrown with tall grass and weeds to the point that nothing seemed out of place at first glance, but when I stepped off my bike and actually started trudging through the reeds, I quickly spotted a large black lump lying on the ground further in. It was the corpse of a man who had apparently keeled over face down.

"Akito..." I muttered. No response came, naturally. His lifeless body was so still, it could almost be mistaken for a discarded mannequin. His ghastly pale skin was what ultimately forced me to accept that there was no longer a person living inside this lump of flesh, at which point I averted my eyes, feeling like I'd seen something I shouldn't have.

I pulled out my cell phone and dialed 119, reported the situation, and followed the operator's instructions. As soon as I got off the phone with her, I opened my Memos app. Sure enough, the note about where and when I had discovered Akito's body wasn't yet written, so I typed it in right then and there for the benefit of my past (or future) self.

"4/2: Found Akito's body @ 6:30 PM in empty lot behind tobacco shop & called police."

Only a few minutes after I called it in, the paramedics arrived on the scene. From this point on, everything started to feel like it was happening in fast-forward. They asked me a bunch of questions, then checked his pulse, breathing, and pupils. A little while later, one of the paramedics came over and talked to me.

"Are you an acquaintance of the victim's?"

"Yeah, more or less..."

"...Well, I'm very sorry to say this, sir, but I'm afraid there's nothing we can do. The police are going to want to examine the scene, so please don't go anywhere just yet," the man explained politely before dialing the police department. Only about five minutes later, an officer from the Sodeshima substation showed up at the empty lot on a moped. He was an older policeman, and the superior of the friendly patrol officer I knew so well. I remembered the latter referring to this older man as a "sergeant" in the past.

The sergeant told me to stay put for a moment before he jogged over to take a look at the body. A little while later, my favorite patrol officer showed up behind him on a bicycle. This was the first time I'd ever seen him with a no-nonsense look on his face instead of his usual affable smile. After checking in with his superior officer for a bit, he came over and spoke to me.

"Well, I'd say it's good to see you again, Funami, but I'm sorry it had to be under these circumstances..." he said, his expression pained and full of worry. "Won't be long before a crowd starts to form here. Let's head over to the substation so we can talk in private, yeah?"

The officer turned and started pushing his bike in the direction of the Sodeshima substation. I raised the kickstand on Eri's bike beside me and followed suit. When we got there about ten minutes later, the officer opened the door and indicated for me to sit down in a simple wooden chair over in the corner of the room.

"Okay, so I'm gonna have to ask you a lot of questions, but it's all just basic police stuff. Gotta cover our bases, y'know? So don't take it personally," the officer explained as he sat down in a rolling office chair across from me.

He proceeded to ask me a bunch of very specific questions about how I'd found Akito's body and what the scene was like when I got there. I answered each one completely honestly and in as much detail as I could. The only white lie I told the entire time was when he asked me why I'd been passing through that area near the empty lot—I told him it was purely a coincidence. In my defense, something told me that saying "I came back from the future so I knew where his body was gonna be" would be asking for trouble. When he was done questioning me about the discovery, he had me verify my current address and phone number, as well as what high school I was attending.

"Cool, so...are we done here?" I asked when that was over.

"'Fraid not. We've got a detective on his way over from the mainland right now. He'll probably want to question you as well. Might grill you a little harder than I did, so it could take a while, just FYI."

"In that case, do you mind if I call home real quick and let them know where I'm at?"

"Oh, by all means. Go right ahead, chief."

With his permission, I called home, and my grandmother picked up. I gave her the rundown and let her know that I probably wouldn't be home until late. She seemed pretty worried at first but appeared to calm down when I told her to make plenty of extra food at dinner because I'd be very hungry when I got back. Shortly after getting off the phone with her, a middle-aged man in a suit walked into the substation, and the patrol officer immediately stood up to greet him. I could only assume this was the aforementioned detective. He was a gaunt and gangly man, about a head taller than me. He seemed like he might not be in excellent health at a glance, but his eyes were undeniably sharp and discerning.

"Hey, folks." he said. "You the kid who discovered the body?"

I nodded, and the detective briefly introduced himself, then sat down in a nearby chair and started asking me a lot of the same questions the patrol officer just got done asking. His tone of voice was equally casual too, yet there was something much more intimidating about him; it made me feel way more nervous. We traded questions and answers back and forth for a little while, until eventually he asked one that made me clam right up:

"And if I might ask, why were you passing through that specific part of town, exactly?"

I knew I couldn't tell him about the Rollback, so my only option was to repeat the same lie I'd told the patrol officer.

"Kinda felt like riding my bike down that street, sir," I said. "Only found him by pure coincidence."

"But the body was pretty deep in there, behind a fair bit of undergrowth, no? You must have awfully good eyes to be able to spot something like that while passing by on a moving vehicle."

"I mean, true... But I guess I *was* riding pretty slow."

"Oh, you were, huh? Okay," the detective said, his eyes narrowing quite a bit. "So you mentioned to my colleague that you knew Mr. Hoshina—is that correct? Was he a friend of yours? What was your overall opinion of him?"

"Well, I don't know if I'd say we were *friends*, but...I certainly had a very high opinion of him. I really looked up to him as a kid."

"And yet you don't seem very shaken up by his untimely demise. Why is that?"

"I am, sir. Believe me."

"So you're telling me that you were just *randomly* out on your bike, just *randomly* happened to ride by that empty lot, and just *randomly* happened to notice Mr. Hoshina's body—do I have all that right?"

His beady black eyes peered down at me, suspicious. I felt a cold sweat beginning to form on my back. I was shaking internally, but I somehow managed to suppress it and nodded in affirmation.

"...That's correct, sir."

There was a long period of silence after that. Neither of us spoke a word. But I refused to incriminate myself anymore, and thankfully, the detective *did* relent and break the silence eventually.

"All right, moving on..."

He resumed questioning me as though nothing had happened.

When the interrogation finally drew to a close, he asked me to explain what my plans were going forward and said that the police might stop by my house over the next couple of days, and I may even be asked to come and answer some questions over on the mainland if need be. I told him I understood, though in reality I wasn't really paying attention anymore at that point. By the time I was allowed to leave the substation, it was already nine o'clock at night.

Despite how utterly famished I had been a few hours ago, now that I was actually home and had a plate of warm food in front of me, I just couldn't work up much of an appetite. Probably because I couldn't get the image of Akito's lifeless body out of my brain. Both Eri and my grandmother were very careful not to ask me anything about it, but I could tell from their expressions and tones of voice that they were dying to know more—and they had a right to know, to be fair. I wasn't in the mood to talk, though, so I took a quick bath and decided to hide out in my bedroom. I felt bad, realizing that I hadn't really spent much time with the family this week—I was either out and about or holed up in my room for most of it. But if they knew what I was going through, I was sure they'd understand.

I rolled under the covers and looked up at the ceiling, where I could almost see a faint image of Akari's face. By now, she'd probably already heard the news of Akito's death. She was probably in a state of shock with her hands clasped over her face, shaking in disbelief. I was obviously worried about her, but I decided to leave her be for right now. With things like this, people usually needed a little time to come to terms with it themselves before they were comfortable talking about it with someone else.

I yawned. It was a little early, but I felt about ready to turn in for the night.

Then I got a phone call. It was my dad. My mind raced back to the day I ran out of the house on him, and that negative association made me hesitant to answer the phone. Still, I knew ignoring him would only get me in more trouble in the long run, so I reluctantly picked up the phone.

"Hello?"

"*Heard you got yourself wrapped up in a bit of an incident. Is that true?*"

No preamble, no nothing, he just dove right in. I assumed my grandmother must have told him about what happened with Akito.

"That's a bit of an overstatement, Dad. They brought me in to ask me some questions and that was it. It was an accident, not a murder."

"*So you really did find a body, huh...?*" my father sighed wearily. "*Sad to hear what an unsafe and run-down place Sodeshima's become. Dead bodies just lying around on the streets...*"

This pissed me off a little bit. I totally agreed that Sodeshima had fallen into a pretty sorry state in recent years, but I could tell my father was hunting for an excuse to trash talk the island and its people. He loved to talk as if they were all a bunch of backwater hicks. I wouldn't stand for it.

"It has nothing to do with what 'kind of place' it is, Dad. This was just a series of unfortunate events, plain and simple."

"You say that now, but I'm telling you..."

"Tokyo's pretty unsafe too, y'know. Lots of less-than-pristine areas in big population centers like that."

"...Yeah, I guess that's true. Fair point, son."

Now this I was surprised to hear. My father almost never acknowledged the value of anything I had to say about social issues and whatnot. I figured that maybe he was feeling a little bad for all the things he'd yelled at me before I left, but it quickly became clear that in actuality, he was just trying to pivot to a different subject.

"Anyway, enough about that. Now listen. I want you back here in Tokyo ASAP."

I groaned. Of course that was the real reason he was calling.

"...Yes, Dad. I'll be home before spring break is over, don't worry."

"You'd better be. Speaking of which, I hope you've been doing your spring break homework."

My heart sank. I'd wanted to completely forget everything to do with school when I ran away, so I hadn't even put it in my overnight bag. I'd need to either finish it really fast after I got back to Tokyo or turn it in a little bit late. Not that I could tell my father that.

"Yeah, I've got it handled. Quit worryin' so much."

"Quit worrying? That's pretty rich, considering how—"

I felt a lecture coming on, so I hung up the phone. *Probably for the best,* I told myself. Still, the thought of having to do homework again after I went back to Tokyo was not a pleasant one. Then the school year would start up again, and I'd have to study for all-new classes, with harder material, and harder exams... Thinking about the unending stream of hard work that was in store for me made my bones ache. I dove face-first into my pillow, hoping to drown out these thoughts before they made me too depressed.

April 3rd, 10 a.m. I climbed out of bed and opened the curtains. It was another beautiful day. Come to think of it, there hadn't been a single day of cloudy weather since I arrived on the island. Weather like this made me itch to go out and take a hike up a mountain or something, but I knew I had work to do here. This was my last day to figure out what happened, and what I was going to do, on the night of April 1st—because in just eight hours, at six o'clock tonight, I was finally going to be sent back there. To the night of Akito's death.

In a certain sense, these next eight hours would be like one final stretch of prep work before the big day. I wanted to be as prepared and as psyched up to save Akito as I possibly could be. That being said, I already knew his approximate time of death, where he died, and what he was doing beforehand. I had to think of other things that I still needed to do... *Oh, right.* I was going to write down the rest of the notes in my Memos app. Not so that I wouldn't forget them, mind you, but so that future me would have them for *his* reference. I pulled out my cell phone and tapped my way to the note in question, then added the remaining two bullet points underneath the one I'd typed out yesterday.

- Est. time of death between midnight and 2 AM that morning.
- Was drinking heavily earlier that night @ the Asuka Tavern, ~9 PM to midnight.

There—that ought to do it. I wasn't one hundred percent sure if I'd used the exact same wording as the way I'd originally seen it written, but I was pretty sure I got close enough. As I closed the app and locked my phone, a thought flashed into my head.

"Oh, right. I was supposed to go ask around at the bar..."

I'd already tried to go there and see what they could tell me about Akito on the 5th, but they were closed for the day. I definitely needed to take care of that before the next Rollback, or I'd have no way of knowing if the notes I just wrote down for myself were even accurate. I recalled that the Asuka Tavern opened at five o'clock most days, which would leave me an hour before the next Rollback would occur. Plenty of time to ask a few questions; there was no need to rush. I decided to take it easy for a while and just try to get myself mentally prepared for April 1st.

I checked my phone—it was 4:30 p.m.—and then slipped it back into my pocket. I grabbed the handle on the sliding door to the Asuka Tavern, pulled it to the side, and it rattled right open. The bar didn't open for another thirty minutes, but I figured there might be someone here early to set up for the night. I walked inside. It was a cozy little joint, with just five or so tables aside from the bar counter seats. Hearing me enter, an older gentleman header

in an airy kimono-style top and loose-fitting trousers sprang out from the kitchen to greet me. Presuming him to be the proprietor of the establishment, I apologized for the intrusion and stated my purpose.

"I just wanted to ask a few questions, if that's all right with you..."

"Questions?" he asked. "Look, I gotta get ready to open up shop here at five, kid."

"It won't take long, I promise. Please hear me out," I begged, bowing my head.

"...Fine, fine. Just make it quick," he said impatiently, so I got straight to the point.

"Well, it's about Akito Hoshina..."

Immediately, the man frowned, and his voice grew deeper and darker.

"...Were you a friend of Akito's, kid?"

"Y-yeah..." I faltered unconvincingly.

"...Well, I sure don't recognize you," he grumbled after looking me over for a moment, then turned away from me. "Sorry, but I already answered a bunch of questions for the police, and I don't feel like talkin' about it anymore. Gonna have to ask you to leave now."

"W-wait a minute!" I cried out as he walked away. "Just one or two questions, I swear!"

The man refused to listen and disappeared back into the kitchen. What was with that attitude shift? The moment I mentioned Akito's name, it was like he turned into a brick wall.

Maybe he was still reeling from the death of a regular like Akito, and that was why he got irritated when a stranger like me came sniffing around asking questions about him. If that were really the case, I wasn't about to back down now. I wasn't some rando; I'd taken Akito's death as hard as he had. I exited the bar temporarily, waited around outside for its standard business hours to begin, and then went back inside the moment it turned five o'clock.

"Hey, come on i—Oh, you again. Don't you have anything better to do, kid?" the owner said from behind the counter, visibly annoyed from the moment he saw me. I remained undeterred and walked right up to the counter to sit down directly in front of him.

"No Akito talk this time, sir," I said. "I'm here as a customer. One iced oolong tea, please."

I was very glad I brought my wallet—the only question now was how long I could ride this bluff. The man sighed, then silently poured my iced tea into a beer mug and clunked it down on the bar in front of me. I grabbed it by the handle and downed it in one go, so fast that I couldn't even taste it. It just cascaded straight down into my stomach. I wasn't even thirsty in the first place. The barkeep looked at me in silent awe as I slammed the empty mug down on the counter in front of him.

"...Gimme another one," I said.

The man frowned but poured me a refill all the same, albeit while watching me very dubiously. He set the new glass down in front of me. I chugged it in one go again, though this time, it was a lot more painful and took me about twice as long to glug it all down. I slammed the mug down once more.

"A-another one..." I burped.

"All right, all right. Don't hurt yourself, kid," he said, scratching his head with a heavy sigh. "What was it you wanted to ask me about?"

Phew, he caved. I was very grateful that I hadn't just forced down two full mugs in vain. I gulped down another burp, as my stomach threatened to return its contents to sender, then asked what I'd come here to ask.

"Was Akito here on the night of April 1st?" I asked.

"Yeah, he was. Got here around nine and stayed till about midnight. Kept to himself, just drinkin' alone the entire time. Not sure if it was exactly nine o'clock or not, but I know for a fact he left at midnight, because that's when we always close. Had to kick him out so I could go home for the night," the man explained. Then his face turned grim. "Probably would've tried to reach out to the poor guy if I'd known this was how things were gonna turn out, but I guess hindsight's always twenty-twenty..."

Now I understood why he'd been so initially hesitant to talk with me. He was probably feeling pretty guilty for having served Akito all that alcohol. I felt bad for asking, but at least now I knew for a fact where he would be and when. Thinking that should be more than enough to save the man's life, I decided to hold off on asking any further questions.

"...Thanks for answering, sir. That's all I needed to know."

I looked up at the menu posted on the wall and saw that the cost of one oolong tea was three hundred yen, tax included.

Pretty pricey, but I stood up in front of the register and handed the man six hundred yen regardless.

"Just three hundred's fine," he said. "I know you didn't *want* to drink that second one."

"Wait, but..." I protested, yet the man had already finished ringing me up for a single glass. He was a good person, I could tell. I wasn't exactly rolling in money, either, so I took him up on his kind offer and told him I really appreciated it.

"Don't mention it," he said. "I mean, what's another three hundred yen, right? That's like chump change compared to the massive tab your boy Akito racked up here."

"Huh?" I replied, seizing up. *Akito had an unpaid tab here?*

"Here's your change, kid. Have a nice night."

"S-sorry, just real quick... Did you say Akito had an unpaid bar tab here?"

"Oh, you bet your ass he did. Hate to speak ill of the recently deceased, but boy, did that guy love to string me along. Same thing happened the night he died, actually; told him it was time to pay up, and he sorta shrugged me off. So I told him again, more firmly this time, and he totally blew up, actin' like I was saying he wasn't good for it, et cetera. It was all I could do to talk him back down."

"Wow, seriously...?"

This was a huge shock to me. I couldn't imagine Akito behaving like that in my wildest dreams. If he really did have massive unpaid tabs like this, like those guys at the festival were gossiping about, then maybe the stuff about him being involved with some shady organizations wasn't mere speculation either.

"Oh, hey! Come on in!" the owner yelled over my shoulder. I turned around to see that a new customer had walked through the door. Seeing this as my cue to exit stage right, I thanked the man politely for his help and left the building.

The sun was already beginning its descent in the western sky. It would probably be dark outside after another hour. There were now just thirty minutes left until the next Rollback, but I had pretty much all the information I needed to save Akito at this point. When I got sent back to 6 p.m. on April 1st, I'd know exactly what I needed to do.

It was pretty simple, actually: I would set myself up outside of the Asuka Tavern before nine o'clock and wait for Akito to get there, then convince him not to drink that night in whatever way I could. That was it. I didn't see any room for error, really...aside from these new and somewhat concerning revelations about his character. While Akito had always been very prideful and competitive, he had always struck me as a good person at heart. According to that barkeeper, at least, my impression of him must be wildly out of date.

I might have been able to shrug this off as an overstatement if not for what Hayase told me at the Ocean's Bounty Festival, that his personality change coincided with some sort of serious shoulder injury. That was one thing that remained a complete mystery to me. How had he injured it, and how had he changed as a result? I couldn't help wondering. I really needed to find out the truth. *If only I could talk to Hayase real quick,* I thought to myself, then realized that I could probably get just as good of an explanation from Akito's little sister. So I dialed up Akari...but she didn't answer the phone. Maybe she was too busy helping her mom out with funeral preparations or something.

It looked like trying to reach Hayase was my only option. Unfortunately, I didn't know her phone number, and there were less than thirty minutes left until the next Rollback. I did know where her family's liquor store was located, but whether I could actually make it there in time was a different story. Maybe I could look up their phone number online, and...

...*No, wait a minute.*

I recalled the previous Rollback. Hayase probably wouldn't *be* at the liquor store right now. She would be out walking her dog in Central Park. And I only knew this because I woke up there in the middle of a conversation with her. If I ran as fast as I could, it'd take me no more than ten minutes to reach the park. While it did mean playing right into the hands of fate yet again, it was crucial that I had a chance to speak with Hayase. And so I sprinted off toward the park.

True to my original estimate, I reached Central Park in just under ten minutes. I scanned the area and spotted a young woman walking a Shiba Inu right by the entrance to the park. Sure enough, it was Hayase. I called out her name from across the park, and she spun around to look at me. I jogged over to her, took a moment to catch my breath, and then got straight to the point.

"Listen, um... There's...something I need to ask you..." I panted.

"O-okay? That's fine, but, uh... Are you all right there, buddy?" she asked, taking a few steps back. I couldn't blame her. Imagine being suddenly accosted by some random guy running over to you, all out of breath and looking desperate as hell. I tried to collect myself some more before continuing.

"I wanted to ask you a few questions about Akito," I said.

"Wait. Akito Hoshina?" she clarified.

"Yes. Could you tell me how he changed after his shoulder injury, by any chance?"

She froze up; I saw the corner of her mouth twitch ever so slightly.

"Sorry, no thanks," she said. "I don't even know who you are, and I really don't feel like thinking about all that stuff right now. You're gonna have to ask someone else."

"Wait, but..." I stuttered, yet Hayase had already turned her back and resumed walking her dog. I didn't have time to find someone else to ask, though, with the Rollback fast approaching. So I ran up in front of Hayase, cut her off, and bowed my head to her. "Please! It won't take long, I promise."

"No means no, kiddo," she responded tersely.

Begging wasn't going to get me anywhere. I needed to find some sort of bargaining chip... *Wait, I know exactly how to win her over! Duh!*

"Aren't you in a bit of a bind right now, though?" I asked her knowingly. "I hear you're short on people for your booth this year."

"How do *you* know about that?" she replied, her eyes wide with genuine surprise.

"Just something I heard through the grapevine. Anyway, here's my offer: You answer a few questions about Akito for me, and I'll help out at your booth tomorrow. I can be your errand boy or do whatever you need me to do. Happy to work from dawn until... well, the early evening, at least."

Hayase looked me over suspiciously for a while. Then, after mulling it over a bit, she began to give me a makeshift job interview.

"What's your name? And how old are you, exactly?"

"Kanae. Kanae Funami. And I'm seventeen."

"And how did you know Akito, exactly?"

"He was...my hero, back in the day. Even saved me from a group of older kids that were bullying me, once upon a time."

"Oh really?" she muttered as she continued to size me up. Finally, after an agonizingly awkward silence, she nodded as if to say I'd passed the inspection. "So you'll really help out at our booth tomorrow, huh?"

"Yes, ma'am."

"It's gonna be backbreaking work, you know. And I can't pay you anything for it."

"Fine by me."

"Okay then. Sounds like you've got yourself a deal. C'mon, let's have a seat," she said, walking over to a nearby park bench. She seemed willing to talk at long last. I thanked her profusely and followed her lead. I took a seat beside her and got right down to business.

"So when exactly did Akito injure his shoulder?" I asked.

"I think it was in September of our senior year," she recounted. "It was right at the tail end of summer, just after we got back from nationals at Koshien."

If Akito was a senior, then...I must have been in ninth grade. I was probably too busy getting ready for the entrance exam for my high school in Tokyo to pay much attention to anything else, explaining why I never heard about it at the time.

"Anyway, I remember him keeling over during practice one day, clutching his shoulder in pain. Then the next day, we all found out that he'd apparently done permanent damage to it. They said it was probably due to overuse and that the inflammation was so bad he'd probably need to stop playing baseball altogether... The whole team was in shambles over the news, I tell ya."

"Wow. It was really that serious, huh?"

"Yeah, none of us could believe it either. But obviously, it was Akito who took the news the hardest. He'd always been extremely careful to stretch before practice and whatnot every day, because he really had his sights set on going all the way to the majors. He was even getting scouted by a few teams, and he loved to talk endlessly about which one he might choose if he had his pick of the litter. So I think it hit him really, really hard. And, well...the fact that he'd put so many years of hard work into refining his game probably only made it that much more crushing."

At this point, Hayase's face grew dark.

"At first, he tried to play it cool, like it didn't even bother him at all. That was really hard to watch. Then, as winter rolled around...that's when he really started to lose it. He was always a pretty short-tempered guy, but now he was downright violent. If he ever heard that anyone was talking smack about him, he'd just go up and punch them right in the face, no questions asked. People were really afraid of him. No one even wanted to say his name anymore, out of fear that he might take it the wrong way."

This conversation was starting to seriously depress me. Akito had been putting in the work toward being a professional baseball player each and every day since I was in elementary school. I could only imagine how devastating it was for him to hear that he'd never be able to wear that pitcher's glove ever again. As unfortunate as it was, I could totally understand how that could turn a man violent. Gripping my knees with both hands, I asked Hayase my next question:

"...I've also heard rumors that Akito got himself involved with some less-than-reputable types of people over on the mainland. Is there any truth to that?"

"Oh, yeah... I've heard those ones too. I honestly don't know if there's any validity to them or not, but let's just say I wouldn't be too surprised. Even back in high school, he had a bad habit of borrowing money from our classmates and never paying it back."

"Wow. Gotta admit, I have a hard time imagining that."

Hayase let out a heavy sigh.

"Yeah, I really don't know what happened to him," she said. "He started making one stupid decision after another, until eventually it killed him..."

There was a heavy hint of regret in her voice, and I had no idea what to say in response. That may have been a good thing in its own way, because she kept on talking to fill the void. It was as though she were at a confessional or something.

"I always looked up to Akito too, y'know," she went on. "Ever since we were in elementary school. I remember I used to bring sports drinks and lemon slices down to him in the dugout way back when he was in little league, just trying to get his attention. This was long before I was ever team manager, by the way. I'd go with him whenever he'd travel to big tournaments or anything, even then. And then in high school, I finally worked up the courage to ask him out, and we became boyfriend and girlfriend, and things were really great...for a while."

Hayase pressed one hand to her forehead.

"But the moment he injured his shoulder and couldn't play baseball anymore, I couldn't figure out how to interact with him. It was like he became a totally different person, and I was starting to get scared... Eventually, I had to distance myself from him like everyone else."

All I could really do was sit back and hear her out. I knew the Rollback would hit any minute now, but I couldn't bring myself to interrupt her in the middle of this heartfelt venting session, no matter the circumstances.

"I couldn't totally turn my back on him either, y'know? Even then. I mean, it was really hard to see the guy I always looked up to and had a crush on growing up reduced to such a miserable wreck... Then the other day, I worked up the courage to reach out and ask if he wanted to help out at my family's festival booth this year. He did kinda grumble and complain about it at first, but I can't tell you how happy I was when he finally said yes. I mean, I still didn't expect him to ever go back to being the *old* Akito again, but it did make me think there might be some hope for him yet... So the fact that he went and died right before the festival? It felt like the universe was playing a cruel joke on me. Still, I mean, it's not like there was any guarantee he'd turn over a new leaf, right? Some folks might argue it was a good thing he left this world before he ever did anything *truly* unforgivable. At least we didn't have to watch him turn into a full-on criminal, y'know?"

"C'mon, don't say that," I cut in, shaking my head. No matter how far off the beaten path Akito's life might have strayed, he didn't deserve to *die* for it. Hayase sort of glowered at me for a second, before sharply turning her face to look straight ahead once more.

"...Yeah, I guess you've got a point," she conceded. "No one deserves to die so young. Man, though, with all the nasty rumors I've heard about him...it's just hard to feel a whole lot of sympathy, I guess. Like, obviously there's the stuff we already talked about. He was seriously in debt, was getting linked to criminal organizations, and so on. Some of the other rumors are way more disturbing than that. Like, for example...

"I heard he's been physically abusing his little sister, Akari-chan."

"...Huh?"

Her words nearly flew right past me. They kept reverberating in my head, but I couldn't parse them. My brain knew each word's individual meaning but refused to accept the implications of what they meant when placed together in that particular order.

"Sorry, did you just say he's been..."

...*beating his sister?* I tried to ask, but before I could get the words out, I was interrupted by the staticky, low-fi melody of *Greensleeves* coming out of a nearby loudspeaker. It only amplified my anxiety. Akito couldn't have seriously been abusing Akari, right...? I refused to believe it; it had to be a rumor, some sick joke cooked up by someone who never liked the guy. But on the off chance that it *was* true, I would—

INTERLUDE V

F OR THE FIRST FEW MONTHS of my high school career, I
floated through life apathetically, without any real sense of
direction. At the insistence of my teachers and upperclassmen,
I did join the swim team, but I was basically running on fumes at
that point, and I didn't achieve any standout records like I had
in junior high. I had a hard time being mentally present during
class too, so I'd often get scolded by my teachers for spacing out.
Without Kanae there to greet me in the morning, going to school
was empty and meaningless. There was a gaping hole in my heart,
through which I could feel his absence each and every day, like an
icy wind. If I could only see him again...or even just hear his voice
over the phone, or get a text from him, then maybe... Well, it
wouldn't fill the void, but maybe it would at least calm that wind
for a while. Too bad. He never got in contact with me.

At first, I gave him the benefit of the doubt, assuming he
probably just needed some time to adjust to his new environment.

Then one month became two, and still I hadn't heard a word from him, so of course I started to get worried. There were multiple times when I told myself I should reach out to him myself, but I could never bring myself to hit that call button or send that text message.

"We're just friends. Don't get the wrong idea."

I couldn't get Kanae's words from that fateful day in junior high out of my head. I knew he was trying to get that other girl to lay off me, but his words still coiled their way around my heart like a serpent that refused to let go. Every time I thought about trying to get in contact with Kanae, that one little remark would rear its ugly head, bare its fangs, and bite down. Its paralyzing venom would course throughout my entire body, rendering me unable to do a thing. So I never did. Instead I staggered through day after day of monotony, constantly teetering back and forth between anxiety and resignation. The only way I could even tell that time was still passing was by the ever-increasing number of drafts in my unsent messages folder.

Then one night, in the summer of my freshman year, my life reached a turning point. For whatever reason, I felt compelled to go out for a run that evening. Maybe I hoped it would distract my brain from the feelings of emptiness and isolation, or maybe it was just that I had an overabundance of energy I needed to expel since we didn't have practice that day. There were any number of possible explanations. All I knew was that I felt a burning desire to go out and run, and so I did. About an hour in, I'd run half the circumference of the island, leaving my whole body drenched in sweat. I needed a break to catch my breath, so I sat down on the seawall and let the cool night breeze blowing in from the open ocean bring my body temperature back down. Across the sea, I could see the dazzling lights of the mainland glowing like fireflies, and a sudden impulse struck me.

That's where I need to be. Over there.

It felt like a flame had been ignited inside my chest. My body was burning up all over again, and I couldn't bear to sit still a moment longer. I sprinted as fast as I could all the way back home, and as soon as I got there, I started looking up information on moving to Tokyo.

After school the next day, I asked my homeroom teacher point-blank:

"What do I need to do to get into the U of I?"

It felt like my only remaining option at this point. Since Kanae was already going to the university's official feeder school, his college choice was pretty much set in stone. And if I could graduate with high enough marks to get accepted to the same university, he and I could be together again at last. Hence why I was asking my teacher about it, even though I knew I was vastly underestimating how hard that would be. I couldn't fight this new urge inside me, and I didn't want to fight it, either. I knew if I didn't start making moves right now, there was a very good chance I'd never see Kanae ever again.

"I'll be honest...you may want to lower your sights a little bit, based on your current grades. And even if you did manage to test in, that's still a very expensive school, you know. Have you talked with your mother about this at all?" my teacher asked. The response was about as unfavorable as I'd anticipated, but I refused to give in.

"No, but I will," I declared.

"Listen, I know this really isn't any of my business, but...I don't think you fully grasp the financial burden you'd be placing on her. Your mother's a very hard worker, but I just don't think a private school like that is in the cards for you. If you really have the drive to study hard and want to get into a good college, there are plenty of reputable public universities that are a lot closer."

"Sorry, but my mind's made up. I want to go to the U of I," I asserted firmly.

"...Okay," my teacher said after a moment's hesitation, not without sympathy. "If you're that dead set on this, then I'll try to help you out. Though all I can really offer is advice."

I was then given the basic rundown on what I had to do in order to make my college dreams a reality. I paid close attention to every word, and by the end, I had a pretty good idea of what my action plan needed to include. It was pretty simple, actually. Everything boiled down to three things: my academics, my extra-curriculars, and my personal finances.

The academics part went without saying. If I couldn't actually get accepted, then the rest would all be in vain. My teacher told me that I should also aim to earn some major accolades during my high school swimming career, because universities took things like that into consideration as well. Such achievements might even help me earn financial aid of some sort. Still, even if I miraculously scored a full-ride scholarship to cover my tuition costs, that wouldn't cover my moving costs nor my everyday living expenses, so I determined that I'd need to start working part-time as soon as I could.

It would be a long and arduous road, to be sure, but now that I at least knew what I needed to do to get there, I was starting to feel a lot more optimistic. I thanked my teacher for the advice and walked out of the classroom. If I managed to outswim the heck out of everyone else on the team, then it would be a piece of cake for me to get an athletic endorsement, and maybe even a scholarship. Thank goodness I'd stuck with one sport for so long. True, I'd been sort of slacking off on it ever since I got to Sodeshima High, but from this point on, I'd need to give it my all.

When I got home after practice that day, I found my brother watching TV on the living room couch with his feet up on the table. I knew Mom had asked him to stop doing that. I chose not to engage and simply walked right past him toward the bathroom. Then he called out to me, stopping me dead in my tracks.

"Hey. Go buy me a soda real quick," he ordered.

His voice was monotone; he didn't even make eye contact with me. Mind you, my brother had always bossed me around, even back when we were little, but he'd only grown more and more demanding since his shoulder injury. It used to be relatively small things like "fetch me the remote" or "go run some bathwater for me," but lately he'd begun to treat me like I was his personal maid, telling me to "go get dinner ready," or iron his laundry, and stuff like that.

To be clear, I definitely sympathized with what he must have been going through after having to quit baseball. But I also deeply resented him for what a loathsome person he'd become. Basically all he'd done since graduating from high school was sit around on the couch and watch TV all day, or go out and do who knows what with his deadbeat friends, only coming home when he felt like it. He showed no interest in getting a job or going to college and yet had the gall to turn around and ask our mom for cash at every opportunity. As far as I was concerned, he didn't have a respectable molecule, let alone bone, in his body.

"Hey. You deaf or somethin'?" he barked, glaring at me impatiently.

Usually, this was the point where I would back down and begrudgingly do as he said, but that wasn't going to fly from now on. Not when I needed to study as much as I possibly could at home to make my dream of moving to Tokyo a reality. If I kept doing every little menial task my brother demanded of me, I'd be wasting tons of valuable time. It was time to lay down the law, I decided, so I tried to tell him no in a way that wouldn't set him off.

"Sorry, no can do. I've got a lot of homework I need to do tonight," I explained.

His eyes shot wide open. Then he grabbed the remote control on the coffee table and threw it right at my head without any hesitation. I shrieked as it crashed against the wall mere inches from my face, sending the battery cover flying through the air.

"Do as I said, you little brat. Don't think you're hot stuff just 'cause you're the fastest doggy paddler in the kiddie pool," he spat, then grabbed his drinking glass and threatened to throw that as well. I whipped both hands over my head as a defensive reflex.

"A-all right, jeez... I'll go buy your stupid soda..." I said, practically running back through the living room. Without even a chance to change out of my school uniform, I scuttled out of the apartment. My entire body was shaking. I never would have expected him to actually start throwing things at me for refusing to be his errand girl. He'd never done anything like that to me before; the brother I'd come to loathe was beginning to actively terrify me. I made my slow way down the steps toward the nearest vending machine as tears of dread and despair welled up in the corners of my eyes.

The next morning, I told my mom that I wanted to go to college in the big city. I explained that I knew our finances were tight, but I assured her she wouldn't have anything to worry about, because I'd handle my tuition costs either through scholarships or student loans. I told her I planned to get a part-time job in the near future, too, to cover the costs of living on my own. She gave me her seal of approval and said she'd see if she could get me a job at a local traditional-style inn that she knew paid a fairly decent hourly wage. Her eyes were full of shame as she apologized for not being able to offer more assistance than that, but I told her it was more than enough.

Now that I'd decided what college to aim for, I had an excuse to contact Kanae at last. With butterflies in my chest, I giddily drafted up a long-winded message to break the news to him... but in the end, I didn't send it. My better judgment told me it might seem a little creepy and overbearing to say I was already planning to go to the same college as him when we weren't even halfway through our freshman year. I decided to hold off until the spring of our senior year, a much more natural time for people to have settled on what their ideal higher education path would be. Whether Kanae knew it or not, though, I'd just taken my first steps toward moving to Tokyo.

The following year and a half, leading up to the present day, were easily the most grueling months of my entire life.

As the summer of my freshman year drew to a close and autumn set in for good, everything started to blur. My only real memories from that time were of being completely and utterly exhausted from the cycle of work, study, swim, day in and day out. I couldn't afford to slack off on any of these three pillars of my life, either, so it was my sleep schedule that took the hit. I started nodding off in the middle of class as a result, often missing a lot of important lecture material. I did okay in the mornings, but after lunch, it was a struggle to stay awake long enough to copy down notes from the blackboard. I persisted anyway, fighting desperately against the urge to sleep so it wouldn't affect my grades.

When the school day was over, I could finally allow my brain some rest. It wasn't much of a reprieve, admittedly, because I had to run straight from the classroom down to swim practice. The format hadn't changed much since my time in junior high. We still swam in the school's outdoor pool during the summer and did physical training during the colder months, with one day a week set aside to go swim at an indoor pool over on the mainland. The only thing that *had* changed was the difficulty. Our new swim coach was a real disciplinarian and would work us to the bone each and every day. There was never a single day when I didn't walk out of practice feeling like a crushed bag of chips.

Even after that, I still had to go to work at my part-time job. I had to wring every last drop of energy from my limbs like a ratty old dish rag to keep smiling as I greeted and served the inn's guests. It was still an unfamiliar working environment to me despite my efforts, and since I was always at the height of my physical and mental exhaustion by that point in the day, I slipped up on the job more times than I cared to admit. Sometimes I would get lectured by my older part-time coworkers, and other times I'd even get yelled at by angry guests on some sort of "customer is always right" power trip. On nights like that, I would lock myself up in the bathroom for a while and have a good, long cry where no one could hear.

Typically, I'd be so utterly exhausted by the time I got off work that I could fall asleep standing up. And yet, even then, my day wasn't quite over. I had to go home and study on my own time to prepare myself for the university entrance exam. As soon as I made it home, I grabbed a bite to eat, took a quick bath, and then tried to hit the books for at least two hours each night. Supplementary studying was essentially mandatory for me, as the core Sodeshima High curriculum was not nearly adequate to get into a prestigious school all on its own. After those two hours were over, I summoned up my final ounce of remaining energy to hobble across the room and crawl into bed, where I immediately passed out. If the next morning was a school day, I would do it all over again, and if it was the weekend, I'd either go straight to work or to swim practice. I never gave myself any days off.

You'd think I might get used to this rigorous schedule after a while, but no. Every new day was like a fresh hell. I carried on living like this even so, never giving myself any time to second-guess my decision or mope about how awful I had it. My mind and body were both equally worn out. Never in a million years would I have thought that it could possibly get even worse.

I remembered having a dream one time. In this dream I walked to school, made my way up to the classroom, and Kanae was there...at Sodeshima High.

"Hey, Akari. How's it goin'?" he said.

"Kanae-kun?! Wh-what are you doing back in Sodeshima?!" I asked in disbelief as I slowly made my way over to his desk.

"Oh, yeah. The high school I was going to shut down, actually. So I decided to come back here."

"W-wow, that's crazy..." I said. Then all the strength drained from my body at once. I collapsed to my knees right there in the middle of the classroom.

"You won't have to push yourself so hard anymore, Akari," he said, reaching down to help me up. "We can just take things slow and enjoy ourselves like old times."

"Yeah... I'd like that," I said, taking his hand and letting him pull me back up to my feet. Then we went up to the roof of the school and ate lunch together. I was so happy, so relieved, and so excited that I couldn't stop talking. Kanae sat there with a smile on his face, listening to every word.

"Akari," he interrupted at one point, staring deep into my eyes as he brought his face in close to mine. I froze up like a porcelain doll, too astonished to move an inch. He brushed his hand gently against my cheek and then pulled it away again.

"You had a little bit of rice on your face," he said.

"O-oh, is that all? Sheesh! Tell me that *before* you start comin' in hot next time! Ah ha ha..." I teased, laughing it off. The laughter quickly segued into tears. Because I knew by that point that it was all just a dream. That sooner or later, I was going to have to open my eyes and face another day of my waking nightmare. And yet, I still didn't want to let go of this moment. I wanted to stay here with Kanae and hold on tight to every last second I could get. Even if it was all a lie.

"Don't cry, Akari," he pleaded.

And I tried. In that moment, I would have done anything for Kanae. The problem was that he'd asked for the one thing that I couldn't possibly grant.

"...Hey, Hoshina-senpai! Wake up!"

Wearily, I became aware that someone was shaking me by the shoulders. I cracked my eyes open and saw one of the younger girls from the swim team staring back at me as though I were causing a public disturbance to embarrass her.

"We're back in Sodeshima. It's time to get off."

"...M'kay," I mumbled drowsily. I thanked her for waking me and rose from my seat. I would often doze off on the ferry ride like this, the slow undulations of the waves beneath the boat lulling me to sleep. I stepped off the boat and out of the harbor, then stretched out my arms and took in a deep breath. All around me were the sweet scents of spring.

I was a sophomore now. Advancing a grade level didn't mean my hectic schedule had gotten any easier, sadly. Every day remained a perilous balancing act between school, swimming, and work...but I *did* feel like I'd started to make progress. Slowly but surely, my grades were getting better, and I had a pretty nice chunk of change saved up. My swimming career was similarly on the upswing.

My teacher said I might even be able to apply for an athletic endorsement from the U of I, explaining that it was an alternate way for students who achieved great feats in specific sports to gain priority admission without enduring the rat race of traditional applications and public endorsements. In my case, all I'd really need to do to qualify was make it to nationals in swimming. The good news was that there was much, much less competition for those applying for athletic endorsements compared to general admission. They usually came with a pretty hefty scholarship, to boot. As someone whose family was strapped for cash to start, this was a pretty attractive option, so I reallocated some of my time and mental resources from studying to swimming. In order to compete at the national championship tournament, I'd first need to win big at the district preliminaries which were held only once per year in the summer. As a sophomore, I had two chances left. I knew I'd have to push myself even harder than I already had been to make it there, but I was determined to claim that sweet, sweet scholarship money.

I worked myself to the bone, getting my crawl stroke time as low as I possibly could. I watched the numbers dwindle smaller and smaller, along with the amount of sleep I got each night. To be fair to myself, that wasn't entirely due to me practicing all the time. It was largely because of my brother. Lately, my brother was bringing his friends back to the apartment about once every three days. Since my mom worked late into the night, he and two or three of his buddies would hang out in his bedroom, getting drunk and cracking jokes until the early hours of the morning. All night, I was subjected to vulgar cackling, juvenile hooting and hollering, and unrepentant stomping. It was so loud that there was literally no escaping it. I'd try to pull my comforter up all the way over my head to shut out the noise, but the walls of our apartment were so thin that their booming voices and howling laughter still made my eardrums throb painfully all through the night. Being unable to get the sleep I so desperately needed, even for the few short hours my stressful schedule allowed, was torture. As the night drew on, and the sleep deprivation got worse and worse, I started to get so agitated and restless that it felt like I might go crazy.

"Ugh, just shut up already..."

I curled up in a ball under the covers and tried my best to think about something more pleasant. Like how when I moved to Tokyo and saw Kanae again, it might be nice for us to go somewhere fun together. Maybe the aquarium or an amusement park. I didn't really care where, honestly, as long as I could be with him. There were so many things I wanted to talk to him about too. I wondered if he'd joined any clubs at his new school, what kind of friends he had, and...whether he'd already found a girlfriend. What would I do if he had? The thought of him having a girlfriend who was way cuter and funnier than me made me sick to my stomach, but it would explain why he hadn't been in contact with me. *Ugh, I hate this. I should just text him and ask so I know for sure. Yeah, I'm gonna do that. But wait... What if he says yes? How will I even respond? Gah, okay, no. I need to stop letting my pessimistic imagination get carried away.* I willed my brain to shut itself off so I could get what meager amount of sleep I could.

A few months passed. Before I knew it, it was June, and the national preliminaries were right around the corner. I remembered coming home one day after eleven at night, totally exhausted from practice and work. But before I hopped in the bath, I pulled my bankbook out of my desk drawer and flipped it open. I glanced through the list of deposits to see that my savings were really starting to add up. Once I deposited today's paycheck, my account would break the long-awaited million-yen barrier. That was more than a year's worth of living expenses already! I did feel a little bit miserly, standing there wringing my hands (figuratively) over how much money I had, but seeing the numbers add up gave me the push I needed to keep going. I did some math in my head, trying to figure out how many more months of work I'd need to do to hit my original goal, when all of a sudden, the door to my bedroom swung open.

"Whoa!" I cried out as I dropped my bankbook on the floor in a startled panic.

"Hey, Akari. My buddies are coming over later," said my brother. "Gonna need you to go out and buy some snacks for us."

I couldn't believe it. The *gall*—the sheer *audacity*. He'd barged into my room without permission—without even so much as *knocking*—and now he was demanding I go play errand girl for him again. I wanted to scream. Who the heck did he think he was? Despite all this, I couldn't bring myself to talk back out of fear that he might start throwing stuff at me again. So I bit my lip and knelt down to pick my bankbook up off the floor. Once I returned it to my desk drawer, I grabbed my wallet and stomped out of the house without a word.

"And be quick about it too!" my brother yelled after me.

I was seething. This last remark nearly pushed me over the edge. Still, I did as I was told, went out and bought the stupid snacks my brother always told me to get, then came back to the apartment. My brother snatched the grocery bags out of my hands the second I came through the door, then immediately returned to his room without even a single word of thanks.

Late that night, right as I finished up my studying and was getting ready to crawl into bed, my brother's friends showed up at the house—almost as if they'd *planned* it that way just to prevent me from getting even a wink of shut-eye with their stupid, obnoxious antics. Only this night, they actually went a little bit further than that.

"Hey, you've got a little sister, don't you, Akito? Akari-chan, right?" asked one of my brother's friends. Again, the walls were so thin that I could hear each and every word.

"Yeah, and? What about her?"

"Oh, I just thought I saw her around town the other day. She's gotten pretty cute, man. Is she over there in the room next door right now?"

My blood ran cold. My body seized up in primal terror. I felt an intangible evil gnawing its way into my chest, tracing its icy tongue along the contours of my heart.

"Wanna invite her to chill for a little while?" said his other friend.

"Hey, good idea. Go tell her to come over here and get wasted with us, Akito. Lord knows we could use some chicks around here."

"Dude, no. That sounds lame as hell."

"Aw, c'mon, man! Fine, I'll ask her myself. Hey, Akari-chaaan! You still awake over there?!"

A burst of uproarious laughter came blaring through the walls from the room next door. Even my brother was laughing now. Meanwhile, all I could do was lie there petrified, shivering in fear with my head under the covers. I didn't even know what I would do if my brother came marching in here right now. The thought alone was so terrifying that I started sobbing into my pillow. Never in my life had I been more frightfully aware of the fact that there was no lock on my bedroom door.

I didn't get one wink of sleep that night. My brother and his friends didn't end up doing anything, but it was still the most harrowing experience of my entire life. I had reached my limit. As soon as my brother's friends went home in the early morning, I ventured out into the living room and confronted my brother head-on.

"All right, look. We need to talk," I said.

"Huh? Whaddya want? Actually, no, save it. I'm too tired right now," my brother yawned as he waltzed away toward his bedroom. His arrogant attitude was the straw that broke the camel's back.

"Okay, no! I've had it up to *here* with you!" I yelled, and he spun around in surprise at once. "All you ever do is treat me like your personal slave and keep me up all night with your stupid partying... Please, Akito. This has to stop. I can't do it anymore."

His cheek twitched angrily.

"Quit blowin' things out of proportion. We were just enjoyin' ourselves a little bit. Maybe you should invest in a pair of earplugs if it bothers you so goddamn much. You're not the boss of this house, so stop actin' like it."

That did it. Something snapped inside of me, and the floodgates burst open. I unleashed all of the fury and resentment I'd been holding back for more than a year now.

"Oh yeah? That's pretty rich coming from a mooching bum who isn't even trying to find a job. How long are you gonna keep milking that busted shoulder of yours as an excuse, huh? Until our mom works herself to death?"

My brother's eyes shot wide open, and his face flared beet red.

"The *hell* did you say to me?!"

He pushed me down with such incredible force that I honestly thought he might have broken my sternum. My legs gave out, and I fell backwards directly into the coffee table—where one of its unforgivingly pointed corners dug deep into the side of my lower back.

"Agh, hngh..."

A sharp pain ran through my hip. I couldn't move. I was stuck grunting helplessly on the floor as my entire body broke out in a profuse sweat. I tried a few times to straighten myself back up, but it only made the pain that much more unbearable. My brother clicked his tongue at me and walked out of the house. A while later, my mother finally got home from work.

"Akari! Are you all right?! What happened?!" she shrieked, letting her shoulder bag drop to the floor in the dash over to help me. She rushed me to the small health clinic here on Sodeshima, and from there, I was transferred to an actual hospital over on the mainland.

I was diagnosed with a suspected "transverse process fracture" of one of my lumbar vertebrae. Essentially, I'd cracked the little protruding nub bone extending off from one side of an individual segment of my lower spine. When they showed me my waist area in the mirror, I saw a big, deep-purple bruise, like someone had smushed a handful of blueberries against my lower back. The doctor told me that surgery wouldn't be necessary, and that there should be no further complications so long as I wore this funny corset-style back brace for a while and took time off to recuperate. The resulting hospital bill wasn't unreasonable at all, and they discharged me that same day.

The problem was that I really couldn't *afford* to take any time off right now. It would be three weeks before I could return to my part-time job, and two whole months before I was allowed to start swimming again. This meant that I had to completely give up on the idea of making it to nationals this year, all while being forced to lie in bed like a cadaver. All I could do to cope with the despair of wasting one of my two remaining chances was weep softly into my pillow. What I truly wanted was to bawl and wail at the top of my lungs, but whenever I did more than gently sob, the contractions of my diaphragm made it feel like long, rusty nails were being hammered into my spine. My only real remaining option was to try my very best to snuff out my emotions altogether.

To stop feeling anything at all. If a random bystander were to look at me, lying motionless in that bed, they'd probably think I was spacing out or something, but on the inside, I was crying out in agony from morning until late at night.

How could all of my athletic efforts go to waste?! I sacrificed all those work and study hours for nothing! What did I ever do to deserve this?! What do I have to show for all those grueling hours of practice I put in now?! Nothing!

I had one more chance to go to nationals, and it wouldn't be for a whole year. The thought alone was enough to put my stomach in knots. Making it worse, only a single person seemed to care I was going through this hell: my mother. She even took some precious time off work to take care of me and sat loyally at my bedside when I was in too much pain to even walk around the apartment on my own.

"Tell me something, Akari," she inquired one day while I was still bedridden. "What *really* happened that morning?"

I had to think for a while about whether I should tell her the whole truth or not, because I knew it was extremely likely to break her heart. My mother worked just as hard as I'd been working, but for the family's sake, and for far longer than me. She didn't deserve any extra stress on her plate. Recognizing that this was one thing I really shouldn't remain silent about, I decided to tell her the truth even so.

"Akito pushed me down...and I fell backwards and hit my tailbone on the coffee table," I confessed.

"I see…" said my mother. "I had a feeling it was something like that. All right. Thank you for being honest with me. And I'm so sorry I allowed such a thing to happen to you due to being an absentee parent. I'm such a horrible mother…"

"No, Mom! It's not your fault at all. Please don't say that."

"Well, rest assured that I'll be speaking to Akito about this. I'll make it crystal clear to him that if anything like this *ever* happens again, he'll be out on the streets."

She sounded like she really meant it. I knew that I could count on her. Or at least, that's how I felt at the time. That night, as I was falling asleep, I heard her yelling over in the living room, her voiced raised to a volume she rarely, if ever, used. Curious, I decided to go and take a look at what was going down. Taking care not to put any strain on my lower back, I hoisted myself up out of bed and stepped out into the hallway. Then I crept up to the door to the living room, which was open just a crack, and peeked inside. My brother was sitting there on the couch while my mother berated him ruthlessly. It was obvious from her frantic yelling how little experience she had punishing her children like this, and yet my brother sat there completely unfazed by any of the words she was saying. If anything, he looked annoyed at how loud she was being, as if he couldn't wait for her to shut up. Then all of a sudden, he and I made eye contact. It was only for a split second, but that single glance was more than enough for him to convey to me that he was going to make me pay for this. *Just you wait.* Panicked, I slunk back into my bedroom to escape from his contemptuous gaze, already regretting my decision to tell my mother the truth.

By the time I recovered enough to return to swim practice, our team had long since been eliminated from the district preliminaries, and all of the seniors on the team had already retired. My remaining teammates welcomed me back with open arms, asking me if I was healing up okay and letting me know how much they'd missed me. Their appreciation of me during what was undoubtedly the most challenging year of my life really did mean the world to me, and I couldn't help but tear up a little bit from how touched I felt. It also made me feel really bad, because I'd been so laser-focused on improving my lap times up until this point that I hadn't made much of an effort to build a connection with any of them. I decided that from this point on, I would go out of my way to engage with them.

I started talking with my teammates a lot more after that, giving pointers to the first-year newbies and making small talk with the other girls whenever there was a break during practice. They were always extremely friendly to me, and whenever I was laughing with them, it allowed me to forget about all the painful aspects of my life for a while. It was probably the most fun I'd had since I entered high school, but it wouldn't last for long. About two weeks after I returned from recovery, I was using the pool restroom when two of my teammates walked in and started gossiping about me. They didn't realize that I was right there in one of the stalls.

"So what do you think Hoshina-san's deal is, anyway?" said one of the girls. "I dunno what's going through her head, but the way she's been acting is pretty rich, if you ask me."

"Right? Like, does she not realize that it was *her* stupid injury that screwed us out of going to nationals in the first place? And then she has the nerve to come smiling back like nothing even happened? It's unbelievable."

"Hey, you wanna know what I heard through the grapevine? They're saying it was actually her *brother* that gave her that injury."

"Wait, seriously? Like, legit domestic violence?"

"Yeah, apparently that guy's turned into a real piece of work lately. Super fragile ego, always asking his friends for money and then never paying it back, beating his sister... Scumbag."

"Wow, what a piece of crap. And you know he's just wasting it all on booze too. How poor and trashy can one family be? I mean, at least Akari's been busting her ass trying to save up money to go to college, I guess, but really?"

"Hey, don't speak so soon. You never know! Maybe she'll start begging *us* for money one of these days. And so the cycle of poverty continues!"

"Ha ha! Okay, but why do I feel like that might actually happen?"

I just sat there stunned for a while, long after the two girls exited the restroom. I couldn't even muster up the will to be angry. All I felt was an intense self-loathing. It was so humiliating to think I'd taken their kind words and well-wishes at face value, even believed them when they said they really missed me... I was a fool to think they actually cared. I started deliberately avoiding all of my other teammates after that.

Thinking back on it now, this was probably where my deep-seated trust issues first began. Anytime I heard someone laughing by the poolside, I would automatically assume it was at my expense, and whenever any of the other girls came up and tried to talk to me, I went into defense mode and told myself they had some ulterior motive. They soon stopped trying to interact with me altogether, and I became a loner on the swim team once again. These trust issues soon started to rear their ugly heads in the classroom as well. While I generally spent most lunch periods face down on my desk, hoping to squeeze a nap in, I *did* try to socialize with my classmates a little bit before this debacle. After it, I talked to virtually no one and ate lunch by myself in silence.

No matter where I went, I felt unwanted. Like I didn't belong.

The only place where I *did* find some solace was up on the school roof. Whenever it felt like I couldn't take being surrounded by these people during lunch, I'd walk out of the classroom and go kill time on the upper landing of the stairwell where the roof access door was. Once I learned the trick to opening that door, I went out onto the rooftop and spent my lunches up there more and more often. I couldn't tell you why, but something about being up there just calmed me down completely. It was the only place I felt like I could breathe. It was like the entire island of Sodeshima was a sunken city, and this was the only place high enough for me to poke my head up out of the water and get some fresh oxygen in my lungs. Whenever I looked down from up there, I felt the same exact thing: *I need to get off this island, and fast.* Then, without fail, the warning bell for fifth period would ring, and I'd sink back beneath the waves again. Forced to hold my breath for yet another day.

After my lower back injury, my brother eased off on all of his demanding and disruptive tendencies for a while. He stopped bringing his friends over to the house, and he didn't order me around like I was his maidservant. Unfortunately, this new leaf of his didn't last for long. By the fall of my sophomore year, his worst behaviors had come back with a vengeance. He was now being even *more* belligerent and obnoxious: partying even later into the night, constantly waking up hungover and in a foul mood, barking insults and throwing things at me again. On particularly bad days, he'd even punch me in the shoulder, or lift his leg up and slam his foot into the small of my back. He seemed to feel no remorse whatsoever for having fractured one of my bones—if anything, injuring me had only emboldened him and made him feel like he could get away with anything.

I didn't have the willpower to fight back anymore, either. I always apologized and acted like nothing happened. My mother would yell at him just about anytime they were in the same room, but this only made things worse, as he would then proceed to take his frustration from being scolded out on me with more physical abuse.

My life was a living hell. And yet no matter how hard things got, I knew I couldn't afford to rest even one minute. I had to pour all of my time and energy into my studies, my swimming, and my job, so that once I graduated, I could get away from this godforsaken place once and for all. That was the one thought I found reassurance in, that this would all end when I made it out of high school. Moving to Tokyo to be with Kanae again was my one and only glimmer of hope through the darkest days of my young life. Still, by completely snuffing out any sense of self-worth I might have had, I narrowly managed to make it through each day. It got to the point where I was completely happy trimming off a few years from my life span if it meant a better life in Tokyo down the line.

And so I worked myself to the bone, praying that the worst of it would soon be over. I resolved not to let any obstacle or hardship get me down again, no matter how crushing. But today, on April 1st, in the middle of spring break before my senior year, and the same day that Kanae came back to Sodeshima for the first time in years... Today was the day the world found a way to rip my heart in two...and break my spirit completely.

I had work until three in the afternoon today. Usually, I worked a full shift on the weekends, but the inn was closed to-morrow, so I got off early. I went home, unlocked the door, and stepped into our apartment. I then headed down the hallway to my room but noticed something was amiss the second I entered; my desk drawer was hanging open ever so slightly. I'd always been very particular about closing it, so it struck me as pretty strange. I shrugged it off and walked over to close it, nonetheless. Right as I was about to do so, I peeked inside, and my hands froze. Both my bankbook *and* my signature-authorization stamp were gone.

"...What the...?"

I stood there for a while, inert. Reflecting on it now, it was something of a calm before the storm.

"W-wait, but..."

Then, finally, came the lightning crash. I yanked open every other drawer in my desk, then slammed them all shut. Finding nothing in there, I proceeded to rifle through my dresser, look under my bed, and reach around inside my purse like a thief gone mad. My bankbook was nowhere to be found. What was I supposed to do now? If someone broke in and stole it, and they had my identification stamp, they could drain my whole account, and then I wouldn't have enough money to...to...

I wanted to start bawling loudly, right then and there. I held it in somehow and racked my brain as hard as I could. If a burglar had actually stolen it, there should have been evidence of a break-in, right? The apartment looked fine on the whole, and the front door was definitely locked. Which meant it must have been either my mother or my brother...and I had a bad feeling I knew which of those two it probably was. I pulled out my cell phone to call Akito, hands trembling. My finger paused a millimeter above the dial button.

What if—and this was a pretty big if—but what if I was wrong, and it hadn't been my brother? Was I prepared for the wrath that might ensue from an accusation like that? He would do far, far worse than just kick me. There was no doubt about that. The thought scared me enough that I chickened out of making the phone call. As I stood there at a loss of what to do, a thought occurred to me. What if it hadn't been stolen at all? What if my mom needed to borrow a little money or needed my account information for some business at the bank? There were several possible explanations that didn't involve losing every last bit of my savings, and this thought calmed me greatly. Maybe I was fooling myself, but I had to focus on these slim possibilities so that I wouldn't vomit then and there. I was determined not to look reality in the eye.

I knew I probably wouldn't be able to get much studying done while this remained an open question in my head, but I couldn't stand sitting around to do nothing, either. I ran out of the house. I ran frantically around town, as fast as I could, hoping the rush of adrenaline would somehow shake the anxiety from my mind. Less than thirty minutes later, I was officially winded, and my limbs were like jelly, so I sat down on the seawall to catch my breath. I spun around and looked across the ocean as I waited for my heartbeat to stabilize. The hazy silhouette of the mainland felt somehow farther now than ever before.

I might have just lost my one chance to move to Tokyo, I thought to myself, and then the tears came streaming down. But then, something magical happened. I heard a voice call out to me, so I turned around, and I saw him. Kanae was right in front of me. Not in a dream, but in the real world. He was here, in the flesh, and only an arm's length away.

"Akari...?"

"K-Kanae-kun?!"

This unexpected reunion caught me so off guard that when I stood up, I nearly fell backwards into the ocean. Thankfully I didn't, and it was because Kanae was there to catch me. He and I then went on to have a whole little dialogue, during which I did my very best to act like nothing was wrong. I didn't want to ruin our long-awaited reunion by talking about my lost bankbook, or my abusive brother, or anything remotely depressing.

Weirdly enough, the more I talked to him, the less it felt like I was acting. After a while, I was genuinely enjoying myself again. It was as if hearing his voice was slowly refilling my cold, empty, desiccated heart with warm waters that soothed my soul. When he revealed that he did not, in fact, have a girlfriend back in Tokyo at the moment, I breathed such a sigh of relief that I nearly fell to my knees right in front of him.

"Have you decided what college you're going to next year?" I asked him eventually.

"Yeah—U of I," he replied. "But you knew that already."

It was exactly the response I expected, but it was nice to fully confirm that I would need to move to Tokyo if I wanted to be with him again. That settled it. It was time for me to stop moping around and tackle my problems head-on. I said goodbye to Kanae and then headed back home. As soon as I arrived, I pulled out my cell phone and called my brother that very instant. I feared if I waited any longer, I might lose my nerve again. And I *had* to know where my bankbook was.

He didn't pick up, which knocked some of the wind out of my sails. Still, I wasn't going to give up that easily, so I planted myself on the living room couch and stayed there until my brother came back home.

When he returned to the apartment at long last, it was around nine o'clock at night. Mustering up all the courage I could find, I stood up and confronted him.

"H-hey, Akito? You wouldn't happen to have my bankbook, would you?" I asked, trying not to sound *too* overly accusatory. He shot me a dirty look, then pulled both my bankbook and my authorization stamp out of his coat pocket and handed them to me. *So it* was *him,* I thought to myself, momentarily relieved that he'd fessed up so easily and returned it. Then I flipped the bankbook open, and I couldn't believe my eyes. After a single withdrawal, my savings balance had gone from over 1,000,000 yen all the way down to a mere 1,200. I stood there, looking down at the numbers in abject horror as all of the blood drained from my face.

"Wh-wh-what have you done...?" I asked. My voice shook in disbelief.

"Pfft," my brother spat, as though he'd accidentally swallowed a fly. "Just borrowed a little money, that's all. Dinged some dude's car the other day, and he forced me to pay for the repairs. Turns out he's actually a bigshot gangster, so I didn't really have a choice."

My mouth hung wide open. I was at a complete loss for words, and yet somehow, the worst was yet to come.

"C'mon, don't be like that," he went on, "you and I both know you probably weren't gonna get into that college anyhow. Besides, if you're really that dead set on moving to Tokyo, why don't you get a job at a strip club or something? Plenty of 'em over there."

"A...a *strip* club?!"

"Yeah, or a hostess bar or something, I dunno. Anyway, hey, I was gonna head over to the bar real quick. Could you lend me five hundred? I know you've got at least that much left in your wallet."

Never before in my life had I known that when your anger surpasses a certain threshold, your blood quite literally runs cold. It was like one of those science experiments I'd seen on TV was being recreated inside my head. That one where they dip a rose petal into a vat of liquid nitrogen, then pull it out, squeeze it, and it shatters into a million pieces. That pretty much exemplified what happened to my sense of reason in that instant.

"Graaaaaaagh!" I wailed, grabbing my brother by the collar with both hands. "How?! How could you do such a thing?! Why do you have to ruin my life at every possible opportunity?!"

"Hey! Let go of me!"

"Do you know how *hard* I had to work to save up all that money?! I worked myself half to death! But you wouldn't know a thing about that, would you?! You don't know the first thing about me!"

"I said *get off me!*"

My brother ripped my hands from his collar and pushed me away. I fell backwards, my back slamming hard against the floor. A stinging pain shot through my spine.

"It's not like you know anything about *me* either!" my brother yelled as I lay there, grunting in agony. "The world's taken everything from me! My dad, baseball—everything I ever loved! I never did anything to deserve that! So why shouldn't I get to take a few things back in return?! Isn't it only fair?!"

"Why are you asking *me*...?! You're not the only one who lost their father here, you know! Just because you can't play baseball anymore, that doesn't give you the right to steal other people's hard-earned money...!"

"Don't lecture me, you little brat!"

My brother clenched his fists and moved in closer. I looked up at him towering over me and saw no trace of sanity left in those eyes. A chill ran through my entire body. I scrambled in vain to get away, crawling backwards along the floor, and then heard my cell phone vibrating on the floor beside me—it must have fallen out of my pocket when I hit the ground. The screen displayed the caller's name: Kanae. I grabbed the phone without a second thought and answered it as fast as I could.

"Kanae-kun, you've gotta help me!" I cried.

"Hey! Who said you could answer that?! Give it here!" my brother barked, snatching the phone out of my hands and ending the call. "Damn you. Tryin' to get me in trouble..."

He threw the phone on the ground, then pointed one finger straight at me.

"You're never getting off this island, you hear me? So just shut up and do as I say like a good girl," he hissed, his spittle spraying out across my face. He stormed out of the apartment without

another word. As soon as he was gone, I broke into an uncontrollable bawl, right there on the ground, as if I'd finally been broken
beyond repair.

I FOUND MYSELF STANDING in front of the miniature wooden shrine looking down at the cracked stone housed within as *Greensleeves* blared out from the loudspeaker behind me. I took a step back to look up at the resplendent cherry blossom tree above and the darkening sky behind it. Nearby were a few pieces of rusty old playground equipment. There was no doubt about it—I was back in the abandoned park again, right where this all began.

I reached for my cell phone and checked the date. Sunday, April 1st, 6 p.m. I'd made it all the way back to the day I first arrived in Sodeshima, the same day that Akito lost his life. After five long and confusing days, I'd get to see how the rest of April 1st played out. I knew exactly what I needed to do next. I'd head over to the Asuka Tavern, stop Akito from drinking by any means necessary, and that would be that. It shouldn't be difficult at all, and I had plenty of time to get over there.

However, I couldn't get what Hayase had told me right before the Rollback out of my mind. It kept gnawing at my chest like a sharp fishbone caught in my throat.

"I heard he's been physically abusing his little sister Akari."

If this was in any way true, it would totally destroy any respect I ever had for Akito...but at the end of the day, it was only a rumor. I couldn't imagine the same guy who'd stood up for me to those bullies way back when beating his own sister, no matter how far he might have fallen. I didn't even want to consider that possibility. For the time being, though, my objective hadn't changed; I needed to focus on preventing Akito's death. I could look into the veracity of those rumors after that.

I ran through the empty, abandoned streets toward the Asuka Tavern. I was aware he wouldn't arrive at the bar until nine o'clock, which was three hours from now, yet I still felt the need to rush over there for some reason. It only took me about twenty minutes to reach my destination. I found myself an inconspicuous stakeout spot a little further down on the other side of the street, where I could keep an eye on the entrance to the bar without alerting or arousing suspicion from the other customers. Now all I needed to do was wait for him to arrive...but as it was only about 6:30 now, I'd be stuck waiting for another two and half hours. I leaned my back up against a nearby telephone pole and settled in for the long haul. Right then, I felt my cell phone vibrating in my pocket. I pulled it out and saw that it was my grandmother calling me, so I answered the phone.

"Hello?"

"Sweetheart, where have you run off to? It's almost dinnertime. Please come home."

Right—this was the day I'd stormed out of the house to cool my head.

"Sorry, Grandma. I'm a little busy right now... Might not be home until pretty late."

"Busy doing what? And how late are we talking?"

I wasn't sure what to tell her. I obviously didn't want to go home now and risk not being able to come back here later, but I also had no idea when I *would* be finished with my business here. So I decided to just be honest with her.

"Sorry, I don't know yet. I promise I'll call you as soon as I have a better idea of when I'll be home. Like I said, though, it'll probably be pretty late."

"You're not still upset at Eri, are you?" she asked reproachfully.

"No, Grandma. It has nothing to do with that."

"...Well, all right."

"And don't worry about saving leftovers for me, either. I'll figure something else out."

"Okay. But do try to be home as soon as possible, dear. I can tell that Eri's quite worried about you, even if she'd never admit to it."

"...Heh. You don't say."

"Anyway, don't keep us waiting too long. Talk to you soon," my grandmother said, then hung up the phone. I randomly recalled that she had been the one who originally told me I'd stayed at a friend's house on the night of April 1st. Yet here I was, decidedly *not* at a friend's house, and I didn't see that changing unless

something very bizarre and drastic happened. It was one of the few things that still puzzled me...but no matter. As of right now, the plan was to get this over with so I could sleep in my own bed tonight. It didn't matter where I might have stayed last time, because *this* time I was going to change the future.

Time passed. The skies overhead slowly turned from hot scarlet to a deep, cold navy blue. *Man, it's freezing out here,* I thought to myself as I rubbed my shoulders for warmth. It was already a little past nine, but Akito was still nowhere to be seen. I even went up and took a look inside the bar a minute ago, just in case I somehow missed him, but he wasn't there. The owner of the bar had said he only remembered that it was "around" nine o'clock, so it wasn't that strange to think Akito hadn't arrived yet, but it made me feel anxious all the same. Where could he be right now, and what was he doing? It would be a lot easier if I just knew his phone number and could give him a call...

"...Hang on."

I could get his number from Akari, couldn't I? I felt extremely dumb. Why hadn't I thought of this sooner? I immediately whipped out my phone and dialed her number. Three rings later, she picked up.

"Hey, Akari? Listen, um..."

"Kanae-kun, you've gotta help me!"

"Hey! Who said you could answer that?! Give it here!"

The call was disconnected from the other side.

"...The hell was that?"

All of a sudden, I got a bad feeling in the pit of my stomach. It *was* Akari that answered the phone, that much I knew for sure. But who was that other person yelling at her? They sounded further away, so I couldn't quite make out their voice. A cold sweat ran down my temples. Something bad was about to happen. She wouldn't have answered the phone begging for my help otherwise. I tried redialing, just in case...but to no avail.

I have to go. Akari needs my help.

I took off running. My destination: Akari's apartment complex. I didn't know for sure if that was where she would be, but it seemed the most likely place. If she wasn't there, I'd have to go try somewhere else. I sprinted as fast as I could down the roadway, tripping due to the lack of streetlights on more than one occasion, and reached the apartment complex in record time. I heaved and huffed as I scurried up the stairs and rang the doorbell. No answer. I knocked loudly on the door. Still nothing. Finally, I tried twisting the knob as a last resort, and the door shocked me by swinging right open. I called inside to ask if anyone was home, then let myself in regardless. This was a potential emergency situation; I didn't have time for proper etiquette. I walked down the main hallway and through an open door into the living room. There, in the middle of the floor, was a young girl curled up in the fetal position.

"Akari! Are you all right?!" I asked, rushing to her side. I knelt down beside her and put my hand gently on her back to try to help her sit up. The moment my fingers touched her, she shot upright and slapped my hand away.

"Stop it!" she cried "Don't you *dare* touch m—"

Our eyes locked, and she froze in place, her jaw hanging wide open. Then, slowly, her expression began to twist into one of grief and despair. Her eyes began to water, and then tears came flooding out like tiny waterfalls.

"*Waaaaaah!*" she wailed loudly, slamming her face into my chest.

This time, I was the one who froze in place, but I only missed a beat before realizing what I had to do. I reached my arms around her and gently rubbed her back, just as my grandmother always did to comfort me when I was little. After cradling her there like that for a time, her sobbing eventually subsided, and she pulled her face away from my chest. Long threads of snot stretched like spiderwebs from her nostrils to my shirt. I reached around and grabbed a tissue box from the coffee table and held it out to her. She took one without a word and blew her nose.

"Feeling a little better now?" I asked.

"...Mmn," she mumbled in a nasally voice. It was hard to take that as a yes or a no. She was still sitting with her shoulders slouched, looking dejectedly down at the floor. What in the world happened to her? I couldn't imagine her breaking down and straight-up bawling like that unless it was something pretty damn terrible. I briefly looked her over, but didn't see any signs of a major struggle or anything. No ripped clothes or visible injuries, at least.

"You're not hurt at all, are you?" I asked, and she just shook her head. So I asked my next question: "What happened here?"

The moment I asked that question, the tears started welling up again. Her face scrunched up, and they started streaming down from the corners of her eyes.

"My mo—he... He took my...my..." she said, sniffling inconsolably between every other word. She was rapidly becoming harder and harder to understand. I decided the explanation could wait for now.

"All right, we can talk about it later," I said, rubbing her back to comfort her again. "You're okay. You're okay now..."

As I continued trying to console her, I glanced up at the clock on the wall. It was 10 p.m., which meant Akito had been out drinking for nearly an hour now. And something told me that demanding he stop drinking over the phone wouldn't cut it at this point, now that he was already intoxicated. I'd need to go back over there and stop him in person. I still had plenty of time, of course, so I could theoretically stay here with Akari a little longer, but Akito's life was on the line. I didn't want to take any chances.

"Hey, Akari, um... Not to be a jerk, but...there's somewhere I've gotta be in a little bit," I confessed. She shot her head up to look at me. Then she grabbed my right arm and squeezed it tight.

"W-wait, don't go..." she pleaded.

"It's okay. I'll come right back, I promise."

"No... I don't want you to leave..."

Having her beg me not to go with a teary-eyed plea tied my heart in knots. On second thought, I couldn't do it. I couldn't just leave her here.

"All right. Then you can come with me," I said, standing up. Akari gradually rose to her feet as well, still grabbing me by the arm as we began to make our way across the living room.

"Wait... Where are you taking me?" she asked.

"To the bar," I replied, stepping out into the hall. "That's where Akito is."

Akari stopped dead in her tracks, still tugging firmly on my coat sleeve.

"Why...do we have to go there?" she asked with bleary eyes.

"Because otherwise, Akito might die tonight. If I don't go over there and get him to stop drinking, that is."

"...How could you even know that?"

"I'll explain on the way there. C'mon, let's go."

"No. I want you to tell me right here."

"But we're running out of time..."

"Please, Kanae-kun."

Akari stubbornly refused to move from that spot. Based on the glint of steadfast determination I could see in her un-clouded eyes, it was safe to say she wouldn't budge until she got her answers. I understood wanting an explanation after I just told her that her brother was going to die, but did she need to be *this* adamant...? There was no time to think about it any longer, though. The only way I'd get her to come with me was by explaining myself.

"...All right, but I'm warning you in advance, this is gonna get pretty convoluted," I prefaced.

"I don't mind," Akari nodded, then let go of my arm.

"Okay. So basically, I'm from the future."

I told her all about the Rollback phenomenon in as much detail as I could.

"So, do you understand now?" I asked.

"How am I supposed to believe any of that...?" Akari groaned, holding her head in her hands as if she had a migraine. I couldn't really blame her; I remembered having a tough time digesting *her* explanation of how the Rollback worked at first. It wasn't until I experienced the phenomenon for myself that I started believing all the things she was telling me. How was I supposed to explain all this in a way that would make Akari believe me, if she would never experience the phenomenon herself? Maybe by making some sort of "prediction" about the future? The only major event I had to predict was Akito's death, and that was one I was trying to *prevent*. I'd watched a little bit of TV and seen a little bit of news on my phone over the past few days, but I couldn't remember anything substantial enough to leave an impact. I checked the time again. It was now 10:30 p.m. We needed to get going.

"C'mon, let's just go," I said. "I can tell you more on the way there. Maybe then you'll start to believe me."

"But..." she protested, gripping the sleeves of her oversized sweater as she hung her head. It didn't seem like I'd convince her anytime soon. I didn't have much of a choice—I'd have to drag her along with me, as boorish as that was. I reached out a hand to grab hers, but this clearly startled her, as she reflexively backed away and tripped over the slight ridge in the doorway where the floor height rose. She lost her balance and fell backwards onto her butt.

"Ow, owww..."

"Oh man, I'm so sorry! A-are you all right?" I panicked, kneeling down beside her as she groaned in pain. "God, that was really stupid of me. I shouldn't have just reached out like that without saying something first."

"No, it's...it's fine," she said, rubbing her lower back as she pushed herself back up to her feet. She looked a little embarrassed.

"Are you sure? You didn't land on your bad hip, did you?"

"...My bad hip?" she asked, puzzled.

"Yeah, you injured your lower back recently, didn't you? You mentioned it the other day. Said it still hurts from time to time."

"Wait, when was this?" she blinked, her confusion now turning into genuine surprise.

"The night we broke into Sodeshima High."

"But we never did that."

"Sure we did. It was your idea! You showed me how to break in through the janky window in the girls' bathroom and everything. Just gotta give it a little elbow grease, and the lock pops right open."

"Wh-whoa, whoa, whoa. How do you know about that? That's something only me and a few of the other girls at school should know how to do..."

"Like I said, I learned from a pro. Namely, your future self."

Akari thought this over with eyes downcast; from what I could tell, she still had her doubts, but she was getting just that little bit closer to believing me. Maybe now she would be more willing to listen to what I had to say about Akito.

"Listen, Akari. Like I was trying to tell you before, I've come back here from a few days in the future. I know what's going to happen over the next few days and when," I explained. She looked back up at me and, after a long pause, gave a little nod, so I continued. "That's why I need you to believe me when I tell you that sometime tonight, between midnight and 2 a.m., Akito is going to die of acute alcohol poisoning. Unless I run over to the bar right now and stop him, that is."

"So...you're trying to save my brother's life...?"

"You got it."

That Akito was in grave danger seemed to resonate with her at last, as her expression changed to one of befuddled horror. Her lips trembled as though she desperately wished to say something but couldn't bring herself to force the words through.

"Anyway, sorry, but I really can't afford to dawdle much longer. Do you still wanna come with me, or no?"

"Y-yeah... I'll go..." she answered meekly.

"Cool. Let's get going, then."

We walked out of Akari's apartment and made our way down the stairs. Braving the frigid night air, we stole away through the empty streets of the sleepy town. I led the way, with Akari following close behind. Neither of us said a word as we rushed across the island to our destination.

The goal I'd worked toward over these past few days was almost within reach. As soon as we reached the bar, I'd waltz right in there and drag Akito out myself if I had to. If he tried to resist, or was already showing signs of alcohol poisoning, I could just call the police or an ambulance. As long as I could get there and confront him, I should be able to change the future and prevent his death from ever happening.

It had been a hell of a week, but it would soon be coming to an end. There were a few things about this whole Rollback process I was still a little hazy on...but they probably weren't worth dwelling on at this point. As long as I could save Akito, that was all that—

I felt an urgent tug on my sleeve. Akari was grabbing me by the arm. I stopped walking and turned to face her; we were standing right beneath one of the few streetlights on the road, so I could see Akari's face perfectly. Then I gasped. She was looking pensively down at the sidewalk with tears streaming down her cheeks.

"I can't do it..." she sobbed, squeezing my arm so hard that I felt her nails dig into my skin through my coat. "I'm sorry, Kanae-kun... I just can't..."

"Wh-what do you mean, you can't? Can't do what?" I asked, desperate. I had no idea why she had stopped me or why she was crying, which made me start to freak out a little bit. She looked up at me and, with tears in her eyes, made a heartrending plea:

"Do we really...*have* to save my brother...?"

It took a few moments for the implications of her words to sink in. You could have given me a million guesses as to what was going to come out of her mouth, and I never would have gotten anywhere close. My mouth hung open in disbelief as I tried and failed to twist my tongue into syllables. Eventually, I started feeling a little bit lightheaded. I could no longer say for sure whether or not my feet were still touching the ground.

"Wh-what are you talking about?" I sputtered. "Of course we do, don't we...?"

"But..." she sulked, gripping the collar area of her sweater with her free hand. She was behaving almost like a pouting child.

"What's gotten into you, Akari? This is your only brother we're talking about..."

"I know, but I just can't do it... I don't *want* to save him, Kanae-kun. I don't even want to be in the same room as him ever again..."

"I mean, fair enough, but this is life or death here. If we don't do something, he's literally going to die. Don't you get that?"

"I do, but... I just... Ugh, I don't know..."

Akari kept on shaking her head, refusing to make eye contact with me. She looked fragile, even paranoid. Like she was convinced something or someone was out to get her, and she was begging me to rescue her from her peril. From my perspective, I couldn't understand what she was so afraid of. Akari hadn't yet expressed her raw emotions in a coherent enough manner for me to wrap my head around.

"Why *don't* you want to save Akito?" I asked.

"I mean...because he's a horrible person..."

"How so?"

"He like...hits me, and kicks me, and stuff..."

"Wha—" I gasped, praying that I'd simply misheard her. "He... actually beats you?"

"Yeah..." she nodded, then began to elaborate, slowly, in a stammering voice.

She told me all about how he was constantly throwing things at her, pulling her hair, and even fractured a bone in her hip. How he would use her as his personal gofer, day in and day out. How he stole all of the money she'd been saving up while working her butt off at her part-time job. How he even suggested she get a job at a strip club to earn it back...

With every word that came out of Akari's mouth, my blood boiled hotter with contempt for Akito, and my empathy for Akari grew deeper. These two sharply distressing emotions overlapped like a massive pair of scissors, snipping away at my heartstrings. Akari was making a cry for help, and as much as I wanted to just cover my ears and block out the sound, I could never do that to her. The more she explained what had been going on, the more a third emotion began to build up inside of me: regret. Regret for two years ago, when I packed up my bags and left Akari alone here in Sodeshima without a second thought. Why hadn't I realized sooner that something had to be wrong? Why had I never once called to check up on her? I slammed my inner conscience with interrogative questions like these, but it didn't have any good excuses. If I had simply stayed by Akari's side, I could have been around for her when...

"So *now* do you see?" Akari cut in, interrupting my train of thought. "Please, Kanae-kun... Can't we just...hold off on saving my brother and let the universe decide...?"

APRIL 1ST, 6 P.M.

I had no comeback for that. After coming all this way, I was now starting to have misgivings at the very last minute. Should I save Akito, or should I not? When the Rollback first began, there was no doubt in my mind what the answer to that question should be. But back then, I didn't know then about all of the things he was doing to Akari. All of the horrible, sickening things. Lest we forget, *Akari* was my best friend here, not Akito, and *she herself* was essentially telling me that her brother deserved to die.

And yet...surely there was still room in Akito's heart for change if we gave him a chance at a second life, wasn't there? If we let him die, he'd never have an opportunity to redeem himself. There were an infinite number of ways his life could change from this point on, both for the better and for the worse, and to let him die now would mean extinguishing each and every one of those possibilities. Was I really prepared to be his judge, jury, and executioner here? I couldn't say.

So what was I to do? My choices were to act against my best friend's wishes as an abuse victim or let a deeply flawed man die. At that precise moment, I admit that the scales weren't tipping in one direction or the other. I was at a loss, and the pressure of the impending decision was starting to stress me out.

Then, out of nowhere, an old memory floated up to the surface of my mind. It was of that field trip in fifth grade, the one Akari and I had reminisced about after breaking into the school the other night. A memory of Akari falling face-first into the mud and me intentionally falling in right after her. At the time, my thought process was that when you find yourself neck-deep in the mud, stuck in a crappy situation you can't break free from, your real friends are the ones who will dive right in and muddy themselves in solidarity to help you out of it. What about now? Was I really willing to bear this mud, this stain on my conscience, and share it with her for the rest of my life?

"...All right," I whispered with a tiny sigh, nodding to myself. I'd come to my decision. "We'll hold off on saving Akito, then."

The moment I said these words, Akari let go of my arm and wobbled as though feeling faint. I grabbed her by the shoulders and supported her back, afraid that she might pass out.

"You all right?" I asked.

"Sorry... I guess I'm just...feeling a little dizzy..." she said. Her pallor didn't look good; she looked so exhausted that she might fall to her knees at any moment.

"...Let's get you home."

We walked right back the way we came, away from the bar where Akito was drinking. Neither of us said a word. I think we both needed some time to process the gravity of the decision we'd just made together. We walked in silence the whole way home, while I supported her back.

We made it back to Akari's apartment after what felt like forever. She unlocked the door, and we both stepped inside. She didn't seem to have the strength even to walk on her own. Right as I thought about finding a place to lay her down, she pointed weakly to a room on the left side of the hallway. Per her instructions, I opened the door and helped her inside. I flicked the light

APRIL 1ST, 6 P.M.

switch on, and the room flashed to life. It was a fairly cramped space—only about eight square meters, give or take—but there was a faintly sweet fragrance hanging in the air.

I assumed this must be Akari's bedroom (I'd never actually been inside it before). Across from the door was a bed in a simple wooden frame, and when I glanced to my right, I saw her Sodeshima High uniform hanging on the wall. I took a quick look around the room to see a bookshelf filled mostly with manga volumes, a plastic chest of drawers, and an old, weathered writing desk piled high with schoolwork and textbooks. Each book had zillions of colorful adhesive page markers sticking out from cover to cover.

"Please don't judge me... I know it's a mess..." Akari whined.

"O-oh, no! Sorry, I wasn't trying to be rude," I apologized.

I quit looking around and helped her totter over to the bed to lie down flat, then pulled the comforter up all the way to her neck and tucked her in.

"You should try to get some rest for tonight," I told her. "We can talk more tomorrow."

"Okay..." she nodded weakly.

I figured it'd be a good idea to stick around, at least until she fell asleep. I turned off the lights, turned on the nightlight, and sat on the floor with my back against the side of her bed. Akari reached a hand out from under the covers and tapped my shoulder, so I turned around.

"Could you...hold my hand?" she asked timidly, reaching it down to me. I was caught off guard by this at first but was happy to oblige.

"Sure, no problem."

I turned around so that I faced the bed and interlocked her fingers with mine. Akari squeezed tight. Her hand was smaller than my own, and every bit as soft, warm, and delicate as it had been when we were kids. So delicate, I was afraid to squeeze too hard in case I crushed it.

We remained there like that, her hand in mine, as the early hours of the night passed quietly beneath our feet. Looking at Akari with her eyes closed made me feel pretty sleepy myself. Still holding tight, I pressed my forehead up against the corner of her bedframe and closed my eyes. The floor was a little too cold for comfort, but I'd probably fall asleep like this eventually... *Wait*. I remembered that I was supposed to call my grandmother back as soon as I figured out what time I expected to be home.

"Hang on, Akari. I've gotta go make a quick phone call," I said, standing up and letting go of her hand.

"Wh-who do you need to call?" she asked tentatively. She sat upright in her bed.

"Just my grandma. Don't worry."

"O-oh, all right... But come right back, okay?"

"Will do."

I stepped out of the bedroom and pulled out my phone. It was already eleven o'clock. I called home at once, fully expecting my grandmother to be pissed. Lo and behold, she was. As soon as I identified myself, she began a magnificent rant about how irresponsible I was and how worried I'd made her. She wasn't letting me get a word in edgewise, and I didn't see her stopping anytime soon, so I blurted out that I was planning to stay the night at a friend's house and hung up the phone. A moment later, I realized what I'd done. The implications hit me so hard that I lost my balance and hit my back against the wall.

Of course.

I felt the biggest lingering question, the one that remained frozen in my mind this entire time, begin to melt away, draining from my every pore like thawing snow. I'd just self-fulfilled my own prophecy. *This* was the friend's house I'd stayed at on April 1st, and in a few hours, Akito was going to die all over again. Then tomorrow, I'd find the body and call it in. I understood now why Akari refused to tell me what happened on the night of April 1st. She couldn't tell me that she and I had willfully allowed Akito to die, not while I was still determined to save his life. The past and future connected anew. Everything had played out exactly as destiny had ordained. In the end, I was powerless to change Akito's fate.

No. I deliberately chose not to.

Without warning, the door to Akari's bedroom creaked open the tiniest bit. I looked over and saw her peeking through the crack, where we made eye contact.

"What's wrong?" I asked.

"Just, you were taking a while... I got a little worried," she muttered.

"Oh, my bad. Yeah, I just got off the phone. Told her I'd be staying here tonight."

"Wait, you're spending the night? ...Right, okay. That makes sense. Duh."

WAIT FOR ME YESTERDAY IN SPRING

She said it as though it took her a moment to digest the idea, but I couldn't check her expression while the lights were still off. I walked back into the room, and we both returned to our previous seating and sleeping positions. My nose chose that exact moment to start to itch, and I let out a sneeze. I rubbed my nose.

"Are you cold?" Akari asked.

"Just a little. Mind if I turn the heater on?"

"I mean, you *could*...but I've got a better idea," she declared, then scooched herself over to the far end of the mattress to make some space up on the bed. "Why don't you just come up here...? Plenty of room under the covers."

"Huh?! Wait, but that's... I mean, d-do you really think that's a good idea?"

"Sure, why not? I trust you. Now, c'mon," she insisted, patting the empty space on the sheets a few times as an invitation to join her. I didn't want her to take my hesitance the wrong way, so I nodded and crept under the covers beside her...but as soon as I felt her lingering body heat in the sheets beneath me, my heart rate shot through the roof.

"Aren't you still hanging over the edge a little bit?" she asked. "Here, come closer."

"O-okay," I said. I wriggled my body toward the middle of the bed as instructed. Now Akari's face was mere inches from my own, and close enough for me to make out each individual eyelash. Her big, dark irises were staring directly into mine.

"Hey, Kanae-kun? Can I tell you something?"

"Yeah? What is it?"

304

APRIL 1ST, 6 P.M.

"I don't wanna sound weird, but...I've been thinking a lot about trying to get into the same college as you and moving to Tokyo after I graduate. I've been working really, really hard for it too... You have no idea how much I've missed you these past couple of years."

"...Wait. Is that what you were saving up all that money for?"

"Mm-hmm..." she nodded bashfully.

"Gotcha... Well, I'm sorry if I made you feel like that was the only way. If I'd known that's how you felt, I would've totally stayed back here with you."

"No, no! Sorry, that wasn't supposed to sound like a guilt trip. Besides, everything's gonna be okay now," she assured me, smiling softly from the other side of the pillow. "Let's just keep this whole thing our little secret and forget all about it, okay?"

Then she brought her right hand up between our faces and lifted her pinky finger.

"Promise me?" she asked.

"...Yeah. I promise."

I interlocked my pinky with hers. When we finally let go, she let out a cute little satisfied chuckle, followed by a long purr of contentment.

"Kanae-kun..."

"What's up?"

"Nothing, just... Thanks," she said, closing her eyes. When she reopened them, a single pearly teardrop rolled out down her temple. "Now don't ever leave me like that again, you hear me?"

305

Then she nuzzled in close, about as close as any two people could ever get, and pressed her forehead into my chest. When I looked down and saw her head there, tucked below my chin, I was struck by a strangely irresistible urge to run my fingers through her hair. So I did. I ran them up the back of her scalp, then back down again, over and over in a slow and methodical motion.

"Mmmnn..." she moaned, a little hesitant at first, but it wasn't long before she relaxed and let herself enjoy the massage-like sensation. I kept tracing my fingers up and down in gentle lines, as if to memorize the contours of her skull. Slowly but surely, Akari drifted off into a deep and restful sleep. Moments later, I stopped stroking her hair and closed my eyes as well. I just wanted to bask in this beautiful, perfect moment and forget the world.

But somehow, sleep eluded me.

Somewhere deep in my heart, I could hear a voice crying out.

Another me—another facet of myself—was making a desperate appeal to my conscience:

So you're really okay with this, huh?

INTERLUDE VI

I T WAS LIKE HEAVEN AND HELL both descended on me in the span of a single day.

Hell came first. When I discovered that my brother had stolen the entirety of my savings, I honestly thought my life was over. My whole world went dark; for the first time in my life, I knew the true meaning of desolation and despair. I couldn't even find the willpower to cry. But then Kanae came along and rescued me.

To be honest, I still didn't fully understand all the things he told me about this Rollback phenomenon, but that wasn't the part that was important to me. What *did* matter to me was that he'd chosen me over my brother. That alone made me happier than I could ever convey in words. Thank you, Kanae. Thanks for hearing out my selfish wish. For making that promise with me. It really did mean the world to me.

How many years had it been since he last ran his fingers through my hair like this? Back then, he would only give me a playful tousle here and there, but his hands had grown large enough now that he could easily cradle my head. It felt so nice, I would have let him keep massaging the back of my head forever if he wanted to. In fact, I wished this whole entire moment could last forever. If heaven truly did exist, I imagined it probably felt like this. Complete and utter bliss.

A dark voice in the back of my mind told me that I would never forget the fact that I traded my brother's life in exchange for this happiness. Probably not for as long as I lived.

Final Chapter

ALL I COULD HEAR was the sound of Akari's steady breathing. Meanwhile, I couldn't sleep a wink for multiple reasons. For one, I was in an unfamiliar bed. For two, Akari was sleeping on my chest. But what kept me up more than anything was Akito's death. It was like the image of his corpse was seared into the back of my eyelids. Every time I tried to close my eyes, I saw his body lying there in the empty lot, his skin white as a sheet, no trace of the boy who once took the mound at Koshien left inside those glassy eyeballs. This was the final resting place of the man who'd once given me the courage to stand up to bullies, the guy who'd led our puny island high school's baseball team all the way to nationals, then broken his shoulder and lost everything. The same man who, in the final years of his short life, had stooped so low that he was beating and stealing money from his own sister.

I didn't know whether we'd done the right thing or not anymore. I wondered if Akari already had second thoughts of her own or if she would regret it in the near future. Thanks to the Rollback phenomenon, I already had memories of everything that would happen over the next five days up to 6 p.m. on April 6th. As though I were following a trail of breadcrumbs, I traced my memories back in search of any indication that Akari came to regret this decision over the next few days.

Tuesday, we had our perfect little picnic in the abandoned park.

Wednesday, we broke into the school at night and shared a tender moment.

Thursday, I thought I was going insane until I spoke to her at Akito's wake.

And Friday, she explained the Rollback to me beneath the cherry blossom tree.

Then I remembered something else. Something her future self told me on that day, before the first Rollback occurred:

"Kanae, I...I want you to save my brother."

Did she really mean that, or was she only saying it to play along with the charade? I couldn't say for sure, but I remembered her saying something else right after that: *"I trust your judgment. So please...take care of past me, okay?"* This was what made me think that Akari could be having second thoughts by that point, like maybe she felt like we'd made the wrong decision. It'd explain why she said the rest was up to me and that she would entrust everything to my judgment.

I had to honor that trust by doing what I alone felt was right.

I slowly sat myself up in bed, then looked down at my side, where Akari was still sleeping peacefully like a baby. *Forgive me, Akari,* I whispered as I silently slipped out from under the covers. When I stood up, I noticed the alarm clock at her bedside read 1 a.m. I turned and tiptoed toward the door, twisted the knob, then took one last look over my shoulder at Akari before stepping out of the bedroom. Slipping on my shoes in the entryway, I left the apartment, hurried down the stairs, and ran off toward the empty lot at a full sprint. Chances were high that Akito would already be there, face down on the ground.

"Forgive me, Akari... This is for your own good... I'm sorry!"

I apologized to her over and over as I ran through the streets. I knew I was yelling pointlessly into the ether, but I felt so bad for betraying her that I couldn't help it. *Forgive me, Akari. I just can't do it. I can't stand idly by and let a man die.* Akito was a bad person, for sure, and I couldn't see myself ever forgiving him for how he'd hurt his sister. I found him utterly detestable in his current state. That still didn't mean he deserved to die. I couldn't sit back and watch a man with his whole life ahead of him pass away and justify it with some huge mistakes he made.

I should never have let my determination to save him waver. Then I wouldn't have had to break any promises. I was an absolute dumbass. A gutless, wishy-washy coward who always took the easy way out. Things would never have turned out this way if not for me and my stupid choices. I was sorry that I had to do this to her—but I needed to save Akito. I needed to believe there was a way we could still find a happy ending in all of this, one where nobody had to die.

I arrived at the empty lot and heaved my way through the tall grass in record time. It didn't take long for me to spot his silhouette lying face down on the ground.

"Akito!"

His face was already bleached with a deathlike pallor, and I could tell that his fire was fading fast. I knelt down beside him and watched his chest. The movements were extremely faint, but he was still breathing. I dialed 119 and frantically explained the situation to the operator. The paramedics from the island's fire department would arrive any minute, so all I had to do now was wait. My personal burden of responsibility now somewhat relieved, the exhaustion finally caught up with me, and I fell to my hands and knees on the ground. I tried to stay focused on breathing in, and then breathing out, spurts of cold night air that burned my throat. When my breathing stabilized at last, I glanced over at Akito again—only to find that his chest was no longer moving. Flustered, I put my hand up to his mouth. He'd stopped breathing altogether.

"You've gotta be kidding me!" I cried as I shook Akito's body. "Hey, wake up! Don't go dying on me now, goddammit!"

No response. I turned him over onto his back to administer CPR, or at least whatever movements I remembered from how they taught us to do it in gym class. I wasn't sure if I did all the steps correctly or anything. I began compressing his chest in steady beats and prayed for the best.

"Come on! Live, damn it! Wake up and answer for what you've done! You can still turn your life around, I know you can! I swear, if you die right now, I'll beat the crap out of you!"

I swore at him as I kept pumping his chest until the small ambulance arrived and two paramedics hopped out. One took over for me, while the other asked me a number of questions.

"Any relation to the victim?" he inquired.

"Yeah, we're friends," I lied, figuring it would make things a lot simpler. "Akito... Sorry, my friend here was out drinking until about two hours ago. He only stopped breathing a few minutes before you got here."

The paramedic looked me over, taking a moment to consider this answer.

"Okay, got it," he nodded. "We'd like to ask you a few more questions about what happened. Mind riding along with us?"

"Sure, no problem."

I jumped in the ambulance after they loaded Akito up into it, and we sped off toward the harbor. The island medical clinic couldn't treat him at this time of night, so we had to take the entire ambulance onto an emergency transport vessel and cross over to the mainland, which took about twenty minutes. From there, it was about another twenty-minute drive to the nearest hospital. Thankfully, they got him breathing again in transit using basic first-aid procedures. He hadn't regained consciousness yet, but it looked like he was going to pull through.

Once we made it to the hospital, Akito was quickly rolled into the emergency room. I had to tell the hospital staff all the same stuff I'd barely finished telling the paramedics, but then my duties as a "friend" of the victim were complete. I sat down on one of the couches in the lobby and tipped my head up toward the ceiling. I'd managed to prevent Akito's death, and that meant I'd changed both the past and the future for the better.

"Man, I'm beat..."

I felt a pain in the back of my sockets when I closed my eyes; a result of all the built-up fatigue, presumably. Too bad, I couldn't rest yet. There were still things I needed to do. First and foremost, I had to get in touch with Akari. She was probably still asleep, so I decided that maybe shooting her a text would be the better play. I opened my phone's messaging app and scrolled down to her name, then froze. I couldn't bring myself to type anything out. I had no clue how to best convey to her that I'd changed my mind and gone to save Akito's life after all, so my fingers sort of hovered in a useless limbo over the keyboard for a while. When I did manage to write something down, I deleted it, started over, then repeated the same process, again and again. I spent about two hours in all sitting there in the lobby and drafting up different ways of saying the same thing, but in the end, I settled on a simple "hey, we need to talk. lemme know when you're awake" and sent it off before I had a chance to second-guess myself again. Something told me this was one conversation we shouldn't have over text.

I ended up napping in the hospital waiting room until about 6 a.m. The staff weren't going to let me hitch a ride back to the island on the ambulance or the emergency boat, so I had to walk to a nearby convenience store ATM and use my cell phone to withdraw some money, then head back to the port via taxi. It was kind of a pricey cab ride for an unemployed student like me, but it would have taken over an hour to get there on foot. That wasn't happening, considering how little energy I had left. When we got down to the port, I paid my fare and left the car.

Thankfully, I arrived right as the Sodeshima ferry was pulling into the docks. I stood at the end of the dock and waited patiently as all of the inbound passengers from the island disembarked, when I noticed that Akari's mother was among them. She'd probably gotten a call from the hospital and was on her way there. She didn't seem to notice me, since she rushed past to the nearest taxi that was stopped on the shoulder of the road and got in. I only saw her from afar, but she looked flustered. I had no way of knowing how she might feel about Akito's recent personality changes, but at the end of the day, he was her son. What mother could keep stoic after hearing their child was in the hospital? Her taxi sped off around the corner as I turned and made my way over to the ticket booth.

Shortly after I boarded the ferry, it departed back toward Sodeshima. I took a seat in the main passenger area and checked my phone. It was half past six, and still no reply from Akari. She was either still asleep or deliberately not replying... Either way, it would probably be fastest to head straight over to her place as soon as I arrived in Sodeshima. I didn't know how to go about breaking the news, but I had to own up to breaking my promise with her one way or another. I mentally steeled myself for that as the ferryboat pulled into the harbor.

I disembarked, then aimed for Akari's apartment complex at a brisk pace through the cool early morning air. About ten minutes later, I was standing at her doorstep, looking up at the HOSHINA nameplate on the door, trying to muster up the courage to ring the doorbell. When I finally did, there was at least a solid minute's worth of silence, after which I finally heard footsteps within. Slowly, the door to the apartment opened, and Akari peeked out from the crack. Her hair was disheveled, and her bangs were all clumped together. There was no light in her eyes. It felt like looking at someone who'd lived for years as a total recluse, despite the fact that I saw her last night. This only exacerbated the guilt already gnawing away at me. I could tell that I was likely to blame for how she looked.

"Akari, listen... I..."

"You went and rescued him, right?" she said casually, as though it was merely an offhand remark. "My mom told me she got a call from the hospital. Figured it had to be your doing."

"...Yeah, it was. I'm really sorry."

"It's fine. No need to apologize. I mean, it's not like you did anything wrong, right?"

"No, but I still broke my promise to you."

"Oh, is *that* what you're worried about? Don't be. I'm the one who wasn't thinking straight," she said, chuckling derisively at herself. "I mean, asking you to be complicit in my own brother's death? What am I, psycho? I can hardly believe I said that. I must be more of a coldhearted bitch than I thought..."

Her amused smirk didn't waver, but then, out of nowhere, fat teardrops began to spill out from the corners of her eyes.

"Akari...!" I cried, reaching out to her in desperation—but she slammed the door in my face. A moment later, I heard the clank of her locking the deadbolt.

"...Sorry, I just...want to be alone right now..." I heard her whimper from inside the apartment. I pressed one ear up to the door and tried to reason with her.

"No, listen to me, Akari! I know you might not believe this right now, but in the future, it was *you* who told me to—"

I stopped short. Say she *did* believe me; knowing she would eventually regret her actions in the timeline where Akito had died was cold comfort. Besides, even that regret was a mere assumption on my part. I stood there, unable to even string together a sentence's worth of reassurance, while Akari wept softly on the other side of the door.

"Please... Just go home, Kanae-kun..." she begged.

I bit down hard on my lower lip. A single door stood between us, and yet it may as well have been an impenetrable concrete wall.

"...All right, I'll go. You better believe I'll be coming back, though. I'm gonna make this up to you one way or another, I swear. I'll never break another promise to you again."

I waited. No reply came.

"...Okay then. I'll talk to you later," I said.

For now, I had no choice but to head home.

I took a hot shower as soon as I got back to my grandmother's house. The searing heat permeated my entire body, all the way to my frostbitten fingertips. I washed my hair and everything else, then stood under the hot water for a while until I was sufficiently warmed to my core. Only then did I step out of the bathroom, put on some fresh clothes, and head down into the living room. I found Eri there in her pajamas, watching TV on a floor cushion while munching on a piece of toast. I guessed she woke up while I was showering.

"Morning, Eri," I said as I walked in the room.

"...Mm," she mumbled despondently, not even looking in my direction.

Taking a moment to think about where I was chronologically, it'd be fair for Eri to feel on edge from our fight the day before. It seemed that way when I rolled back to April 2nd the last time, at least. Maybe now that I had changed the future, though, she would be in a different frame of mind. Last time, she approached me first, but I decided to break the ice myself now.

"Hey, sorry about yesterday," I apologized. "I definitely said some things I really shouldn't have. It was pretty immature of me."

Eri took a big bite of her toast, chewed it well, then swallowed before answering me. Her eyes never once left the TV, mind you.

"Nah, it's okay," she said. "I kinda crossed the line too."

"All right. So are we cool, then?"

"Guess so."

Hardly the most emotional heart-to-heart of all time, but we'd buried the hatchet. I sat on one of the other floor cushions, rested my elbow on the low dining table, and casually changed the subject.

"So hey, what would you say if I told you I was gonna drop out of school and move back here to Sodeshima?" I asked.

Eri dropped her piece of toast on her plate—buttered side up, thankfully—then turned to face me. Her eyes were wide with surprise.

"W-wait, you're dropping out?"

"I'm, like, eighty percent sure, yeah."

"...It's not because of all that mean stuff I said yesterday, is it?"

Her expression turned so grave that I almost chuckled.

"No, it's got nothing to do with you. Don't worry."

My reasons were a lot more self-centered than that; this was the only way I could think of to make it up to Akari. If Akito went back to his old ways after he got out of the hospital, which he very well might, I couldn't risk leaving her alone with him again. I was the one who broke my promise and saved his life, after all, and though I didn't regret my choice, I did still need to take accountability for it. So I would drop out of my high school in Tokyo and stay here with her in Sodeshima instead. Having to sacrifice a portion of my educational career was a small price to pay to see her smile again.

"If you say so..." Eri said, obviously still a little concerned. "Well, to answer your question, I think it's safe to say our deadbeat dad will be pissed...but I bet Grandma'd love to have you back here with us."

"What about you?"

"I...I dunno. But...having someone else around to clean out the tub so it doesn't have to be me every day might be kinda nice, I guess."

"That's all I am to you, huh? A glorified janitor?" I teased.

"Hey, it was *your* job up until two years ago."

Right, I guess it was. She'd always get on my case whenever there was so much as a stray hair left in there when she wanted to take a bath.

"Well, if cleaning the tub's all I've gotta do to earn my keep, I guess that doesn't sound like such a bad gig."

"...You're really serious about this, huh?"

"Just about."

"Did something happen, or...?"

"Eh, it's kind of a long story."

I couldn't possibly tell Eri about any of what I went through this past week. Instead, I stood up to make it clear that the conversation was over. I turned to head back upstairs to my room, which was when Eri stopped me.

"W-wait, Big Brother!"

I whirled back around, caught off guard. She'd always called me that back when I lived here, but she hadn't used it once this whole week. Sure, it sounded a bit childish now that she was in junior high, but it felt good to hear. Like she was finally warming up to me again.

"Um," she stammered, "if you ever need someone to talk to or anything, I'm always here. Not trying to be nosy, but I mean...it's not healthy to just bottle things up inside, and..."

Her face was as earnest as could be as she sat there looking up at me from the floor. *What a sweet kid,* I thought to myself; her kind offer raised my spirits a little.

"Thanks for the offer, but I think this is just one of those things I have to deal with by myself. Sorry," I apologized, before turning and walking out of the living room.

I crashed down onto my bed. I barely got any sleep at all last night, but I didn't feel particularly tired. Perhaps that hot shower had woken me up a bit, or maybe I was just too worried about Akari. Yeah, probably the latter. Every time I remembered how distraught her face looked through the crack in her apartment door, it felt like someone was driving a stake into my heart. I was beginning to feel like I hadn't made the right decision after all. Here I was, struggling with the same dilemma again. Would it be better if I hadn't saved Akito? I let out a deep, heavy sigh of regret.

"...Man, I have *gotta* get my act together," I said, then slapped my cheeks with both hands to snap myself out of this pessimistic spiral. It was far too late for me to be getting cold feet; the damage was already done, and now it was my responsibility to fix it so that Akari could be happy again. Simple as that, no need to overthink it. I'd prioritize whatever was best for her from now on.

The calm spring morning came and went like a light rain that was gone before you were aware it had arrived. Next thing I knew, it was midafternoon. I'd already tried to check up on Akari, but she still refused to see me. I heard the words "go away" come from behind the door, and after that, there was only silence. I called and texted her as well, but to no avail. I wondered if I might need to take more drastic measures, like camping out in front of her apartment or trying to force my way inside...but neither seemed like a very good idea. They were more likely to hurt her further, if anything, and extend the healing process unnecessarily. Despite all that, I felt uncomfortable leaving her alone with her thoughts right now...

"Man, what am I supposed to do...?" I groaned.

I looked up at my wall clock. It was 3 p.m. Ideally, I'd like to salvage my relationship with Akari somewhat before the next Rollback hit in three hours. I assumed that would be the final one, as then I'd have filled in the entirety of the ninety-six-hour blank space in my memories. I wondered then if I would be sent back to 6 p.m. on April 6th, when Akari first explained the Rollback to me, since that was the furthest point in the timeline I had experienced. On second thought, though, that timeline was also broken now that I'd saved Akito's life...so maybe all bets were off. Maybe there wouldn't be another Rollback. Or maybe my consciousness would repeat these same four days over and over for the rest of my life, my body never growing older than seventeen as I slowly but surely went insane. Now there was a scary thought.

After successfully giving myself chills, I figured I'd better not dwell on questions I had no way of answering. It would be six o'clock soon enough, and then I'd find out for myself...whether I liked it or not. Still, given that I couldn't even guess what might happen, it was all the more important that I talk to Akari while I had the chance. I resolved to go try to talk with her one last time—but I would have to be quick about it.

Right as I shot up in bed to get going, I felt my phone vibrate next to my pillow. Someone had sent me a text. I picked up the phone and looked down at the screen. It was from Akari. The words she had written, however, made my heart sink all the way into my stomach. A moment later, my mouth went dry as the desert, and I broke into a full-body sweat. I tried to call her, hands trembling, but it didn't go through. The robotic voice of her answering machine told me she was either out of range or had her phone turned off. I jumped up and raced down the stairs so fast that it was a miracle I didn't trip and fall, then shot out the front door like a speeding bullet. There was no time to explain the circumstances, so I grabbed Eri's bike without permission and sped off in the direction of Akari's apartment complex, riding as fast as my legs could take me. I had a very bad feeling about this; if I'd interpreted her message correctly, then it was vital that I reach her as fast as humanly possible.

"Goodbye, Kanae. I love you."

How could I be such a stupid, worthless piece of crap? I'd spent several hours lying around in my bedroom, talking a big game about how I was gonna make things up to her, while she was already neck-deep and drowning in the worst depression of her entire life. Alone, with me nowhere to be found. Who the hell did I think I was?

"God, I'm such an *idiot*...!"

I pedaled so hard that the pedals themselves threatened to come flying off, and the chain screeched metallically as though it might snap. I pressed on even so, spinning my spokes as fast as they'd go all the way to Akari's apartment complex, where I slammed on the brakes and ditched the bike in the parking lot. I booked it up the stairs and rang her doorbell. Nothing. I tried twisting the knob and found that the door was unlocked.

"Akari, you there?! I'm coming in!"

I bounded into the hallway and swung open the first door on the left. Akari wasn't in there. Her bedroom seemed a lot cleaner than I remembered it being last night. All of the textbooks that had lain out on her desk were now filed neatly away in her bookcase.

"Wait, what's this...?"

A single folded-up sheet of notebook paper lay atop her desk. I grabbed it and opened it up. It was a handwritten letter in which Akari thanked her mother at length for everything she'd done for her. There was no signature at the bottom, only the words "I hope that one day you can forgive me." My gut feeling was all but confirmed at this point.

"Damn it, no...!"

I set the letter back down, then called out for Akari again as I searched the rest of the apartment. I checked the living room, the kitchen, the bathroom, and even the back deck, but she was nowhere to be found. Clearly she had left the house, but where could she have gone? With a gulp, I finally had no choice but to confront the word I'd been intentionally avoiding this entire time: *suicide*. If Akari was going to make a serious suicide attempt, where would she do it? I guess it would depend on her intended method. Drowning was probably the easiest option with the ocean right nearby, but she could just as easily plan to jump from the top of a tall building, or step in front of an oncoming train, or hang herself...though none of these options did much to narrow down her potential whereabouts. *Damn it, I've got nothing. She might not even be on the island anymore, for all I know.*

I considered whether I should call the authorities. What would I even tell them? That I suspected a friend of mine was about to commit suicide, but I had no idea where or how? Could they do anything at all with that information? I didn't know, but it was worth a shot. I pulled my cell phone out of my pocket and started pushing buttons, all while racking my brain for any potential hints from the past few days I'd spent with Akari. I tried to untangle every last knot remaining in my mind.

All of a sudden, I saw something glimmering at the bottom of my mental abyss, like a gold nugget buried deep in the mud. My gut told me this was not a lead to ignore, so I put my cell phone down and tried to home in on it. I closed my eyes and focused my mental energy on dredging up whatever lurked in the depths of my brain. Time seemed to crawl by...and then I heard an echo of Akari's voice.

"You know, this is my favorite spot in all of Sodeshima."

My eyes shot open. Could that be where she was? It met the criteria; she could theoretically kill herself there. I didn't have time to think twice. I tore out of the apartment, hauled Eri's bike up off the pavement, and sped off toward Sodeshima High. I ped-aled as fast as I possibly could, huffing and puffing up the hilly streets. I felt sweat drip down from my chin onto the handlebars.

When I reached the final ascent leading to campus, I shifted into low gear and tried to power my way up—but then there was a loud *thunk*, and the pedals started spinning with zero resistance as the bike lost all traction. Unable to maintain my balance, I fell down hard on the asphalt.

"Yeowch..."

I winced in pain as I looked over at the fallen bicycle. The chain had snapped.

Screw it. I'll run the rest of the way.

I started hoofing it up the hill, ditching the bike where it had fallen. My throat hurt bad enough that I worried it'd split open, and my heart was beating so loud that I could hear it booming in my eardrums. But I hadn't the time nor the right to slow down. I'd happily endure any bodily harm, permanent or otherwise, if it meant the difference between Akari committing suicide or not.

At long last, I made it to Sodeshima High. The gates were open, but I didn't see anyone out on the athletic field. As for whether there was anyone up on the roof...it was impossible to tell from down here. I made a beeline across the track and let myself inside through the main entrance. I knew that if any faculty members were to spot me, I'd be thrown out, but there was no time to try to play it cool and blend in.

I dashed up the stairs, praying internally that my hunch was correct. Sure enough, when I reached the uppermost landing, I found the padlock from the door lying discarded on the ground, along with two flattened-out hairpins. My hunch was now a certainty. She was here.

I swung open the door and stepped out onto the rooftop. A strong wind attempted to blow me over, and I had to squint my eyes from the glare of the setting sun. Then I saw it. A figure stood beyond the protective fence spanning the perimeter of the roof and was leaning out over the edge. The person wore a Sodeshima High uniform, its skirt blowing in the wind.

It was her.

I'd made it in the nick of time, but it was way too early to breathe a sigh of relief. Her hands were gripping the metal railing behind her for now, but she looked as though she might let go and jump at any moment. I didn't want to frighten or provoke her in any way, so I called out her name in a calm and measured voice:

"Akari."

She whirled around. She looked genuinely surprised to see me.

"K-Kanae-kun? But...how did you know I'd be here...?" I took a moment to catch my breath before answering.

"Let's just say your future self gave me a hint."

"You're kidding..."

"Nope. It's your favorite spot on the whole island, right? You even made a point of bringing me up here to show me one night."

"...When was this?"

"Let's see... It was the night of the 4th, so...two days from now, I guess?"

Akari furrowed her brow and cast a forlorn glance to the side.

"Wish I could've gotten to experience that future," she said.

I got chills. The heartache in her voice stabbed me like a knife through the chest. I swallowed hard, then asked the question I'd come here to ask.

"Akari. You're not planning to kill yourself, are you?"

"I am."

"...Is it my fault?"

She gave a slight smile. It neither confirmed nor denied my assumption.

"I'm...tired, Kanae. Tired of everything," she said, her voice measured and slow. "I mean, I've worked *so hard* to try to get into the same college as you. Each and every day, I push myself harder than the last. I stay up late every night, studying until I literally can't keep my eyes open any longer. I swim laps until I'm so exhausted, I throw up. I keep working the same job even though my supervisors make me cry pretty much every day... It's like I've been living in hell, Kanae. On top of everything else, my brother's been harassing me and treating me like a slave. The one time I tried to stand up for myself, he pushed me down and fractured a bone in my lower back so I couldn't swim. And when he stole all of the money I'd been saving up for so long, I thought my life was over for good. There was no way I could ever recover from that. But even then, I still didn't want to die, because you came back to me. Because when I called you in my time of need, you came running to my rescue. And...because even when I made the most selfish request imaginable, you still heard me out. But in the end, you broke that promise and chose my brother over me."

The pain in Akari's voice was palpable, but I had no reply for her. All I could do was stand there, clenching my fists until she finished speaking. Then, finally, I offered a few words in response.

"You're not wrong," I said, choosing my words very carefully. "I did break my promise to you, and I did save Akito against your will. But...that doesn't mean I 'chose' him over you, or that I did it specifically to slight you or anything like that. I don't hate you, Akari. Hell, if anything, I—"

"You wanna know what hurt more than anything, though?" she interrupted—though it surely didn't feel like an interruption from her perspective. I was certain she wasn't even listening to me anymore. "It wasn't having my money stolen, or you breaking your promise, or anything like that."

"Then what was it...?" I asked.

Akari hung her head as though trying to hold something back.

"It was the realization...of what a horrible person I really am, deep down. I mean, I *deliberately* chose to stand by and do nothing while my brother was dying, only to turn straight around, go home, and cuddle up in bed with the boy I like. If that doesn't make me a psychopath, I don't know what does."

"Akari, you're not a psychopath...!"

"Yes, I am," she replied, her voice shaky. "You made the right choice, Kanae-kun. I can't hold that against you. It's me who's crazy. Which is why...I should just kill myself and spare everyone else the misery of having to live with me."

She looked up at me again. Her eyes now bore an unmistakable glimmer of desperation.

"Akari...!" I cried, putting one foot forward to run to her side.

"Don't come any closer!" she snapped, and I froze in place. "Tell me one last thing, Kanae-kun: Why did you do it? Why did you change your mind and betray me?"

I paused. My mouth went dry, and cold sweat dripped down my forehead. I knew if I made the slightest misstep with my words, Akari was at a real risk of taking her own life. I wet my parched tongue with fresh saliva and then proceeded to say my piece.

"...Because your future self asked me to. She explicitly told me to save Akito. She even told me where he'd die and when. I can't see you ever doing that unless you came to regret your decision for real... And trust me, you're not the only one, Akari. I was all in on letting him die for a while there, before I remembered what you told me in the future. I thought in way more depth about the long-term repercussions from all of this. Only after that did I rethink it and decide I needed to save Akito's life after all."

Akari didn't say a word. She stood and listened quietly as I continued.

"A minute ago, you called yourself a horrible person...a psychopath. I disagree. You've got a good heart, Akari, a better heart than anyone I know. That's why I knew you'd come to regret it sooner or later. The fact that you'd let your brother die would eat away at you for the rest of your life... Even after you got married, and had kids, and lived happily ever after with whatever lucky guy got the pleasure, it would always be there—lurking in a dark corner of your mind. I didn't want that for you. You can earn back lost money and people's trust, but you can never take back a life. I didn't want this to forever cast a shadow over your future."

"What 'future'?" Akari scoffed, her face contorting in distress. "Quit preaching to me like you're my dad... All you're doing is throwing together a bunch of empty reassurances and speculation to convince me not to jump. You're only trying to stop me from dying so *you* won't feel guilty."

"It's not speculation," I shot back. "Akari, I was there. You literally came to regret it in less than a week."

"Oh yeah? Where's your proof? Show me one piece of evidence to support your little theory that I'm not rotten to the core."

My words caught in my throat. Obviously, I had no way of proving something that happened in a now-severed timeline. Recognizing this, Akari's expression turned cold, as if she'd given up her last hope that I could prove her wrong.

"See? Nothing but empty words. Heck, I bet *you* don't even fully believe the stuff that's coming out of your mouth. Like, can you honestly say with one hundred percent certainty that *you* did the right thing?"

She had me totally figured out. I didn't know what to believe; I'd waffled back and forth ever since last night. Was it really right for me to save Akito? Was I really acting in Akari's best interests, or pouring salt in her wounds for no reason? Had her future self truly come to regret what happened, or did I only save Akito's life because it would make *me* feel better? The more I pondered, the deeper I was consumed by my own misgivings and regrets. I couldn't see anything clearly anymore. I knew, though, deep down, what I had to do. I needed to believe in the path I'd chosen without letting my doubts dissuade me. There was no turning back now.

"You're right," I admitted. "There are lots of things I'm not sure about...but one thing I can say for sure is that you aren't supposed to die here. Akari, if you step back from that ledge right now, I'll do anything you ask of me. I'll drop out of high school and move back to Sodeshima. I'll find a way to make back the money Akito stole from you. I'll do everything in my power to make sure you never have to go through anything like this again. Please don't end it all here. I need you, Akari."

"Oh, give it a rest, already. You're just trying to talk me down and you know it."

Her words were harsh and cold, and I had no angle to counter them from. So deep was Akari's despair that she'd basically made up her mind by now, and nothing I could say would convince her otherwise. She was determined to jump. The impact from a fall from this height would kill her. I could only stand here and watch, helpless, as my best friend took her own life. Such was my punishment for breaking my promise to her.

...*No, screw that.* I wasn't giving up yet. I came here prepared to put it all on the line in order to save Akari. Now I needed to put my money where my mouth was. Slowly, steadily, I approached Akari. It was time to make my final gambit.

"Stop!" she yelled "If you come any closer, I'll..."

"Go ahead. I'll be right behind you."

"Huh?!"

I hopped over the railing to join Akari out on the ledge, standing immediately to her right. Akari looked at me with suspicious eyes that told me she was prepared to jump the moment

I tried anything fishy. I was careful not to make any sudden movements that might alarm her while making it clear I had no intention of backing down. My toes were already sticking out over the edge. One step forward would send me plummeting to my death. A glance down was enough to give me vertigo; it sent a rush of adrenaline and fear through my entire body. My palms were already sweating against the cold metal railing.

"Y'know, when it comes down to it," I began, gazing up at the deep magenta sky, "this is really all my fault. I mean, this whole thing could've been avoided if I hadn't told you about Akito's death or the Rollback. Then you wouldn't have been complicit whether I chose to save him or not. You could've stayed blissfully unaware."

"...What are you trying to say?"

"Nothing. Just that I need to be held accountable for all the pain and suffering you're going through right now, and that I can only atone for it by finding a way to make things right again. If you die right now, I'll be forced to live with that guilt forever."

"So you'd rather kill yourself too?"

"You got it."

A strong wind blew past, sending my bangs aflutter. The smell of sea salt wafted into my nostrils. My footing wavered a little bit; I gripped the railing even tighter.

"...You're a real jackass, you know that?" she scoffed. It may have been the first time she insulted me and actually meant it.

"Believe me, I'm aware. This past week has made it abundantly clear what a worthless piece of crap I truly am."

"Are you using scare tactics on me or something? FYI, I really *am* going to jump. Right now. Whether or not you do too won't change a thing."

"That's fine. What I'm saying is, if I can't convince you otherwise, I'd rather join you and end it all myself."

"Just checking, Kanae-kun: Do you seriously think that threatening to commit suicide is a good way to talk someone *else* out of committing suicide?"

"Probably not. Like you said, I'm a stupid jackass. I'm afraid that's the best I could come up with."

Akari was staring daggers at me now.

"...You expect me to believe you're gonna jump for real?"

"Oh, I am. Make no mistake."

"Stop bluffing. I see your knees quaking."

She had me there. I was literally shaking in my boots. I'd hoped she wouldn't notice.

"N-no, that's, uh... That's because my legs are tired from riding my bike all the way up that big hill."

"Oh, is that why? How come your voice is shaky too?"

"I mean, it's chilly out here. You felt that breeze that just blew by."

"Then explain the sweating."

"People sweat when they're hot, Akari. It's called homeostasis."

"You said you were cold?"

"...Okay, fine!" I yelled at the top of my lungs. "You got me! I'm scared out of my goddamn mind! Happy now?!"

I couldn't deny it. The thought of actually taking that next step and falling to my death scared the hell out of me. Sure, it may be a relatively painless, instantaneous death, but the thought of my blood and guts splattered all across the asphalt filled me with nausea, and imagining how the world might move on without me made me want to cry. The thought of my own death terrified me. Wasn't that only natural?

"...Thing is, there's something I'm even more afraid of," I continued, readjusting my grip on the railing. "And that's the thought of losing you, Akari. That's what really scares me, far more than my own death ever could. I know full well I couldn't bear to go on living in a world without you. I'm not strong enough for that."

I took a brief pause after this mild self-rebuke.

"You know, I never told you this, Akari, but the real reason I'm back here in Sodeshima right now is because I ran away from home. My dad caught me skipping out on my spring break supplementary courses and gave me the scolding of a lifetime. Said he wished he never brought me back to Tokyo to begin with. So I left. And yeah, I know that probably sounds like small potatoes compared to all of the agony and suffering you're going through, but I think it just goes to show what a weak little coward I am. I mean, if I was willing to run away from home over something as trivial as that, what makes you think I wouldn't want to run away from life itself after losing you? Even if you took my own blame out of the equation, I don't think I could cope with that."

"...What's your point?"

"No point. I'm explaining how serious I am about this. If you die here, then I die too. Simple as that."

I wasn't bluffing. That was where my head was at right then.

If I could place complete and total confidence in anything, it was my ability to run away when the going got tough. I had to be upfront about that with Akari, regardless of how hard she was treading water in her own pain and suffering. It was my only method of conveying to her that this wasn't an act.

"...If you want me to live so bad, then why not drag me away by force?"

"I mean, would that really do anything to change your mind?"

"Nope. I'd go do it the next time you took your eyes off of me."

"...That's what I thought."

She truly did have her mind made up. What options did I have now? How could I make Akari want to keep on living? I tried with all my might to wring one last idea out of my frazzled brain but still came up empty. We were at an impasse. Worse, as I thought on it more deeply, dying began to seem like the right answer to our conundrum. Somehow convincing her to live wouldn't magically put an end to all of her struggles. Plenty of hardships lay in her future. Heck, from a general perspective, there was far more to be sad about in the world than to be happy about, and our backwards society tended to reward evil more readily than good. Like we learned back in junior high, trying to stand up for your morals only put a target on your back. Life... wasn't fair. Akari knew that far better than I ever could. The will to live exited my body in one abrupt swoop. I turned to face her.

"So we're really doing this, huh?"

"Yup. I am, at least," she responded in no time, her eyes steady and assured.

"...Okay then."

I grabbed Akari's right hand.

"Hey, what the—"

"I'm not stopping you. If we're gonna go, then I want us to go together."

Her palm was cold and drenched with sweat.

"I'm serious about this, you know," she reiterated.

"Yeah, I know."

"You...really don't have any regrets?"

"I mean, I'd be lying if I said I didn't..." I admitted after mulling it over a little. "But all I ever wanted was to grow old and die with you, so one out of two is good enough for me."

"...I see," she said, then interlocked her cold, dainty fingers with mine. "Guess we're on the same page, then... Because I'm not afraid of dying either, as long as I'm with you."

I didn't say a word. I nodded at Akari, and Akari nodded back at me, as though we'd both made our peace and were ready to kiss the world goodbye.

"Okay," she said. "Here goes nothing."

"Ready when you are."

I exhaled all of the air from my lungs with deliberate slowness. The strong wind blowing by felt pleasantly bracing, like it was cleansing my entire body. I took in a deep breath through my nose, and I could smell the ocean, along with the slightest hint of plum blossoms. All told, I was as afraid to die as ever. Somewhere deep inside, I felt a certain contrasting calm; I attributed it to holding Akari's hand in mine. With her by my side, I could look my fears in the eye undaunted. I wished I had the chance to use this newfound courage for something other than ending it all...but no matter. Everything would be over soon. Knowing I wouldn't have to worry about the future any longer was strangely comforting, in its way. Feeling about as close to content as I could get, I closed my eyes and waited.

I waited for quite some time. Nothing happened. Akari's little hand remained firmly clasped within my own. I opened my eyes and turned to my side, only to find her hanging her head with her shoulders trembling.

"Akari...?"

A sound came into focus at last. Sobbing. Akari was crying, and I didn't even realize.

"It's not fair..." she whimpered through the tears. "Why'd you have to do this to me, Kanae-kun...? How am I supposed to die when you say stuff like that...? I can't do it... I can't..."

I nearly fell to my knees right then and there. The words "I can't do it" washed over my entire body like a wave of relief. All the tension built up inside me started to subside, and my legs went limp. *Oh, thank goodness.* Akari chose to live. I was happy enough to burst into tears myself.

"...C'mon, let's go back inside the railing," I suggested.

Akari complied, throwing her leg over the railing as she wept. Once both of her feet were back on solid ground, I turned and hoisted myself up onto the railing as well. A powerful gust of wind picked up at that exact moment and knocked me off balance.

Uh-oh. I desperately clutched for purchase at everything in reach, but my hands were too slippery with sweat. My body tottered backwards, and my stomach dropped.

I'm gonna fall.

It all seemed to happen in slow motion. The railing receded before me while the skies above expanded before my eyes with a tremendous *whoosh*. My body bent further back, sealing in the realization that I was about to die as it did so. Strangely enough, I didn't feel a lick of fear. Maybe it was because I mentally pre-pared myself to die a moment ago, or maybe I felt satisfied after achieving my goal of saving Akari's life. Either way, all I felt in that instant was that if the universe decided to kill me off here, then so be it. I did what I came here to do, so fate was welcome to take my stupid life. As I came to terms with my fate, however...

"Kanae-kun!"

Akari reached out and grabbed me by the hand. The sense of weightlessness vanished altogether as she gripped my right arm with both hands. She held me far more firmly, far more *impera-tively* than she had when she stopped me on our way to the bar last night. She hauled me back over to safety on the other side of the fence, whereupon she and I both fell to the ground—me directly on top of her, in an accidental aggressor position. Her face now mere inches from mine, I saw my reflection in her wide-open eyes.

Now, here, the belated fear of death hit me like a truck. Had Akari not grabbed my hand when she did, I would have been gone forever. I shuddered at the thought, and my legs got weak enough that I couldn't lift myself up off the ground.

"H-holy hell, Akari. You just saved my—"

Before I had any chance to thank her, she wrapped her arms around me from below and pulled me in close. I was now quite literally on top of her. I could feel her heartbeat pulse against my chest.

"Oh, thank god... I was so scared you were gonna fall..." she sniffled between sobs, her breath hot against my ear.

"Thank god" was right. We were both still here, still breathing, after one near-suicide and one near-fatal accident. As far as I was concerned, that was nothing short of a miracle. How could I not be ecstatic about that?

"Hey, Kanae-kun...?" she whispered in my ear. "Remember what you said to me earlier? About how you'll never break another promise to me again...? Did you really mean that?"

"One hundred percent. I'll never betray your trust again. I swear."

"Okay then... See, there's this one little thing I want you to promise me."

Akari pulled away from me. We both sat up straight, facing each other directly. I lowered my gaze from her tear-drenched eyes to her trembling lips. They shaped sounds together to form six little words:

"Make me a happy woman, okay?"

"Oh, you bet I will," I said, then wrapped her up tightly in my embrace. Akari hugged me right back, and we both sat there in each other's arms while the faded melody of *Greensleeves* rang out over the island. It was already six o'clock. I braced for the worst— but even after the chime was over, no Rollback occurred. Time was back in its proper order, and for the first time in what felt like forever, I was living in the present again. The future awaiting Akari and I was a total enigma, but one that she and I would face together, hand in hand.

It was now April 3rd, the day after Akari's suicide attempt at Sodeshima High. On that bright and sunny afternoon, I made my way down to Sodeshima Harbor. The warm sunbeams upon my face heralded the beginning of spring, promising that winter's lingering specter would soon disappear from the last few shady pockets that lent it sanctuary.

In truth, this was the *second* April 3rd of my seventeenth year on earth. This time, I intended to take it slower than the last. Nothing happened at 6 p.m. last night, leading me to believe that the Rollback was over. While I never gained a proper understanding of its mechanics or what triggered it, the 6 p.m. thing was a rigid rule throughout the phenomenon. I felt safe in assuming the phenomenon had truly ended.

That wasn't a guarantee that I was free from its clutches altogether. I knew that. Still, I figured it wasn't healthy to live in constant fear of otherworldly time hiccups; I would cross that next bridge if and when I came to it. It wasn't like I could do much to prevent it, so why stress myself out in the meantime?

I soon arrived at the harbor and made my way to the ticket office. Inside, I found Akari sitting on one of the benches, wearing a knit sweater.

"Wow, you're here early," I called out as I approached. She turned to look up at me.

"Yeah, sorry. I felt antsy all morning..." she said, fidgeting with her fingers down near her belly button. A fragment of darkness endured in her expression, but I sensed none of the instability from when we were up on the rooftop yesterday.

"Well, don't push yourself," I said. "If it gets to be too much for you, we can always quit and go home."

"I think I'll be okay. Especially since you're coming with me... And I'll have to face him sooner or later."

Akari's voice was tense with either fear or trepidation, or perhaps a combination of the two. We were on our way to visit Akito at the hospital he was staying at over on the mainland. It was Akari's idea. She called me up this morning and said that it was something she couldn't avoid forever if she wanted to go on living. I thought that was a mature way of looking at it and agreed to go as her escort. Admittedly, I had my reservations about this meeting between a victim and her abuser, but they *were* siblings. It wasn't like they could realistically go the rest of their lives without talking to one another, at least not until Akari graduated from high school. Some amount of reconciliation was necessary, I assumed.

"Don't worry," I reassured her. "If he tries anything funny, I'll put a stop to it."

"Yeah, okay... Thanks," she said. A little of the tension left her shoulders.

I checked the big clock inside the waiting area. The ferry was supposed to arrive at any minute, so I got in line at the ticket window. After paying for our fare, I walked back over to where Akari was sitting. Our boat arrived a short while later, so we stepped aboard and embarked on our little voyage to the mainland.

We left the ferryboat and got on a bus that took us all the way to the hospital. After checking in at the front desk, they gave us Akito's room number. We went up the stairs, down the hallway, and around the corner, before eventually arriving at his hospital room. As we stood in front of the door, I looked over at Akari out of the corner of my eye. She looked pale and was biting her lip with a frown. Her hands shook slightly. When she noticed my gaze, however, she turned toward me with a forced smile.

"Ah ha ha... Sorry, I guess I'm more nervous than I realized."

"You still wanna do this?"

"I mean, we're here now. I can't turn back."

"...Okay then."

I took her hand and held it tight. Akari recoiled in momentary surprise, then gave my hand a brief squeeze in reciprocation. She took a deep breath, knocked lightly on the door, and then opened it without waiting for a reply; it was a shared hospital room with multiple occupants, so she must not have felt the need. Akito's bed was on the right-hand side, over by the window. Still holding hands, we walked in and made our way across the room

WAIT FOR ME YESTERDAY IN SPRING

to the privacy curtain partitioning his bed away from the rest of the patients.

"Hey, it's your sister," Akari said. "We're coming in."

No reply came, but someone was clearly in there. Akari slid the curtain aside and walked in, and I followed suit. Sure enough, Akito lay there in his bed, wide awake. He had an IV drip hooked up to his arm.

"I didn't say you could come in," Akito scoffed, glaring at Akari. He noticed me enter right after her, and his eyes widened a little in mild surprise.

"Hey, you're...Funami, right?" he asked.

"That's me," I said.

"Heard from my old lady that it was you who found me and called the ambulance. I really owe you one, man."

"Nah, it's cool... Don't worry about me. It's her you should be thinking about."

I signaled Akari with my eyes. She took a deep breath.

"Akito, we need to talk," she said.

"...Yeah? About what?" he replied. His voice instantly turned hostile.

"About what you did two days ago... No, what you've *been* doing for the past couple of years. All of the harassment, all the late-night partying, all the grunt work you've made me do, all the money you've stolen... It all needs to stop. I don't want to catch you doing any of that again," she declared. Akito was visibly uncomfortable, but Akari persisted: "I've already told Kanae-kun about everything you've done to me too."

"...Hmph. What, are you guys going steady now? Explains why you're holding hands. The hospital ain't the place to be flaunting your relationship status, guys," he snorted derisively.

This was the straw that broke the camel's back. The image of Akito I'd fought to maintain in my mind, my concept of him as a stand-up guy, a hardworking pitcher, crumbled to dust once and for all. I knew damn well that there was no way he'd forgotten all the horrible things he'd done to Akari—and yet here he hadn't only shrugged it off but made wisecracks at her expense. My blood began to boil. I let go of Akari's hand, walked up to Akito's bedside, and looked down at him from above.

"Man, you've turned into a real douchebag," I said. "What the hell happened to you?"

"Beg your pardon?" Akito said, his face flaring up with rage.

"You heard me. You're a douchebag. All this crap you've done to hurt your little sister, and you can't muster up one little apology? Do you seriously feel entitled to act like a complete asshole because you lost your shot at being a star athlete?"

"You tryin' to say somethin', pal...?"

"Yeah, I am, actually. Listen up: Try to mess with Akari again, and it won't end well for you, 'pal.' I'll come running with a big ol' rock and chuck it right at your head—just like how you taught me to deal with bullies."

"No, *you* listen, dickhead... I don't think you know who you're dealin' with."

Akito's eyes flashed with anger. He sat up and made a grab for my collar...but whether due to the alcohol poisoning or the fact

WAIT FOR ME YESTERDAY IN SPRING

that he hadn't been an athlete in years, his grip was weak. I shook him off no problem, causing him to lose his balance and fall out of his hospital bed.

"Grgh..." he grunted as he hit the floor.

His IV tube fell out, and a trail of blood began to trickle down his arm. I had no intention of trying to kick a hospital patient while he was down, so I reached out a hand to help him up. He slapped it away.

"Don't touch me," he barked, still on his hands and knees, his nails scratching at the floor. "You and everyone else are always lookin' for excuses to talk down to me... Ever since I had to quit baseball, it's like I'm one big disappointment. It's bullcrap... It's not fair, goddammit..."

He lifted his head and looked at me in distress. His expression was full of hate, and yet I found something strangely pitiable about it.

"Do you have any idea what it's like?" he demanded. "To have the one thing you've dedicated your whole life to ripped out from under your feet? Do you?!"

"...Nope, can't say I do. But there's more to life than baseball, man. Not every single person you meet is gonna judge you based on how good of a pitcher you are."

I reached out my hand again, but he ignored it and sat up straight without assistance. Not a moment later, I heard a woman's voice at the door announcing her arrival. It was a voice I thought I recognized. My hunch was confirmed as soon as she slid open the privacy curtain.

350

"Hey, sorry that took so long, I had to—Wait, huh?"

Sure enough, it was Hayase, holding two cans of coffee precariously in her right hand. She must have been here to visit him even before we arrived.

"Whoa, Akito! Are you okay?! Did you fall out of bed?"

She set the coffee cans down on the bed and squatted down to help Akito up, looping his arm around her shoulders.

"Knock it off," he growled.

"Oh, don't be like that. You're still recovering, it's fine," she said, helping him back up onto the bed before turning to look at us. "Hey, Akari-chan! Good to see you! And who's your friend here...?"

Ouch, I winced. *Forgotten already.* Then I realized that she and I actually *hadn't* met yet in this newly revised timeline. *Duh.* Right as I was about to introduce myself, Hayase gave a short, high-pitched shriek.

"Akito! You're bleeding! Damn, we need to call the nurse!"

"Aw, save it. It's not even a big deal..." Akito said in an attempt to downplay it.

"Oh no you don't, buster. We gotta get that looked at, pronto," she said. She pressed the nurse call button next to his pillow while giving him a disapproving look. "I swear, you've always been like this. Stubborn about the dumbest of things. This is why everyone ends up distancing themselves from you sooner or later."

"So what? Who cares?"

"*I* care. You need to learn to take good advice when it's given to you, for cryin' out loud. Open up a bit more, why don't you? You're only making things harder for yourself by shutting folks out. What do you think would've happened if you weren't lucky enough to be found by someone the other night? Did that even cross your mind?!"

Suddenly, there were tears in her eyes. Akito got a little flustered at that.

"Psh, c-c'mon... It ain't that big a deal. I mean, look at me. I'm fine, aren't I?"

"You could have *died*, Akito!" yelled Hayase.

Akito shrank back. His eyes wavered uncomfortably for a moment, unsure what to do, but eventually he threw up his hands and scratched his head.

"...All right, I'm sorry. Sheesh."

It was almost too quiet to hear, but he *had* apologized. We stood in shocked silence around his bed for some time, until the nurse we'd called showed up to ask Akito how he was feeling. He mumbled a few begrudging answers at first, before Hayase smacked him on the back and told him to explain in greater detail. Incredibly, this was all it took for him to start being more cooperative. I was standing there watching their little back-and-forth when I felt Akari gently poke my sides with her index fingers.

"We should get going," she suggested.

"...Good idea," I agreed.

At least he'll be in safe hands with Hayase, I thought to myself.

Akari and I briefly said our goodbyes to the two of them before we excused ourselves from the hospital room.

The boat ride back to Sodeshima was practically empty; I chalked it up to the fact that it was in the middle of the work-day. You could probably count the number of other passengers on one hand. Akari and I sat side by side right in the middle of the seating area.

"Thanks again, Kanae-kun," she said at one point, with zero lead-in.

"Hm? For what?" I asked.

"For coming with me to the hospital, silly. And...for standing up to my brother."

"Oh, yeah... Don't mention it. Shame I didn't manage to wring an apology out of him..."

The main objective of the day was to draw a line in the sand, after all—and I wasn't confident we'd accomplished that goal.

"Well, it made *me* happy, that's for sure. I never could've done that on my own," she said. The corners of her mouth twitched upwards. It was only the slightest hint of a smile, but I'd take it. Seeing her happy again was enough of a reward for me on its own.

"Feel free to let me know if he gives you any more trouble. Luckily for you, I'll be just down the street from now on."

"Wait, huh?" she said, staring blankly at me. "You mean you're not going back to Tokyo?"

"Nope. I'm dropping out so I can stay right here with you in Sodeshima... Didn't I already tell you this up on the roof the other night?"

Her eyes widened in astonishment.

"I totally thought you were just bluffing about that to talk me down..."

"Hell no. I wouldn't lie in a dicey situation like that."

"Have you already filed your withdrawal paperwork?"

"Nah, not yet. I figure I can call the school and take care of it over the phone."

I knew it wouldn't be quite as easy as that in practice. I expected some firm resistance not only from my father but from my teachers as well. Still, I was fully prepared to fight for my right to withdraw myself from school.

"Forget it, then. You don't have to drop out," Akari said.

"Huh?" I gawked, knocked thoroughly off-kilter. Of all the people I expected to face opposition from, Akari wasn't one of them.

"I mean, that'd only make things harder for you in the long run, right? Like, what would you even do after moving back here?"

"Uh... Probably enroll at Sodeshima High, I guess?"

"And after you graduated from there?"

"Haven't really thought that far, to be honest..."

"You're already on the fast track into a great college, Kanae-kun. You shouldn't waste that opportunity. I mean, don't get me wrong, I really appreciate the sentiment, but I'd feel horrible if you were to give all that up on my account."

"Urgh..."

On second thought, she had a point. Maybe dropping out of high school *would* be too drastic. I had reservations about the idea myself, of course, but Akari's doubts made me wonder if I should just scrap it entirely. Some part of me did feel like a bit of a coward for skulking off back to Tokyo by myself after talking a big game up on the rooftop the other night, though. How in the world was I supposed to make up for that? While I sat there stressing myself out about it, Akari gave a soft, simple smile.

"It's all right, Kanae-kun," she said. "You sit tight and wait for me in Tokyo, okay? I'll come join you as soon as I graduate."

"But what about..."

"I'll be fine. If anything bad *does* happen, you'll be the first to know. I promise," she said, then reached out and held my hand like a parent trying to reassure an anxious child. This conversation flipping around to concern for *my* emotional needs did make me feel like a pathetic loser. Akari was right, though. I may not have thought my little plan through as well as I should have. There was only one year left until we both graduated. If we could make it through this next year apart, she and I could be together again, even if it was after far too much time separated. That thought alone gave me the strength to squeeze Akari's hand back.

"Okay," I said. "Still...try to stay in touch even if everything's going well, yeah? I'll be sure to call you up from time to time too."

"Of course."

"Don't overdo it, either. It doesn't matter if your school stuff doesn't work out. You can come and live with me anyway, y'know."

"I know..." Akari nodded bashfully.

I knew full well the implications of the words that had come out of my mouth. I might as well have proposed to her. But I didn't feel embarrassed at all, and not only because this was my second time dropping that exact line on her—but because it wasn't even an exaggeration. I really did see the two of us sharing our lives together in the long run.

"Welp, guess I'd better start saving up money again if I ever want to make it over there," she mumbled halfheartedly.

"Oh, you don't have to worry about the financial aspect of it. I've got it covered."

"What? No, no, no. I couldn't possibly borrow that kind of money from you, Kanae."

"I wasn't offering to lend it to you. You're gonna earn it yourself, and it'll be a piece of cake. I promise."

"...What are you talking about?" Akari asked, tilting her head in curiosity.

"Well..." I said nonchalantly. "Ever played the lottery before?"

The next year came and went.

I woke from my peaceful slumber to the sound of sprightly footsteps bounding across hardwood flooring in the other room. I creaked my eyes open and gazed up at the white ceiling above me. This was neither my grandmother's house in Sodeshima, nor my father's condominium. This was *our* new apartment, right in the heart of Tokyo.

Picking myself up out of bed, I left the bedroom and headed out into the living room. Over in the kitchen, a slender figure with shoulder-length chestnut hair darted back and forth, clad in a comfy cardigan. It was Akari, age eighteen. It wasn't until she stopped in front of the stove to drizzle oil in a frying pan that she noticed my presence and turned to face me with a welcoming smile.

"Well, look at you, sleepyhead! Woke up all by yourself for once, huh?"

"Yeah, guess I did. Can't keep using you as my alarm clock forever."

I walked into the kitchen and offered my assistance in getting breakfast ready. I set the table with chopsticks, tea, and a small bowl of rice for each of us. A little while later, she came out to join me on the carpet with two sunny-side-up eggs on a small tray. We sat across from each other and set out our modest little breakfast upon our modest little dining table. We clapped our hands together in unison, picked up our respective pairs of chopsticks, and dug in.

Two weeks had passed since Akari and I started living together. As I leisurely ate my breakfast, I thought back on everything that had happened over the past year since the end of the Rollback phenomenon. There was a lot to say, but the single biggest event had to be Akari winning the lottery—even if it wasn't due to luck in the slightest. I'd memorized those winning numbers I looked up during the Rollback and told her what they would be. At first, she was pretty opposed to the idea, comparing it to cheating, but I bent over backwards to assure her that we weren't doing anything illegal, that we probably deserved *some* amount of restitution after everything we'd been through, and that at least this way the money would be going to a good cause and wouldn't be frittered away on needless luxuries. I managed to convince her in the end, so she begrudgingly went out and bought the lottery ticket. With that, all of our financial needs would be taken care of for the foreseeable future.

As far as schooling went, Akari got accepted into the university on nothing but her own merits. She worked her butt off and won the district preliminaries last summer, then went on to make an admirable showing at nationals and secured the requirements for an athletic endorsement. She cleared the required application process with flying colors and was admitted to her dream school with priority status. I could still remember the emotional phone call she gave me when she first heard the news. Now, a few months later, she and I were finally reunited in Tokyo and had begun cohabitating. It had been smooth sailing so far—we were way more compatible than I ever would have thought. Almost freakishly so.

"Phew. That hit the spot, thanks," I said, finishing my meal and carrying my dishes over to the sink. When I returned to the living room, Akari had set her chopsticks down and was staring fixedly down at her phone. "What's up? Something happen?"

"Yeah, my mom just texted me. Get a load of this," Akari said, holding her phone out in front of my face. On the small LCD screen was a picture of Akito and Hayase smiling in each other's arms, beneath which hung the caption: "Guess who's getting hitched!"

"Well, damn. Now there's a shocker," I said, though I wasn't especially surprised. Akari told me Hayase took a renewed interest in getting Akito back on his feet after the whole alcohol poisoning incident. From what little I'd heard, I wouldn't go so far as to say he'd turned over a completely new leaf, but it sounded like his behavior had made a marked change for the better. He now had a full-time job at Hayase's family's liquor store and was working to steadily pay back the million yen he stole from Akari.

"I know, right?" Akari replied. "Talk about hitting the ground running, jeez."

"Yeah, those two sure didn't waste any time... They've been together for what, a year?"

"If that. I've gotta say, though...there's something else that surprises me more," she said, looking me in the eye as though she'd just had some huge epiphany. "See...if I'm honest with myself, I still haven't really forgiven my brother for everything he did to me, right? But when I read this text just now, there was a moment where...for a split second...I felt genuinely happy for him, from the bottom of my heart."

From where I was sitting, Akari looked a little confused, as though she wasn't sure how to interpret these unfamiliar emotions. How could she feel happy for the same man who'd once abused her, who she'd hated so much that she nearly condemned him to death? I thought this was a poignant testament to just how much she'd grown.

"Hey, good for you! Go ahead and be happy for him! Nothing wrong with that. I think that's pretty mature on your part, actually. I'm proud of you."

I flashed a broad, wholesome grin over at Akari, who smiled right back at me—with the sort of reinvigorated smile of a person who'd just overcome impossible odds.

Akari and I worked together to clean up after breakfast, then got ourselves ready for school and stepped out of our apartment. It was a nice, warm day without a cloud in the sky. We made our way down to the nearest bus stop and got on board. About twenty minutes later, the bus dropped us off right outside the main entrance to the U of I. As I took a step off the bus, a single cherry blossom petal fluttered past me, flitting right in front of my nose. I turned my head and tried to follow it with my eyes, but it was soon picked up by the breeze and sent careening upward into the sky, where I lost track of it.

"C'mon, Kanae-kun! Let's go!" Akari beckoned me, reaching out her hand.

"Right, sorry. I'm coming."

With Akari's hand in mine, we took our first steps onto campus—together. The brick road leading in wasn't particularly wide, lined on either side by rows of magnificent cherry blossom trees. I looked up to a beautiful soft pink canopy; an endless shower of petals came fluttering down to the ground like powdery snow. I read in a brochure that this footpath, which ran from the main entrance up to the central university building, was affectionately dubbed the "Tunnel of Cherry Blossoms" by the students and teaching staff. They were long past full bloom by now, but it was still a gorgeous sight to behold.

Akari came to a stop without warning. Wondering why, I turned to face her, and her gaze met mine. There were tears in her eyes, and a warm, natural, completely uninhibited smile spread across her face.

"What's wrong?" I asked.

"Nothing, I...I'm just really happy right now. Y'know?"

I felt her hand grow warmer in my own.

"Yeah? Well, just you wait," I declared, "because the best is yet to come."

Akari nodded enthusiastically, and we set off once more, walking hand in hand toward the rest of our lives. With heads held high, we trained our eyes firmly on tomorrow—never once looking back.

Afterword

SOMETIMES, the more we love and admire someone, the more likely we are to distance ourselves from them so we won't come away disappointed or heartbroken. And yet, in the vast majority of cases, people won't know how you feel about them unless you put it into words. This can make establishing intimate relationships with others a tricky business when you aren't prepared for rejections that might hurt both them and you. But it still feels a little unfair, doesn't it? Seeing someone's most heartfelt emotions go unrequited, I mean.

We know deep down that it's not rational to expect the other person to be a mind reader, and that it's borderline toxic for the would-be suitor to tell them one thing and expect that they'll interpret it a different way, when in reality, we should be able to take someone's word at face value. Still, when a person has such strong emotions that they literally can't act on them or put them into words, we still empathize with them—we want those wild and uncontrollable feelings to be rewarded, to mean something. This essentially sums up how I felt about the female lead, Akari, throughout the entire duration of writing this novel—more than anything in the world, I wanted her to get her happy ending.

With that said, I'd just like to make a few acknowledgments before I sign off.

To Mr. Hamada, my loyal editor: I know it was an awfully hard road getting this one from the initial planning stages all the way through final revisions, and I'm eternally grateful to you for sticking with me through it all. Something tells me we'll have another uphill battle on our hands with this next book; I hope I can continue to lean on your guidance.

To KUKKA, my incredible artist: just as I felt like I had no future as a writer, and I should hang up my pen and move to Hokkaido to eke out a meager living on a farm or something, I received your first piece of concept art, and it gave me the inspiration to get my messy manuscript in order and see this thing through to the end. This book probably wouldn't even exist right now if it weren't for your jaw-droppingly gorgeous illustrations. Thank you so much for gracing these humble pages with your artwork once again.

To my extremely supportive readers: it's thanks to all of you that this second novel of mine was able to come to fruition, so thank you for that. And thank you for all of the fan mail and the love you've shown me on social media—it really does help keep me going from one day to the next. I have every intention of continuing to write until I physically can't anymore, so I hope at least some of you will follow my continued works and come along with me to wherever it is I'm going next.

Finally, I'd just like to give a huge shout-out to all of the other incredible people in the editing department, my proofreader, my designer, and everyone at the printing office who had a hand in making this book possible.

And on that note, dear reader, I leave you. Until we meet again.

MEI HACHIMOKU

2020

ABOUT THE AUTHOR
Mei Hachimoku

Born in 1994. Leo. I've been living in the same place for so long, yet I still don't know the name of whatever song it is they use for the evening chime. If I have any stalkers that happen to know, please shoot me a message on the DL.

ABOUT THE ARTIST
KUKKA

Super excited to have the opportunity to work on another Mei Hachimoku novel! Been stanning COBIHAMU-CHAN hard lately. Still playing Splatoon 2 in TYOOL 2020. Come find me online! TWITTER HANDLE: @hamukukka